DALE MAYER

A Psychic Visions Novel

A MOTHER'S LOVE

A MOTHER'S LOVE
Beverly Dale Mayer
Valley Publishing Ltd.

ISBN-13: 978-1-834083-58-2
Print Edition

Books in This Series:

Tuesday's Child
Hide 'n Go Seek
Maddy's Floor
Garden of Sorrow
Knock Knock…
Rare Find
Eyes to the Soul
Now You See Her
Shattered
Into the Abyss
Seeds of Malice
Eye of the Falcon
Itsy-Bitsy Spider
Unmasked
Deep Beneath
From the Ashes
Stroke of Death
Ice Maiden
Snap, Crackle…
What If…
Talking Bones
String of Tears
Inked Forever

Insanity

Soul Legacy

Coveted

Endgame

A Mother's Love

Remnants

Boxed Sets and Bundles

https://geni.us/Bundlepage

About This Book

When Eden and her best friend, Debbie, embarked on a three-day retreat for some much-needed relaxation, Eden never anticipated the whirlwind romance that would ignite between Debbie and Richard, the leader of the retreat. Nor did Eden foresee her best friend's sudden personality change and subsequent betrayal, shattering a fifteen-year bond in mere hours.

Even more shocking was the discovery that, before the weekend concluded, Debbie would be found dead under mysterious circumstances.

Detective Eric Kent, a man with a keen intuition and a knack for unraveling the unseen, was assigned to the case. While waiting for the autopsy results, he dove in and quickly found himself entangled in a web of questions. Eden's account of events was riddled with emotional pain and confusion, yet something deeper seemed to pulse beneath the surface—something much darker …

This was no ordinary case; it required a perspective that transcended the obvious, a journey into the unknown, where love and danger intertwined.

Sign up to be notified of all Dale's releases here!
https://geni.us/DaleNews

CHAPTER 1

"**G**OOD RIDDANCE," DEBBIE called out, as Eden stormed from the hotel.

It was the final straw as far as Eden was concerned. She threw her bag into the front of her car, determined to leave the retreat.

She snorted. *Retreat.* A three-day meditation retreat, supposedly *to get you back to normal, to break up the stress in your life, to just take a breather, to find time for yourself.* She and Debbie had both come with the intention of taking time for that little bit of self-care that they needed, but then something went wrong right off the bat. Somehow Debbie's gaze had landed on the leader of the retreat—somebody who had organized it, somebody who had a decent name in the meditation industry.

And his gaze had fallen on Debbie.

Eden wasn't the jealous type, wasn't the kind to begrudge her friends getting good things in life. However, her bestie was already a little too loose and fancy-free with her affections, at least as far as Eden was concerned. Anyone looking from the outside in might call it jealousy, but it was not. Eden just preferred to actually know the name of the person she was sleeping with, whereas Debbie had a *life is for the living* attitude. Thus, while you were living, you should enjoy everything about it.

Eden turned and took one final look at the hotel and prepped for the two-hour drive back. Her friend stood just inside the front door of the lobby, staring at her. Debbie's expression, almost a mocking look, left Eden unsure of who the hell Debbie had become or how quickly her friend had switched into this other person who Eden didn't recognize.

Eden was about to lift a hand and wave, then thought, *Screw it.* Absolutely no reason to. Besides, Debbie would probably give her the finger in return, so Eden steeled herself and tried to avoid one last glance back.

Without success.

She looked up, and there was her supposed friend, literally giving her the finger. Shaking her head, and mad at herself for looking back against her better judgment, Eden got in her car, started the engine, and pulled away. It had been one of the craziest situations, and she still didn't quite understand how it had happened.

Friday night had been awkward, since Eden was unexpectedly alone, but they were both on their best behavior at that point. Then somehow the next day, it had all become about Debbie and *him.* He still conducted the planned meditations and everything else as scheduled, but Debbie had been right by his side, for every damn moment.

He flaunted Debbie right in front of everybody, and it had been unbelievable, but Eden couldn't do anything about it. At first, it had been fine, whatever—do whatever you want to do. She believed in free will and all. Her friend was apparently just having one of those lovely little moments with the meditation guru, but then Debbie quickly changed. A point came when she no longer appeared to be the Debbie who Eden knew.

Instead of joining Eden for a meal or just laughing and

giggling about the relationship in the ladies' room, Debbie had been all in.

"I'm his favorite girl, and I'm going to stay here and be with him forever."

Eden was surprised, but she really started to worry when Debbie added, "I already quit my job via text, and I gave notice on my lease as well. I'll be out of my apartment by the end of the month."

Eden had stared at Debbie in shock. The end of the month was in four days. "You did what? Debbie, this is way too fast. No, no, no, you can't just up and do that. Think about this before you go jumping into a relationship on a whim."

"I can do anything I want," Debbie declared, with a smirk in Eden's direction. "You're just jealous."

Eden hadn't been jealous. She had been stunned, never having seen her friend make such a snap decision, not liking the way she had gone about it. Eden had been without a clue as to how to make Debbie see the folly of her actions, see things with clear eyes and common sense.

Debbie had been adamant about Eden taking a hike, while Debbie declared she would spend the whole weekend with *him* anyway. Debbie added how their boss had insisted that she come back in for the standard two weeks' notice, or there would be issues.

Eden wasn't sure what those issues were, but they both worked at the same place. Eden worried this would affect her own work relationships.

Debbie was being so ridiculous about the whole thing. In addition to resolving things at work to their boss's satisfaction, Debbie also had to get rid of her stuff in her apartment, pack it all and move it. Debbie needed to take care of these things. Surely she couldn't get it all done in the next four days.

Eden didn't know what to think, she really didn't. But, as she drove away, fuming mad, she wasn't sure she cared anymore.

Fifteen years of a friendship down the tube, all because of some man. A man Debbie had barely just met. Like, what the hell?

Debbie had done this before, but that was minor compared to whatever this was. Usually she would get a boyfriend, and you wouldn't see her for the first month, and everything was *him, him, him, and him.* She had never been a moderate personality type. It was all or nothing, and she dove in headfirst, usually to come right back out again, bawling her eyes out because her most recent Prince Charming had turned out to be a frog, not that Mr. Right she was looking for.

When Eden had tried to talk to her friend this time, Debbie had been beyond insulting about the whole damn thing, something that, for Eden, would never fly.

She shook her head, tears in her eyes, as she drove home, wondering what the hell had just happened. She was mad the whole time she drove, but, by the time she got home, she was just sad and more or less disgusted to realize how quickly her friend had morphed into this new personality and had ditched their long-term friendship they had shared up to this time. It was heartbreaking and absolutely devastating.

Eden pulled into her garage, parked, grabbed her gear, then headed into her home. She had bought her small bungalow a couple years ago, when the owners, an older couple, had decided it was time for them to move into a senior facility. The house had to be updated, inside and out, but she was happy to do all that, since she'd gotten it dirt cheap, and, for that, she would be forever grateful to them.

There was just something about having your own space, knowing you didn't ever have to leave or to deal with something unexpected, like a problem with a landlord, roommates, whatever. She walked into the main part of her house, dropped her bag at the foot of the stairs to take whenever she went up, then opened some windows to get some fresh air in—maybe to soothe her own soul too. She felt very much like she'd taken a beating, which was shocking, since she hadn't even realized she was on the docket to get one.

Shaking her head, she went to her kitchen, put on the teakettle, and prepared to wait for the water to boil, stepping out into the backyard, taking several deep, calming breaths.

Here was the one place she had put a lot of time into. Most of the inside was done, so she was finishing up the backyard. The old pergola had a couple rotten beams, which she had replaced, then finally refinished the whole thing, as it had weathered badly.

She had gone whole hog on digging up the grass and learning to level off a mixture of sand and gravel to put down patio blocks, something that she had done slowly, over time. Now she had this beautiful pergola patio area, with great big garden terraces all around that were still pretty new, but they were growing beautifully. In the not-too-distant future, these garden beds would give her an even better oasis out here.

It was the one place of hers that Debbie absolutely loved, and she and Eden used to sit out here all the time, just relaxing. It was exactly what Eden needed for herself on a daily basis. Most people didn't understand the need for a peaceful space, or maybe everyone just didn't need it the way she did.

Every day when she came home from work, it was all about finding that Zen space, a chance to just sit back and relax. Their work had been even more frustrating and stressful than usual, with a new manager who was making everybody's life miserable. Plus, Eden had to get a grip on her never-ending thoughts running wild in her brain. The plan for a weekend away had seemed perfect to her. She intended to go alone and to focus on herself, but Debbie decided she would go too. She was a force to be reckoned with at times. The retreat had been for Friday, all day Saturday, and the better part of Sunday, ending around 2:00 p.m. However, the problems with Debbie had literally started on Friday night, when they had attended the initial meet-and-greet event.

Eden found it unbelievable to watch Debbie and *him*. While Eden was all for love at first sight, she was not one for becoming a different person who nobody could even recognize within hours of a relationship beginning. Even now, Eden was completely struck by how disastrous that whole event had been. To add to the insult, Eden had actually paid good money for the weekend that resulted in an early boot in the ass.

Groaning, she returned to the kitchen to pick up her tea, which had now steeped, then wandered around the garden for a little bit, trying to shake off the horrible feeling in her gut. She worried about returning to work tomorrow, knowing everybody would pester her with questions— questions she couldn't even begin to answer. *If Debbie quit, would she show up or not show up for her required notice period?* Eden didn't know.

And, if Debbie didn't show, it would put even more pressure on the rest of them to get the job done, until

Debbie was replaced. That was just one more thing Eden was having a hard time coming to terms with about this whole mess. Was Debbie this selfish? Would she care, when she came out of the trance of it all?

Maybe.

How far would she take it?

That's debatable.

Until right now, Eden hadn't realized just how little Debbie would care, how she was completely willing to let everybody else pay the piper, just so she could do whatever in this new relationship.

Eden shook her head. It had all just been too much, too damn fast.

She cried out, "Why? Why so fast? Why not take a moment and savor the growing relationship? Why jump like a crazy woman into this chaotic mess?"

Eden didn't know.

There just didn't seem to be any rhyme or reason to it, and that, as much as anything, scared her. She wanted to pull out her phone to see if Debbie had texted her, but no way she would, not after all that craziness. Debbie was dug in and good.

Honest to God, Eden wouldn't even know what to say to Debbie now anyway. What her friend had done seemed to be such a foreign concept, including the way she had treated Eden. She wasn't entirely sure that she could ever go back to the way they were.

So many things had been said—awful things, nasty things, insulting to the core. How did one move past all that? I mean, it was easy for people to say, *Oh, she wasn't in her right mind,* but, if Debbie wasn't in her right mind, whose mind was she in? Because it was an unbelievable display of meanness. Some of the stuff Debbie had said was downright cruel. Sipping her tea, Eden felt the tears collecting in the corner of her eyes.

When her phone rang, she looked at it and snorted because, of course, it was Debbie. Eden shook her head at that and didn't answer. She was still too hurt, still in far-too-much pain from all Debbie had said. At this point, the call seemed like adding salt to the wound. It was impossible for Eden to even imagine exposing herself to such an irrational and unpredictable person right now.

Debbie phoned one more time a few hours later, but Eden didn't answer. She'd done her laundry and got ready for work the next day but hadn't done anything related to this horrid weekend or to her misguided friend. Eden was still very, very upset. She crawled into bed and, after a very difficult time, eventually crashed.

She woke up early in the morning to a phone call. Groggy, she answered it without thinking. "Hello?" A crackle came first on the phone, followed by a man who said, "Hello, is this Eden Landon?"

"Yes," she said, shifting into a more upright position, trying to wipe the sleep out of her eyes as she gazed at her phone, not understanding the time, even as it glared right back at her.

"My name is Detective Eric Kent. We have your number from a friend of yours, a Debbie Kingston."

"Yes," Eden replied, her tone hardening. "What about her?"

Then came an odd silence, before he said, "Are you two friends?"

"Well, we were until this weekend," she stated, "but yes." She pinched the bridge of her nose. "Why? What's the matter?"

"I need some information before I can say anything."

She stared down at the phone, not comprehending. Who was this person, and why was he asking questions about Debbie?

"I need to know what happened this weekend."

"Well, that's nice," she said. "I would like to know what happened too."

After a moment's hesitation, he added, "I need to come speak with you."

She groaned. "It's six o'clock in the morning."

"I know. My apologies."

"You want to tell me what this is about?"

He read off her address over the phone, and she confirmed, "Yes, that's me."

"I'll be there in ten minutes," he noted and hung up.

She stared down at her phone in shock. Would this mess ever be over with? She had to be at work all too soon, without an unexpected visitor to tend with.

She didn't even want to think about work, but she got up and managed a very quick shower, as much to wake herself up as anything, and had just got the coffee on when her doorbell rang.

Glaring, she walked over and opened the door to the detective standing in front of her. He held up his badge, and she looked at it and said, "Eric Kent? Police?"

"Yes. I'm a detective," he clarified, with a nod.

She frowned, not sure what this was all about. "What can I do for you, Detective Kent?"

He motioned at the door. "May I come in?"

She hesitated and then shrugged. "I guess." She let him in and added, "I just made some coffee. Would you like some?"

"I would love a cup," he said quietly.

She tossed a glance back in his direction, not exactly sure if he was being facetious or not. Such an odd tone filled his voice. He followed her into the kitchen, but his gaze was searching, looking around constantly. "Look. I'm not sure why you're here," she said. "Maybe you could explain that first."

He hesitated, looked over at her, and asked, "How long have you known Deborah?"

She frowned, thinking it over. "Known her? Probably close to twenty years. Been friends with her for fifteen, and that just ended."

He was in the process of lifting his cup, when he looked at her in surprise. "Can you tell me what happened yester-day?"

Eden shrugged. "I mean, for a lot of people, it would probably be very normal," she said, "but, for me, it wasn't normal at all."

He stared at her and just waited.

She sighed. "We went to this retreat to take a break from all the chaos. Work has been extremely stressful lately, and I was feeling overwhelmed and just needed to get away."

"So, this retreat, what was it about?"

"A pretty standard off-grid kind of thing. Not un-plugged but limited slots. The leader was a well-known meditation expert, a kind of self-help guru," she said, trying hard to hide her distaste. "I just needed a break."

He remained silent, letting her vent.

"I was going alone. Then Debbie decided to come with me, and now I wish to God she hadn't."

He stared at her, one eyebrow raised.

She shrugged, frowned, and added, "She fell for him ... really badly."

"Him, being—"

"The meditation guru and, from one minute to the next, he was her whole life. He was everything to her. Nothing else would be in her world but him—way over the top. I couldn't believe it. She gave notice on her lease and quit her job via text, without proper notice apparently," she shared, raising her hands, "even though she knows we're completely swamped."

"Are you saying you two work together?"

"Yes, different jobs but at the same place," she said, groaning. "Anyway, yesterday, when I heard all that, I was trying to get her to slow down a bit, but she completely went off on me, saying a lot of horrible things. I ended up leaving early."

"Alone?"

"Yes, I left her there, even though we drove together, and it was …" She frowned as she stared down at her coffee. Then she sniffled. She looked up at him in horror because the threat of tears was coming again. "I will not cry. Just … gimme a minute."

He nodded but again his gaze was odd.

Rubbing the tears from her eyes, she continued. "Anyway, she was being so ugly and so mean that I just came home. And I don't really know what happened to make her act that way, but apparently we're no longer friends," she said. "There it is, the whole story. Does that answer your questions?"

He frowned.

She frowned back at him and nodded. "Clearly it doesn't, but that's okay because none of this makes any sense to me either."

"You mean, her relationship with the new man?"

"Yeah, her relationship with *him* for one thing," she said, taking a sip. "Honestly, she's always tended to go crazy over men, especially whenever her relationship is new, but not like this. Usually when she meets a new guy, she gets overly excited about it, but she's never been like this, never turned … mean," she added.

"So, she plays it kind of loose?"

"Always, as long as I have known her. She meets a guy and is immediately smitten, over the moon, but usually, within a short time, like one month to six weeks, she's back to herself, acting as if nothing ever happened, except that her heart has been broken all over again," she explained. "So, I don't know what to tell you, and I really don't know why you care."

When he looked directly at her, something churned in her gut.

"Because she's dead."

CHAPTER 2

EDEN STARED AT the detective, her bottom lip trembling, then sat down on the kitchen chair hard. "You have to be wrong," she cried out in disbelief. This wasn't possible. Couldn't be possible. She tried to pick up her coffee, only her hands were trembling, and some coffee spilled. She set her cup down, her gaze focused on it. "When I left the retreat, left Chattanooga, she was totally fine."

"We have a confirmed ID."

How? The question reached her mind before she could finally get it out. "How did she die?" Did her new lover kill her? What if Debbie had ended up dead because Eden had left her behind? She couldn't breathe as all these thoughts went through her head, her gaze now locked on to the detective's face. At least now she understood why he was here.

She shook her head and looked away. "No, it just can't be." She glanced back, as she picked up her coffee cup, then put it down right away since her hand trembled even worse than before. She spun to look at him. "You didn't answer my question. How did she die?"

"That's unknown at this point. Potentially suicide. Pill bottles were close by, but we'll have to wait for the findings from the medical examiner. We are still waiting for an official cause of death. Her records do point to a longstanding heart condition though."

She stared at the spot of coffee she had spilled, fascinated by the puddle still morphing. It was something for her mind to focus on, rather than thinking about Debbie. Eden turned her gaze to the detective and said, "The heart condition started as a childhood thing. As for suicide? That's not Debbie. I told you what our fight was about. No way she would commit suicide—especially not right after finally meeting her *perfect partner.*"

She said it again, but this time there was more sorrow than shock in her tone, more bewilderment than anything. She bit down hard on her lip and said, "Please, I need to know more."

He nodded quietly and said, "She was found at her own home here in Nashville. In her own bed. Alone. The house was locked, and we found no sign of forced entry."

Her eyebrows shot up. "Well, I guess she got home somehow then." He frowned. "But who called it in? How did you know? Someone must have—"

"A wellness check was called in for her by—" Eric looked down at the notebook in his hand, a small compact pad, and he read off, "Richard Santino."

"He's the guru guy. He led the meditation retreat," she said. "Him and his brother, Richard and Rinaldo Santino. They ran the program we signed up for." She frowned again. "So, Richard wasn't with her?"

"No. He said that she was supposed to call in as soon as she got home, but she never did." He reached out a hand and then slowly withdrew it when Eden instinctively pulled hers away.

She stared at him and shook her head. "I need information, more information … please."

He sat still for a moment and sighed. "We don't have a whole lot of information at this time, but I can tell you that we found no easily definable cause of death. We're waiting for the final report."

She blinked. "What does that mean?" she cried out, staring at him in shock. "I thought you said she took pills."

He frowned. "We found pill bottles near her body, but, without the autopsy, we don't know if that was a factor at all," he said. "We saw no obvious indication of a cause of death otherwise."

"So, she wasn't hit over the head?"

"Not obviously, no."

"She didn't fall down the stairs?" He shook his head. Yet Eden's mind couldn't make sense of the lack of information and couldn't stop thinking of probable scenarios, even if impossible.

"As I told you, she was found in her own bed. The wellness check was called in by Richard."

Eric kept his voice calm, even as she stupidly continued to question him. "How did he know?" Another stupid question. God, she needed to just shut up. Yet couldn't.

Eric replied, "That's the point of a wellness check. He didn't know. He just said that he hadn't heard from her as planned, and, as far as we know, he was very concerned. She was supposed to contact him as soon as she got in, and there was no reason why she wouldn't have."

Eden sat back in her chair and said, "No, there wasn't. She was absolutely head-over-heels bonkers about him. I can't even believe she left him and came home. She told me that she wasn't going to."

"What do you mean, she wasn't going to?" he asked.

"Well, her story changed a few times, but, at one point,

she told me that she had quit her job via text with no notice. However, the boss was making her come back in, something about needing to give proper notice or to give time to finish up jobs or something. But then Debbie said she wasn't going to."

"That's two different things you are telling me."

"That's what I am telling you. Debbie was off her rocker, smitten with the guy, and wasn't making any sense. You'll have to check her phone. By the end for her ranting, I wasn't exactly listening," she said. "I was too livid, and I assumed she would come home and move at some point because she also said that she ended her lease on her rental and that she was moving in with *him*. I don't even know where he lives," she cried out, staring at him. "I mean, he was there for the weekend retreat. For all I know, he could live in a whole other country."

"He has a home in Seattle but is always traveling. He has regular seminars across the country including Nashville," Detective Eric confirmed, "and he was supposed to see her today, but he was off doing something else for a different business trip."

"So how did she get home last night?" she asked, her gaze narrowing. "Maybe he killed her and then waited a few hours to call in for a welfare check."

His lips twitched, and he said, "Until we get a detailed autopsy report, we won't know much more."

"You better check him out."

"We already did. He has an alibi for the night. He was back home, and apparently his brother was with him."

"Yeah, but then they just alibied each other," she pointed out immediately.

He stared at her and said, "You really don't like them."

She groaned, closed her eyes, and said, "Look. I don't have any reason to like or dislike either one of them. I'm just telling you that the whole thing was beyond odd, and this just continues that reality. And, other than her heart murmur or whatever that seemed to be controlled with her prescription, she was otherwise very fit and healthy. So I can't believe her death would be from natural causes."

He nodded. "All I can tell you is that she was dead in her bed, and, for all intents and purposes, she went peacefully. It appears she passed in her sleep."

Eden just stared at him.

"Hey, it happens. Not very often, but it does happen."

She shook her head. "I don't believe it."

"And that may be the case," he said, "but I was hoping you could give me information about any trouble she may have had at the retreat."

"Yay, *me*," she said bluntly. Eric looked at her, his eyebrows shooting up. "Like I said, it was a pretty wild case of love-at-first sight, followed by *I'm completely flipping my life around, and, by the way, I hate you for ruining my moment of true love.*"

"So, you said you two had words?"

"Don't get me started on that," she said, then sobered, her flare of anger immediately draining away to be replaced by sadness. "I was trying to talk her out of leaving her job and giving up her apartment, you know, to give the relationship some time. But she blew up and basically told me that she hated everything about me. *You're not my friend,* and *Everything about me is wrong.* That's what she said to me."

"Anything else?"

"Yeah, plenty more where that came from. She told me that she was just with me because she was lonely and needed somebody, but now that she found her soulmate, *blah, blah, blah*, I was no longer needed. That was pretty much my weekend." She took a deep breath and said, "It was godawful. She didn't hold back a bit and made some raw, ugly comments."

She turned to stare off in space, her mind still blanking on the concept that Debbie was dead. She turned and looked at him and asked, "You're sure it's her, right?" She grabbed her phone and pulled up one of the most recent pictures of her former best friend. She held it up. "This is Debbie. Is it her?"

He nodded. "Yes, that's her." And he gave the address for her apartment, and Eden's mind buzzed with shock again.

"Yeah, that's—that's her apartment."

"How long has she lived there?"

She grimaced. "Only two months now, I think."

"And was she month to month?"

"I think so." Then she frowned and added, "I'm still in shock over the weekend as it is. I hardly got any sleep. I was so upset, and I don't really understand what happened to her. However, I believe whatever happened to her happened to her much earlier."

He frowned at her. "What do you mean by that?"

"She wasn't herself. She was not in any way, shape, or form the person who I drove there with. And I know that it sounds like jealousy."

"It does," he agreed, with a nod.

"Yeah, that's what she told me all weekend long too," she confirmed, trying hard to calm down. "Yet I'm telling you that whoever was there was not Debbie. She didn't look like her. She didn't act like her—not at all."

His gaze intensely drilled into hers. "And you do know—"

"I know," she interrupted. "It sounds as if I'm absolutely nuts. I get it. And I'll probably never say it again because obviously nobody'll believe me, but I'm telling you. It's like she went through a personality change, just as soon as she met him."

"Was it reciprocated?" he asked.

She thought about it and shrugged. "I don't know this Richard guy anywhere near as well as I know Debbie. I'd not met him before the weekend, so I don't know if he went through the same kind of change or not. He did appear to be just as smitten with her as she was with him. That much I'm sure of." She sighed.

"At the beginning, I was thrilled for her. It seemed as if she'd really made a connection, but then this demon child inside her emerged, as if it had been waiting for the right circumstance to finally get out and to be the absolute worst person she could be."

Eric studied her closely.

Eden shook her head. "Yeah, I know. I sound as if I'm the worst person ever, saying something bad about Debbie, now that she's dead. God help me, that'll be brutal when I go into work. I just won't say anything. That's probably the best way to handle it."

"Not say anything about what?"

"About the personality change," she replied. "Although my boss is likely to ask a million questions as to why Debbie quit on him, and then he'll be looking for more of an explanation. I don't know what I'll tell him."

"Since she is now deceased, I don't think there'll be very much in the way of explanations for anybody."

She stared at him, and it suddenly hit her. This person she had spent so much time with, this best friend who she had had a huge falling out with, was dead—even though Eden still now hoped they could get beyond it.

Not just ill, or missing, but dead. Debbie was gone.

Eden sat back, tears welling in her eyes. "I know that you don't believe me and that you have absolutely no reason to, but I'm telling you something is very wrong here."

He tapped his finger on the table, but it was more of a thoughtful I'm-thinking-about-this kind of thing.

She couldn't even be sure that he was thinking as much as he was figuring out how to exit the house of this crazy woman. "I don't have any answers for you. I haven't a clue what happened to her," she added.

"But you do know that I have to ask."

"Ask what?" she said, bewildered. "Go ahead and ask."

He nodded. "Where were you last night? Up until I called you?"

She stared at him blankly for a moment and then flushed, knowing exactly what he was asking her. "Meaning, did I kill her?" she asked baldly.

"Meaning that, if foul play were involved and if what you're saying is correct, you're the one with the motive."

"What?" she asked, shocked at how quickly that had turned around on her. "Because she chose a man over me? Good God." She laughed, sounding a bit hysterical. "Women have been doing that since the beginning of time." She took a deep breath. "And, just to let you know, if I would kill anybody, it probably would have been him."

"You don't like him?"

She wasn't even sure how to explain the reaction she had to Richard. "I don't know if I don't like him because I don't even know him. I don't have any idea who he was as a person, but I had an off feeling about him. The way Debbie responded to him was alien to me, even for her, and it was just compounded by the strange way that it escalated."

"And yet you told me that initially you were thrilled for her."

"Yes. Because she was so happy, and it looked as if she had met somebody who thought well of her, the same as she thought of him. But soon enough it seemed that it was going way too fast, and she needed to slow down and to take a step back."

Then she stopped, took a deep breath, and continued. "As I told you earlier, she has done this before. Fallen fast, I mean. To the point that she's given up her previous spaces and has moved in with various boyfriends, only to have them beat the crap out of her, dump her outright, or bring another girlfriend home and throw Debbie out on the street. I just wanted her to slow down and to confirm this wouldn't be a repeat of those relationships."

"How many times would you say that's happened?"

"Three recent breakups. I know at least two of her other friends would back me up on that because we've all pitched in to get her moved on from bad situations." Eden took a deep breath to calm herself. "I don't know how to explain that part of her life. It's as if she vibrated at a level where she attracted a certain type of men." She frowned. "Sounds stupid, right?"

"Are you trying to say that she attracted men who mistreated her?"

"Is that even possible?" she asked, staring at him.

"You tell me."

"What's that saying about water? Something about water

finds its own level. I was hoping, because she's been free and clear for the last few months—as in not dating—that she saw things more clearly now," she explained. "We just thought that maybe she was working on herself and looking for men who were a little more stable, a little more normal. Not the kind who would put her in the hospital again."

"Did she ever press charges on the ones who put her in the hospital?"

"Oh God no." Eden rolled her eyes. "She never wanted to be the kind of person who would do that, and I think the men knew it too."

Eden continued. "Debbie's also never had kids, for which I am grateful. I was always there for her," she whispered, her tears welling up again. "But I feel like this time I failed her somehow, though I don't know what I was supposed to do. I tried to get her to slow the hell down, to give them some time to get to know each other before she quit her job and moved in with him."

Eric nodded in apparent sympathy.

"I couldn't believe it when she told me she'd already texted her boss and quit. Who does that?" she asked, staring at him. "She hadn't even known Richard a whole weekend."

"When did this relationship start?"

"Right after the meet and greet. Debbie and I spoke a couple times, and she was already making life-changing decisions. Considering her history, I couldn't trust him or her. I was never invited to share coffee, a drink, or a meal with them or anything. In fact, she used my warnings to point out that I was bitter and jealous instead."

He pulled out a notebook and wrote down something as she continued.

"I was really concerned for her. She seemed hypnotized

or something." Eden raised her hands, her palms showing. "I was hoping that this Richard guy—who was promoting self-care, wellness, and all these good things—might be a different sort than the men who Debbie normally hangs out with. But I couldn't possibly tell you if he is a good man or not. This all happened over the course of a weekend. That's all it took for Debbie."

Realizing that she was starting to babble, she shook her head. "Look. I was here last night. I was alone. I don't have an alibi. I talked to my mom at—" She pulled out her phone and showed him her call history. "There, it was like nine o'clock last night. She laughed at me and told me it would all blow over. To give Debbie six weeks and she would come back, crying again, like she does every time. Debbie did call me twice ..." She again checked her call history. "I didn't answer," she admitted. "I was too upset and didn't want to hear any more ugliness."

"I'm sorry about that," Eric replied, putting down his notebook. "I'm also sorry for the fact that she won't be coming back after six weeks. This time her disappearing act is permanent." With that, he stood and walked to the front door.

Eden trailed behind him, not even sure what to say in response to that last comment of his, which struck home in a way that she hadn't really expected it to. And of course it was true, but Eden didn't have anything to do with her friend's death. All she could think about now was the fact that, if she had been more overjoyed about the new relationship, Debbie would be alive today. She looked over at Eric and asked, "Will you let me know the autopsy results?"

He frowned and asked, "Does she have any family?"

"No." Then she winced. "Debbie told me that she had

named me as the executor of her estate. This was years ago. I presume it remains the same."

"In that case," Eric noted, "I will see that you get a copy of the autopsy, if and when we get to the bottom of this. Did she have anything worth giving away?"

"I don't think so. I never saw any signs of wealth."

"There might be something in her bank account. She's been working for a few years, hasn't she?"

"Yes, but it won't be very much. She had a spur-of-the-moment boyfriend who thoroughly cleaned out her bank account. The last one actually," she clarified, "and we all lent her enough money to get into another apartment, away from him."

"And she never paid you back?"

"We didn't ask for it back. At least I didn't. I assumed she didn't have it." She took a deep breath. "So, when I go to work today, am I to tell my boss, or will you contact him?"

"I will be contacting him as a matter of course," Eric shared, "but you can tell him the news. I'm here because you're about the only name in her address book."

She stared at him, shook her head, and muttered, "We got her a new one after she got a new phone. After the last boyfriend, it was necessary because he was a … Let's just say that it was pretty ugly."

"So that's another question. If this is foul play—and I don't know that it is, so keep that in mind—but would this last boyfriend have done anything if he found out Debbie was head over heels with this new guy?"

She stared at him in shock, then sank down into the nearest armchair. Nodding slowly, she said, "Honestly, he might. I just … don't know how he would have known about her new apartment."

"People do strange things when they're in love, when they think they're finally safe and happy. Would Debbie have texted him, taunting him with *I'm finally free of you. I've got a man who's decent and who treats me wonderfully?*"

"Oh God." Eden closed her eyes. "Yeah, Debbie absolutely would do that. A part of her can be, … let me just say, a little vindictive. And, if she felt she was doing really well and someone like him who had done her so wrong was still out there, Debbie might very well have let him know."

"You mentioned a phone, but no phone was with her. At least we couldn't find one."

Eden stared at him, pulled out her phone, and quickly called Debbie's number to see if anybody would answer. Together, they listened as it rang and finally went to voice mail.

He wrote down the number and asked, "Do you know what kind of phone it is?"

"An iPhone but I don't know the model. It's fairly new, as we just got it for her."

He nodded. "We'll look into it." As he stepped through the door, he turned back to her, then handed her his card and added, "If you think of anything else, give me a call."

"Sure, but I don't know what you're expecting."

"You're the one who seems to know her the best."

"Debbie had a few other friends, but, yes, I would probably be the closest one to her."

"I will need to get their names," he stated with conviction.

Eden brought up her contact list and showed him the contact info on Debbie's other girlfriends. "Shirley hasn't known her all that long, but Mary and Dolores have known her for years."

He nodded. "I'll contact them."

"So," Eden began, as he wrote down the information, "you'll tell them about her death then? I also need to get to work." She checked her phone and noted how late it was. "I need to go like now."

He nodded. "I will tell them about Debbie's passing. I suspect these three friends will call you immediately after I speak to them."

"I'll send them a text once I get to work." She quickly walked back to the kitchen, grabbed her purse, and headed out the door, locking it, turning to find him still standing there.

He studied her for a moment. "I can let you know when the body is ready to be released."

And, with that parting statement, he turned and walked away.

DETECTIVE ERIC KENT waited until Eden pulled away, then he drove off behind her. He would need to go to her office and talk to her boss and a few of her coworkers anyway. Suspicious deaths required a certain amount of investigation.

And since there hadn't been any particular evidence of foul play, he wasn't sure if this was a waste of time or not, but Eden had certainly brought up some interesting points about her best friend's personality changes and about Debbie's impulse to constantly go overboard in a relationship. He drove to her office and waited until Eden got inside. Then he checked the time.

It was almost 8:00 a.m. He sent her a text, asking what time her boss would be in.

She responded within minutes. **Not until nine usually.**

It was a long time to wait idly, so he turned around and headed back to his office. As he walked in, his partner, Cody, looked up and greeted him with a smile.

"How'd you make out?" Cody asked.

Eric shook his head. "It's a weird one, but, until we get the autopsy, we don't really have anything to go on."

"*Nothing* means that it could literally be nothing, right?"

"It could be a natural death, but, according to her best friend—or her ex-best friend," he clarified, the emphasis making Cody's eyebrows rise, "our victim went through a complete personality change during this weekend retreat and fell head over heels in love with the leader of the retreat, who just so happens to be the guy who asked us to do the welfare check."

"Are we sure it was love?"

"No, it sounds more like obsession to me—to the point that Debbie quit her job and terminated her lease via text over the weekend, and blew up at Eden, saying all kinds of mean things to what appears to be her best friend of many years."

"Oh, that's something," Cody noted. "Any leads?"

"Yeah, but we need to find Debbie's phone. Then we might see if she had sent a text or had any contact with her most recent ex-boyfriend, who apparently was violent, the kind of person to take away her phone and to leave her without it, just so she couldn't contact anybody."

"Is that information credible?"

"That still needs vetting. According to Eden, he could be a person of interest if we have foul play in Debbie's death, just because he appears to lack character and has been violent before. Debbie's friends pitched in to get her away from him and helped with her first month's rent because she had no place to go. Debbie had been staying with them while they found a place and got her settled. Then she moved into her new place, got her act together for the past couple months, and everything seemed to be fine."

Cody frowned. "Until this retreat?"

"Yeah, apparently—though it's not the first time Debbie has done something like this. The girlfriend—Eden Landon—was upset that Debbie was doing it again, and so Eden was trying to get her best friend to slow things down. That's when the victim blew up and got ugly enough that her best friend left and came home early from the retreat without her."

"So Eden could be a suspect."

"Yeah, if foul play is involved, Eden would be the logical prime suspect. However, I don't have a clue what her motive would be."

Cody shrugged and shook his head. "It could just be the fight. People do all kinds of things in a moment of passion. Besides, it could be anything from, *Hey, we're done picking up the pieces behind you* to *If you go with him, we're done with you.* Then again, jealousy could be a motive. Maybe Eden liked the guru guy herself, which may have come into play in the argument."

"Could be."

"While we are tossing ideas around, Debbie could have realized that Eden was not happy for her."

"*You just want them all for yourself,*" Eric mimicked.

Cody asked him, "What do you make of all this?"

"Although Eden and their other friends had helped Debbie in the past and had acknowledged that Debbie had a history of whirlwind romances, she had never used that kind of language with Eden nor accused her of interfering in

Debbie's life and in Debbie's decisions. As far as Eden's concerned, it isn't a natural death, and she doesn't know what the hell went on because Debbie just wasn't herself, like she had been hypnotized or possessed or whatever. The whole jealousy angle is something to check out, but I don't really have anything to substantiate it, other than it came up in the argument, according to Eden," Eric explained.

"So, what's the next step?"

"I need to talk with Eden's boss—who is also Debbie's boss—and get an idea of the character of both women. Then I need to talk to Richard, the meditation guru."

"That's the guy who called in the wellness check?"

"Yeah, and hopefully he is still at the retreat center."

"It's worth mentioning that, if he had anything to do with this, calling in a wellness check and not being in the area would be a great way to have an alibi and to keep himself out of this."

"Why would he do that though?" Eric countered, loving sparring with Cody regarding various theories on a daily basis.

"Maybe this Debbie chick just flung herself all over him and was making all kinds of plans that he didn't know how to get out of, and he just wanted to shut down the whole thing. Like, … remember Kathy?" Cody whistled and gave Eric a wolfish grin. "I have had my own share of psycho girlfriends but—"

"I would rather not think about my psycho ex and would prefer to focus on the victim here instead. I can understand the urge to kill, but killing seems extreme in this case."

"Maybe." Cody rolled his eyes. "But we also don't know what kind of guy this Richard is. If he has a name in this industry, he probably has a lot of women throwing themselves at his feet. Maybe it wasn't as mutual as it appeared, and he just really needed to get out of it. For all we know, he has a wife somewhere, and she was already making waves, having found out about it after your prime suspect came home."

Eric nodded. "I hadn't considered that."

"What about the body?"

"No visible marks on her. Thirty-two, visibly healthy, yet with pill bottles near her body. So, to think she would have been involved in any drugs is hard to believe. She sure didn't look to be a regular user."

"It might be hard to believe, but we also know that it happens."

Eric nodded. "I know this is a strange one, but, until we get the autopsy results, we don't know if we even have a case or not."

"And we could also end up with no results," Cody reminded him. "*Cause of death unknown.*" Cody gazed at his partner with a sigh.

Eric knew what his partner was thinking. Cody was goofy, intuitive, and extremely observant. And Eric had the feeling himself that this case would be a mystery to unravel. "Yeah, well, … we'll do the investigation and, if it goes somewhere, great. If it doesn't, you and I both know it ends there, which would really suck if something criminal went on here."

"Absolutely," Cody muttered and shook his head. "But we also have to remember that we have God-only-knows-how-many other cases to work on, plus more that just came in last night."

"Like what?" Eric asked.

"Got a couple actually. One looks to be a gang shooting, and we have another rape and murder. It could be connected to that other case we still have open."

"About six months ago," Eric added ruefully. "And we never found him. And then likely connected to another one we haven't been able to solve, also with a similar MO."

"Thanks for the reminder," Cody pointed out, his tone dark. "Apparently we're not doing great on this front."

"It's not even that," Eric noted. "It's more about doing what we can. We're extremely short-handed, so take pleasure in what we can close, and don't let the rest of it wind you up."

"I get that, but, if we can't find any information and if there's no forensics—"

"We don't have much to go on," Eric admitted, his tone matching Cody's now.

"I know. I wasn't trying to—"

"To bitch?"

Cody had a goofy smile all over his face now.

"Yes, you were," Eric declared cheerfully, "and with good reason."

"But, if you're okay to run this down as far as you can take it, then put it in front of somebody else, get fresh eyes on it. See if anybody has anything to add."

"And if not?" Eric asked.

"We park it, unless forensics comes back and says she was drugged or something equally bad," Cody replied. "Then we have a whole lot of other things to work on. The forensics team is still at the rape-murder site."

"What's the latest on that one?" he asked.

"The police are canvassing the area. I should look at doing that on this one too," Cody suggested. "I need to check with the neighbors to see if they saw or heard anything during the evening hours last night."

"Right, so go do what you can do this morning, then park it until we know more. I will still be a couple days," Eric shared.

"Yeah, but Debbie is also important."

"Other cases become more important when we don't have any other leads or a direction to take," Eric noted, with a heavy sigh, as he looked down at his notebook. "I'm running names on the rape-murder case then will go back to the crime scene."

"I'll go run this down and talk to the people I need to talk to. And then I can help you," Cody offered.

"Good." With that, Eric turned and headed to his desk. Picking up his phone, he made appointments to go talk to the people on his list.

He figured he could just talk to Debbie's boss on the phone. So, when the clock turned nine, Eric called her workplace and had a quick talk with him. He confirmed what Eden had already told him in terms of the two women being the best of friends.

They appeared to have been close friends for decades. Eric didn't see any real issues between them, but he had no way of knowing for sure yet.

He did confirm that Debbie had submitted notice that she was quitting, which she had done by text, something her boss most definitely did not appreciate. And, when the boss tried to talk Debbie out of it, to give it some time, she had been adamant.

"Honestly, Detective, she was quite belligerent, and I had never experienced that side of her. I'm not at all sure how I feel about it, now that she is dead, but nothing quite like people quitting and airing grievances to bring out aspects of their personality which you hadn't seen before," he explained. "I was quite surprised. Stunned, really, and I was also terrified that Eden would quit too."

"Would she have done it?"

"They tended to do a lot of things together, although Eden is typically quite stable."

"Do you think Eden would have been jealous of her friend having this new relationship?"

"Jealous? No, I think she would have been more wary than anything," the boss clarified. "Debbie had a history of making poor relationship choices and some very flamboyant decisions."

"So, Debbie has done this before?"

"Not that I want to share details that are not mine to share, but I have given her several days off in order to settle up some relationships that had become, … let's say, very difficult," he replied. "So, I imagine, from Eden's perspective, it was more about trying to stop Debbie from moving too quickly and from getting in over her head again."

Which is just what Eden had said. Eric marked that down in his notebook, thanked the man for his time, then called to speak to the man who had set all this in motion. *Richard Santino.*

When Richard answered, Eric explained who he was and heard another agitated voice whispering in the background. When he asked what was going on, Mr. Santino told him that he was putting his phone on Speaker because his brother, Rinaldo, was also with him. Eric introduced himself again and asked both men to take a moment to explain who they were and how they came to know Debbie Kingston.

Richard sounded distraught. "It's absolutely awful," he

muttered. "I called in for a wellness check. I was worried when she didn't call me after she'd gotten home, and then I couldn't get an answer, but to hear she was dead?" He left it at that.

Eric did note a lot of emotions were packed in his tone.

Richard sniffled once, twice, and his brother mumbled something to him, sounding tense.

"Look," Rinaldo added, "this is an absolutely horrible thing. I have no idea what happened to her, but I can tell you that she was a lovely person."

Eric listened intently to see if anything was in their voices that sounded off. Either they were professional liars or they had no knowledge of Debbie's death. Considering that they were in the business of sales—essentially selling themselves—Eric imagined the brothers couldn't afford any blemish on their reputations and likely would do a lot to keep themselves out of it. Eric could certainly understand that, as long as they were free and clear. They both had alibis, but, as Eden had pointed out, those alibis weren't strong, since they had each provided an alibi for the other— which in Eric's mind crossed both out.

He asked Rinaldo a few questions, and then talked to Richard specifically.

Trying to get his brother Rinaldo to stay out of the conversation was a little hard because he kept jumping in, trying to answer for Richard.

"Can you tell me exactly the nature of your relationship with her?" he asked Richard.

Richard sniffled a couple times, before answering. "We had just met that weekend, and she was the loveliest person whom I have ever known. I had really hoped it was the start of a beautiful relationship." Then tears erupted once again.

Not a lot, just a few, enough that gave the impression of being sincere, but also gave the impression that everything was on par and yet maybe a little superficial.

"I don't know what anybody has told you," Richard added, "but I can tell you that she had a big argument with a friend, and that was very difficult for her. But we fell in love. And when you fall in love," he stated, "you have to follow your heart."

"And what were your plans from here on in then?"

"We were going to take it slow and steady. We obviously wanted to spend as much time together as we could. I had planned to go to her place the following weekend, so we would spend as much time as we could getting to know each other. We weren't making any definite plans for the future," he pointed out, "but I didn't really want to let go of an opportunity—in case she was the one."

Rinaldo spoke up. "Obviously this is very stressful for my brother. I'm also very concerned about our name. I know it may sound cynical, but any association of our company with a case such as this, … it can tarnish our reputation."

"Yeah, but, if you haven't done anything, it shouldn't matter," Eric replied.

"Public perception is a fickle thing," Rinaldo stated, his tone pointed. "I'm sure you can understand that we want to confirm this is kept very low-key."

"Of course," Eric noted in a noncommittal voice. "At the moment, we're not even sure that a crime has been committed."

At that, Richard whispered, "I really hope not. She caught a ride with another attendee because Debbie had a bunch of stuff to sort out, and I perfectly understood that. It had been a whirlwind for me too." He choked back a sigh.

"This is our company, after all," he said, with a heavy sigh. "Sometimes doing this work takes a toll on us, and sometimes it's pure joy. And right now, when something like this happens, I have to be very aware of how much negative energy is surrounding me."

"But it's not necessarily negative energy surrounding *you*," his brother clarified. "We just have to confirm we meditate, stay in our own bubble, and try not to let this affect us. Plus sending as much loving light energy to Debbie and her eternal soul."

Eric's eyebrows shot up. Was that even possible? If you fell head over heels for somebody, and she suddenly died, how could that *not* affect you? But he didn't say anything. It wasn't his place to offer anything, just to get answers. He sat silent, waiting to see what would happen next.

"You're right, Rinaldo," Richard murmured, followed by a heavy emotional sigh. "When we go home, we can light a candle for her."

Again it was on the tip of Eric's tongue to ask what good that would do, but he also didn't want to sound like an asshole. That could potentially shut down the very lines of communication he was working on building. There may not be any need for any of this, but he also couldn't be sure, and he may well need the little rapport he had established with these men for future communications.

With the contact information on the attendee who drove Debbie home that weekend, Eric ended the call and then placed the next one.

"She was silent almost the whole way home," Susan offered. "I was okay with that as I was pretty chill myself. I dropped her off outside her apartment and left to go home to my husband and kids."

Eric asked several more questions. Susan hadn't met Debbie before the meditation weekend but had been happy to give her a ride home as they lived near each other. Once home, Susan hadn't gone out again and thankfully her husband confirmed it.

So, all in all, another dead end.

CHAPTER 3

EDEN COULDN'T HELP herself. She picked up her phone, and, as soon as Eric answered, she asked, "Did you get the autopsy results?"

"Good morning," he muttered, yawning.

She winced and quickly checked the time. "Sorry, I guess it's a little early."

"Yes, it absolutely is a little early," he confirmed, "particularly when that is also not my only case. I was out working on another case into the wee hours last night."

This time she really did wince. "Okay, … well, I'm really sorry."

"Hey, don't let me pressure you into feeling sorry," he quipped, but enough laughter filled his tone that she realized he wasn't angry with her.

"I should have at least looked at the clock."

"What time is it?" he asked, as another yawn engulfed him.

"It's seven."

"Is it really?" he asked. "Dang, I guess I got some sleep then after all."

"Good, I'm glad somebody did," she muttered. "So what about my question?"

"I have no idea if we have the autopsy results back or not," he admitted. "Again, I'm not awake, and, as of last night, we did not have them. If they're in now, I don't know yet because I haven't had a chance to check my emails, because—"

She groaned. "Let me guess, because I just woke you up and because you're not up and moving yet?"

"Nope, I'm sure not," he stated, with a chuckle. "I will do my best to get there soon though."

"Right," she muttered. "Will you call me back and let me know?"

"I will," he said, his voice gentling, "and, just so you know, I won't even call at seven in the morning."

"You could though," she pointed out. She needed him to understand what she was going through, without telling him that. "I haven't had a good night's sleep since."

"I'm sorry to hear that," he replied, "but remember that we don't know that the autopsy will give us any definite answers."

"I understand, but that in itself will be an answer."

"But not an easy one," he noted. "I mean, we want answers. We want to know how, why, when, and by whom, but we don't always get that. Particularly in the world I live in, we often don't get anything even close to that."

"I don't think I could do your job," she muttered.

He paused, and, when he spoke, his tone was serious. "I never did ask you what you did for work."

"I'm a graphic designer and work part-time at home but go into the office for one to two days a week."

"Does that give you enough work to survive?"

She gave a brutal laugh. "What constitutes making a living can be subjective these days, but there is more than plenty of work, as long as my brain is functioning enough to do it," she clarified. "I used to work remotely, until everybody was ordered back into the office. I decided I didn't want to burn the midnight oil anymore, but, of course, the work-life balance thing comes at a cost," she conceded. "And now, when something like this happens, the cost is even higher because it's much harder to get my act together and to produce, especially when I'm devastated over a turn of events that I'm not ready to accept."

"Of course," he acknowledged. "However, I don't want to sound the alarm, but you do need to be prepared for the fact that there may never be any answers, other than just the reality that she's dead."

Eden considered that and then sighed. "I know that's a possibility," she acknowledged, "but you're right. I'm not at all ready to accept that."

"I hear that," he said. "I have seen enough to know that grief is a hard thing to make peace with. Anyway, let me wake up, have some coffee, check my emails, and get into the office." She heard him moving around on the other end. "Then I will give you a call."

"Fine," she muttered, ending the call. She wasn't exactly the nicest to him, considering she needed his help. However, she wasn't doing very well at currying any favors right now.

It was so damn hard to sit here and wait, knowing that other people had access to information and didn't seem to be particularly bothered to share it. Then she chastised herself for that assumption.

"Don't be an idiot," she muttered. "You don't know anything about what Eric was doing or about the other cases he's working on." He was a detective in a big station. Of course he would be working on multiple cases at the same time.

She got up and poured herself a second cup of coffee and

sat back down, staring at the work in front of her. She really did have work to do, but it was so darn hard to focus, and yet she *abso-fucking-lutely* needed to because this would not be an easy week if she couldn't get her act together.

She had things that needed her attention, and dealing with work wouldn't come easy when she didn't have any interest in doing it.

Knowing she needed to do something to switch this all around—and realizing just how far behind in her work she was—she got up, walked into her living room, and turned on the music that she preferred. In this case it was sound bowls. Then she dropped herself onto a yoga mat and into a light meditation, her entire focus on trying to get back on track with her work. She couldn't do anything for Debbie at this point, but Eden definitely needed to do something for herself. When she finally pulled back out of it, she heard her phone ringing.

She glanced down, surprised to see it was Eric. "Hello," she said, her voice still almost disengaged from the world around her.

"Are you okay?" he asked sharply.

She gave her head a shake. "Yes, yes, of course."

"Did I ... disturb you or something?"

"Or something," she replied, a note of humor in her tone. "I was literally just coming out of a meditation."

He paused, then asked, "You do that too, *huh*?"

"What do you mean *too*?"

"Every once in a while, when I can't get any work done," he began, "I drop into a meditation in order to clear my head and to change everything going on around me."

"Yes, that's exactly what I was trying to do. I've been unable to focus on my work, and I needed to pull it together.

I've still got bills to pay, and I have a commitment to my employer, but Debbie's death has all been so very distressing. It's been difficult."

"It might be distressing, but having your own life fall to pieces because of what happened to Debbie won't help anyone."

"You can preach that all day long," she countered, "yet it doesn't change the fact that I still need answers. My mind won't quit churning this over and over." She didn't tell him how her mind always did this, filling with thoughts seemingly out of nowhere.

"I did get a partial autopsy report back."

"Anything you can tell me, and why partial?"

"We don't yet have the tox screen back, but no obvious cause of death was found, which we told you already. Nothing suspicious was found in the autopsy. For all intents and purposes, her heart just stopped, which—considering her pre-existing heart condition ..."

Eden stared down at the phone, not sure what to say to that.

"Are you okay?" Eric asked.

She shrugged, trying hard to shake off the feeling of despair. "Does that really happen?" Her voice shook and broke.

"Yes, not often, but we do sometimes have autopsy results where we find absolutely no cause of death. However, considering the number of pill bottles beside her, we're assuming that will be the cause, but we won't know until the tox screen results come in."

Eden was silent for a long moment.

"Obviously, at this point, we're waiting for the tox screen to know exactly what she took or ... was given."

"It just never occurred to me that this would happen.

She was the opposite of suicidal. Someone else must be involved."

"If we can't prove it," he began, "then this goes nowhere."

She was stunned and could only stare down at the phone. "But that's so … wrong."

"It might be wrong," he conceded, "but again it all comes down to what we can prove. So, if we find no proof of any wrongdoing, I can do absolutely nothing about it."

She closed her eyes and sank back, tears wanting to rip through her. Yet, for the most part, she was able to hold them back as she contemplated everything he just shared.

"I know that's not what you want to hear, and, until we get that tox screen, we won't have anything more conclusive to go by."

"So, what then? It's just *case closed*? What does that mean?" she whispered.

"Not necessarily," he clarified. "You need to wait and let us figure it out. I do have to talk to the team and see if anything pops up, but I will need a cause of death first." He took a deep breath and added, "And I can't just create that out of nothing."

"So, you can't prove murder if you don't have a cause of death?" she asked.

He thought about it and replied, "Murder may have been done here, but we would have to prove that they did something first, and then try to find the way that whoever may have done this … if somebody did this," he corrected emphatically. "It is something that I would have to look at from a completely different angle. Nothing about this is easy."

"No, it's not," she grumbled. "Believe me that I know

that." She heard his heavy sigh and added, "I'm not trying to make this a bigger deal than it is."

"Are you sure?" he asked, with a note of half-hearted humor. "I mean, I get it. She's your friend. She's dead, and you can't quite accept what happened here."

"It's got nothing to do with the way of it all," she declared, "but it would be very hard for me to accept that she's just gone, with no reason, with no explanation as to what happened."

"And I get that. I really do. You're not the first person to have somebody die and to not know how or why."

"No, I might not be the first, and I understand that." She paused. "So now you'll try and tell me that this happens, and, yes, it's a shame, but you can't do anything about it?"

"Don't jump the gun just yet. I will do whatever I can do, … if there is anything I can do," he stated, his tone firm. "I'll get off the phone now. If I have news, I will contact you." Without saying anything else, he ended the call.

She sank back, tears collecting in the corners of her eyes. She looked around the room. "I don't know what the hell happened, Debbie," she wailed, "but I'm not giving up yet."

She sensed a soft, gentle wind blowing through her space, yet knew it wasn't real. When she meditated, she knew to always expect the chance of something much softer, much gentler coming toward her. So this feeling of a soft, gentle wind was meant to soothe her soul. However, right now, all she felt was conflict, so harsh and hard to even contemplate that her friend had been murdered.

But then again, her "peaceful" death didn't make sense either. How did somebody, just thirty-two years old and in her prime, up and die?

People had to die from something, and the doctor saying

her heart just stopped wouldn't cut it, no matter how true it might appear to them.

ERIC WALKED INTO the office, and his partner looked over at him. Cody Kar, while brilliant, was not the most considerate. He was rough around the edges, abrasive even.

"Hey," Cody greeted him. "Got the preliminary autopsy report on your one case." He waved a file at him.

"Yeah, I saw it. I called her friend."

"Yeah, I'm sure that was fun."

"No, it sure wasn't. She's of the opinion that her friend was murdered."

"She might think that, but that doesn't mean we have anything to go on to prove such a thing," Cody pointed out. "With no indication of a clear path to move forward, you and I both know there won't be funding to continue this case."

"No, there sure won't," Eric conceded, with a nod, "and the department will stick to that."

"You're not kidding," he muttered. "So, barring new information, we need to focus on my case anyway."

"I know. I can't even believe the shit we get up to. So, we've got some asshole walking into women's bedrooms, even though they've got tight security, raping and murdering them while in their own beds."

"Not to mention that they are then tucked up way too nice. Safe in a way."

"And yet not safe apparently," Eric muttered. They both just looked at each other, frowning, because this was the case everybody hated.

"We have no idea why these individuals were selected.

We have no idea if the rapist had some process to his crimes, which we don't understand yet. No idea about anything really."

"What about forensics?"

"No forensics either."

"Figures," Eric muttered. "How the hell are these guys always getting away without leaving any forensic information behind?" he muttered. "Just a little bit to help us out would be great."

Cody laughed. "Yeah, just a bit would be great, but you and I both know that a little bit won't necessarily show up. These cases are getting a little harder every time, it seems."

Captain Louis interjected, as he walked past, "Which makes us believe that this guy has done this before."

"Agreed," Eric muttered, "and that just makes it even more imperative to catch him this time."

"Yeah, well, where are you at?" A crease formed in the captain's forehead.

Both Eric and Cody had an idea what was coming if the answers weren't just right.

Eric began, "We went through all the case files last night."

Cody added, at his side, "And we talked to the neighbors, who had nothing to say. Basically they heard nothing, saw nothing, and the latest victim wasn't the kind of person to invite trouble."

"Nice lady is all you got?"

"She was a teacher, and nobody has any idea why she would have been targeted," Eric replied, knowing full well that it would piss the hell out of Captain Louis. Eric continued. "She lived alone, had no enemies, and never caused a ruckus. Nobody would have thought to even worry about her because she was always home, safe and sound."

"But somebody noticed her," the captain barked, "and somebody kept an eye on her, and somebody decided that she would suit quite nicely." The captain's tone was harsh. "We need to catch that somebody before he turns around and does this all over again."

"I'm not arguing with you," Cody noted, "but, so far, it's too early in the investigation to say much of anything about it, Cap."

Just then Meghan walked by, nodding at him awkwardly. "I'm about to broaden this quite a bit more for you," she began.

"And how is that?" Cody asked.

"I found similar cases in the last two years." She turned to Cody. "You did ask me to look."

"How many?" Cody asked sharply.

"Three."

"Could be just a coincidence," Eric suggested, his gaze moving from Cody to Cap, then back at Meghan, and she just shrugged. Eric frowned. "So, are we really thinking this guy has done this at least three other times plus our two open ones and not been caught? How? Why?"

"I don't know," she stated, as she stared at him. "That's for you guys to sort out. All I can tell you is that I went looking for anything potentially connected, like, *too clean*, and this is what I came up with." She handed out copies of the files to each of the three men.

Eric glanced through these files and groaned. "That would be really, really shitty if these are all connected."

"It is possible. They were all young women, all lived alone, and all in town."

Eric interjected, "But they weren't all in the same boat,

from what I recall."

"There are a lot of different circumstances," Meghan pitched in, her tone critical. "On one, the boyfriend was a very good suspect, which you'll see when you read the case, but they never could come up with the evidence to charge him. So, maybe, maybe not." She half shrugged and pointed. "I think these are all viable."

"If you think they're viable," the captain noted, "then we need to take them seriously. Better get to work reading those cases." He gave a nod to Eric and Cody.

Eric took the stack of paperwork, walked over to his desk, and sat down. If these three were really connected cases, that was bad news. He looked over at Cody. "How the hell could we have missed all these?"

"If they're all connected," Cody replied, frowning, "then it's not the kind of connections we're usually looking for. It's got to be something different."

"But one was a suspected boyfriend, John Jones—which that name alone always seemed fishy to me—so I remember reading the initial investigation on that case. Plus, his mugshot, with all that facial hair and the messy long hair, made him look as if he was wearing a disguise, don't you think?" He frowned as he opened the file in his hand. "They had a really ugly breakup, and the boyfriend had an alibi, but it was his brother, so nobody really trusted his alibi. Yet they also never found any connection to John Jones. No forensic evidence, no criminal history, no nothing. He's still got eyes on him periodically and is still considered a suspect."

"Okay," Cody noted, "but being a suspect is nothing. Outside of being in a very shitty situation, it doesn't prove anything, and it's not something we can ever take to court."

"Agreed, and we have absolutely nothing viable to present in court on this current one of mine either," Eric pointed out. "We have to take another look at each one of these cases. So let's go back to the beginning and start with fresh eyes."

He got up, walked over to a large map on the wall, and pulled out a few pins because he needed to see Debbie's murder in relation to these three rape-murders that may somehow all be connected. "I know there's no visible connection but… Let's map the locations for Debbie's death and these three other victims just in case. Add in the one from six months ago and our new one. These killers hunt in a certain area and won't change that, as long as they are still finding victims. Also I'll set up a whiteboard with these three other cases and their suspects, if any. Let's see what they have in common."

It didn't take long for them to realize that all the cases were committed within a few miles of each other. Including Debbie's case…

As a matter of fact, it formed a nice, neat, and tidy square when they looked on the map. "Well, crap," Eric grumbled. "Looking at these cases in this way, it does seem that we have a connection."

Staring up at the wall, Eric quickly added sticky notes with time of day, age of the female victim, occupation, and the fact that they were or were not in relationships, and that resulted in several more easily identifiable links. The two detectives stared at it and shook their heads. Then Eric added pictures of the victims—all young, short-haired brunettes, just like Debbie. "So, now we can possibly see Debbie as our fourth victim of this same guy. However, no rape was involved here which makes it an anomaly and that's concerning."

"I would agree with that," Cody stated.

Two other men in the department walked over and took a look. Then the discussion got hot very quickly. They were pretty fired up, their voices raised and faces red, when the captain joined them.

"Okay, so it looks as if we have a serial rapist and killer here," Louis stated, as he stared at the data. "But why the hell did it take us so long to put that together?"

Eric looked from him to the wall, shaking his head. He offered, "Because the cases cross different precincts. Only one of these prior rape-murder cases is one we handled. That's deliberate. And now the current murder—no rape— on Debbie is a timeline difference. Each of these are almost a year apart only now they are getting closer in time. The next one could be only four months away. Just finding out that we didn't even know about these others, and now here we are, with potentially a fourth victim, is pissing me off."

"Gentlemen, this is a hot mess," the captain declared, his tone sharp. "Figure out this shit, and be quick about it."

CHAPTER 4

EDEN HEADED TO bed that night, weary and weeping, her grief warring with her anger at how things had been left between her and Debbie.

Eden had spoken to several of their mutual friends about it, and they had reminded her that Debbie's personality changes with her other relationships—although minor compared to this blowup—had been very similar. It seemed that Debbie thought, if she sent away all her female friends, she wouldn't have to worry about them competing for her new heartthrob's attention. As Eden looked back, she realized that she'd never been around at the onset of Debbie's other love affairs either.

Having these difficult thoughts at bedtime was never a good idea, and Eden's sleep was anything but peaceful. She got down on the floor to meditate because she needed some time to herself.

Soon she walked calmly in the pasture, determined to let her meditation mantra in her head surround her, waft all over and through her, becoming something that just drifted away, along with all the other monkey mind thoughts that were driving through her.

She wasn't asleep; she wasn't awake. She was caught in between, in a meditation where she was trying to let go of all her thoughts that would never leave her alone, particularly this one.

That's because I'm not a thought, Debbie's meditative voice whispered, soft and gentle, so unlike the voice that screamed into Eden's nightmares. *That's because right now you're reaching out for me, but you're not hearing me.*

This isn't happening, Eden muttered and groaned.

It is happening, repeated the same voice, in the same tone, but there was an edge to it now.

Groaning, Eden tried to shove her thoughts further away from her brain, so she could sink deeper into the meditation. It was so hard, and meditating was never something that came naturally to her because her mind always moved a mile a minute. She was typically twenty steps ahead and kept her life organized because she liked the order, the grounded assurance, and the calm that came with preparedness. Debbie's way of life was more one of chaos. And grief was hard, but this seemed to be getting worse instead of better, as Debbie seemed to be dominating Eden's world.

That's because you're not paying any attention to me, so I have to keep bugging you.

And yet that wasn't true because the one thing Eden was doing right now was giving Debbie attention, even though Eden was trying not to. The more she tried to stop, the more it seemed to get worse.

Laughter resounded in the background, and, for the most part, she recognized it as Debbie's laughter, and that was killing Eden. At times she wondered if she was losing her mind.

She finally swiped down the meditation app that had been guiding her deeper and deeper into the unknown, where she would relax and de-stress. She was trying, but relaxing wasn't easy for her. Her thoughts always took over.

Yet it was a foreign concept that anything would help.

What in the world helps you deal with the death of a friend, but keeps you hearing her voice even after she is gone?

Eden got up and walked to the kitchen. Just then she heard laughter behind her, and she froze for a moment. Then she turned and looked around. "That's a new trick." She glanced down to see the goose bumps on her arms. She wasn't sure this was progress or a good step forward. In fact, it was on the creepy side.

She picked up her pace into the kitchen and put on the teakettle, standing close to it, hovering almost. It seemed as if the warmth helped a little to ease back the chill settling around her almost constantly now.

She glanced around the small kitchen, wondering if she had imagined the creepy sound in her house. And why was it creepy when it was Debbie's laughter? That made no sense either.

None of this did. Eden wished it would all go away.

I'm not going away, Debbie's voice snapped. And, as if on cue, the kitchen door opened, then slammed shut, right in front of her. Eden spun around in shock.

I was murdered, and it's up to you to prove it.

Papers she had on her coffee table in full sight in the nearby living room now lifted and swirled in the madness, as if a huge wind had joined the party. She bolted toward an exit, opening the front door, when it slammed shut in her face, stopping her in her tracks.

She was stunned, partly from her contact with the door, but, even through all the chaos, she heard Debbie's final words.

Or else …

CHAPTER 5

THE NEXT MORNING Eden woke up tired and worn out, with a small bruise on her face from hitting the door, but also with a determination to move forward. Her sleep had been rough, but she'd managed short bouts, only to wake up and look around in fear. Now that morning was here, she knew she needed help. This couldn't continue. She also had to deal with Debbie's estate. Even if there was no clear path, nothing to explain the chaos she had experienced last night, she had to deal with Debbie's worldly items.

Debbie didn't have any possessions of value, so Eden didn't think probate was needed. However, she would need to consult somebody about it. Debbie just had a rented apartment, and, if she had actually canceled the lease, chances were, she was due to be out of the apartment soon.

A couple phone calls later, Eden had the grim news. Frank, Debbie's apartment manager, had given Eden three days to clean out the apartment, if she planned to remove anything. The landlord wanted her to remove all Debbie's belongings. Otherwise he would bring in a cleaning company, charge her for that expense, and everything would go to the dump. The thought of Debbie's possessions hitting the dump without a care was traumatic to Eden.

When she explained that Debbie had passed away, a moment of silence came from the manager.

"Interesting, but you still have only three days left."

He didn't seem to be bothered at all by Debbie's passing. But then again, why would he even care? Eden got that, but it still stung like hell.

Frank continued. "She canceled the lease—without prior notice. She only had the place month-to-month, but she was supposed to give me one month's notice, so I could charge her for that as well."

"She didn't have any money," Eden pointed out.

"No, of course not," he muttered in disgust. "When do they ever? Clean it out by the end of the three days, or else I'll have to do it myself and will charge you for it and for the extra month." With that, he ended the call with her.

Eden didn't know what the renter's rights were in this case, but, with these additional fees and a three-day deadline, it didn't make any sense to prolong things. It wouldn't make this easier. On the contrary, it would literally just extend the suffering and pain.

She hadn't yet heard when Debbie's body would be released, so she sent a text to Eric, asking if he knew. She got a text back about thirty minutes later, telling her to expect two days. She wasn't even sure why they needed Debbie's body for an extra two days but whatever. Eden had enough on her plate right now anyway. She headed over to Debbie's apartment, and, as she walked upstairs, she stopped, not sure if she was allowed to go in. She phoned Eric just to confirm it was all aboveboard. "I'm over at Debbie's apartment right now. Can I go in? Is there any reason not to?"

"No reason not to. I presume you have a key."

"Yes, I have a key, and the landlord wants everything out within three days. He basically told me that he would dump whatever I don't remove and would charge me for it, plus for the added month that she was supposed to give as notice."

A moment of silence passed on Eric's end, and then he said, "I don't know what his rights are."

"Debbie canceled her lease, and I guess they had a hell of a rip-roaring fight about it. She's losing her deposit, but the manager agreed that she could go, so I don't know. Anyway, I'm tired, worn out, and already … Well, I've just arrived, but it occurred to me that it might still be considered a crime scene."

"No, you're cleared to go in."

She had to fight the urge to protest, but he was right.

"I've got to go."

When he ended the call, she stared down at her phone. He thought this wasn't a crime scene because no crime had been committed. But he was wrong. Definitely a crime had been committed here, but she had no way to prove it.

Tired, she pulled out her key and quickly opened the door. The neighbor popped her head out as soon as she got the door open and asked, "Hey, what's going on? I saw cops and an ambulance here. Is Debbie okay? I'm Kali, by the way."

Eden looked back at her, opting for a variation of the truth. "Debbie went to bed one night and never woke up. So, I am here to clean out her apartment."

Kali's face widened in shock. "Oh my goodness, oh my goodness, oh my goodness!"

Eden nodded. "I'm feeling very much that way myself right now."

"Of course you are." Kali had tears in her eyes, but the last thing Eden needed was pity. "Oh, that's horrible." The neighbor lady came closer. "I just don't understand."

"Neither do I," Eden conceded. Then she gave her a

small smile and added, "But I only have three days to get her apartment cleaned out. Otherwise it'll all go to the dump." When Kali's eyes widened in horror, Eden nodded. "That came directly from the landlord this morning. On the other hand, apparently Debbie abruptly turned in her notice without the required thirty days' advance notice, so he needs to get it available to rent again."

"You poor thing."

"Yeah, not something I ever expected to be doing," she muttered. "I don't even know what I'm doing here, but"—she shrugged—"it seemed wrong to just leave Debbie's things for the landlord to send to the dump. I basically came to see if anything needed cleaning out."

"You should just take what you want, dear," she suggested, patting Eden on the shoulder, "then leave the rest to him. If he'll act like that, he might as well just pay to have it all cleaned out."

Eden nodded. "If I have further arguments with him, that's exactly what I'll do."

"I would do it anyway," Kali noted in a confiding whisper. "It's not as if he cares about any of us." The neighbor lady returned to her apartment.

Eden muttered, "Right. I do know that."

In fact, she and Debbie had laughed about her landlord many times. Never in anybody's corner, always cranky, miserable, and acting as if the world owed him—which Eden had little patience for. Yet that's just the way her life was right now.

Inside Debbie's apartment now, Eden felt the tears welling up in her eyes.

A bottle of wine remained on the counter that the two of them had split several nights ago, as they had discussed plans for the future, such as possible trips to take this year, anything to break up the boredom of their lives. As Eden picked up the wine bottle and walked it over to the garbage, she wished she could have any of those moments back again, anything that would help her recoup the relationship she had had with her best friend.

Debbie had been very special in so many ways, but the way she'd acted at the weekend retreat, so adamant and so sure that she was doing absolutely the right thing—with zero room for doubt, for change—was just the way it was with her. Eden went to work in the kitchen area, tossing all the food into the garbage and lugging multiple bags down to the trash chute to get rid of.

By the time she had a box of stuff to take home and multiple other boxes dumped—literally upended into the chute—she began to feel as if she were getting somewhere. Still, a couch and a couple chairs remained, plus a coffee table and a lamp. She didn't know if anybody locally needed them.

She certainly didn't, and no way she would lug them out of here. That was way-too-much work, weight, and pain. That's what it all came down to, the pain.

She resolutely headed to the one room she had been avoiding the entire time—the bedroom, where Debbie had died. Eden went through the kitchen first, got the living room emptied out next, except for the larger pieces of furniture, and then worked on the bathroom, full of so many girly things that kept her in tears. The special shampoos Debbie bought so religiously the conditioner she spent God-only-knows-how-much money on—that she didn't really have—yet she always had to have that conditioner. Eden knew another woman would understand, but, for a lot of people, it was way too confusing to sort out. The bathroom was emotional but fairly easy, since most of it just needed to be upended into the garbage.

With that done, Eden stepped into the bedroom, and there she stopped, feeling the biggest onslaught of tears of the day. Clothes were on the bed. Clothes were on the floor. Clothes were everywhere, as Debbie had obviously packed, unpacked, and then packed again, as if not knowing exactly what she would do with anything or how to get the right clothing packed for this new life of hers. Yet her bag packed for the weekend seminar seemed to be untouched. Eden frowned, then realized that her own bag remained unpacked too, even though she had done some laundry. That was how messed-up Eden had been when she reached home.

Determined to get through this project before she completely broke down, she went through the clothing in Debbie's closet. Some of the clothes were Eden's, and she shook her head as she noted just how many of them were here at Debbie's.

Grabbing a couple suitcases and anything else she could use, Eden opened them up and packed them with things going back to her house. Anything that she wanted to keep as a remembrance, she packed. At the end, Eden still had several bags of extra clothing that she would take to charity.

Eden loaded up her car, making multiple trips with suitcases and all the rest, then headed back up for the bedding, with so many things still on her mind.

The landlord caught her on the last round and asked, "Are you done yet?"

She stared at him, blank for a moment. "No, I'm not," she replied, when she finally could speak. "I'm not moving the furniture out." When he glared at her, she shrugged.

"You could always rent it as furnished."

"Let me come see." He walked upstairs, took one look, and snorted. "It's hardly decent."

"It might not be decent by your standards, but it's all Debbie had," Eden stated. "So, a little bit of niceness from you would go a long way."

He shrugged. "She wasn't my friend. What do I care?"

Eden winced at that because he was right. Debbie wasn't his friend. But then he obviously wouldn't have any friends with that attitude either. She didn't say anything, just grabbing two more bags from the bedroom and bringing them out. "I think this will be it."

"You have to clean it out."

"The bottom line of breaking the lease is that Debbie loses her deposit and you end up cleaning it with those funds. I've already removed her personal stuff."

"Not this furniture though, have you?" he snorted, raising his voice. "Somebody's got to clean this place, and it ain't gonna be me."

She didn't say anything, just stared at him. She was so exhausted that no way she could even contemplate getting involved in moving furniture too. She shrugged and grabbed the other bags, but he stepped in her way.

"You have to clean it. Otherwise you're not going anywhere."

She frowned at him, trying hard to let go of her anger. "Keep the furniture," she suggested, "as payment in lieu of anything you may feel she still owed you. Other than that, you are welcome to go to her grave site and to scream and rant at her because God knows I have nothing more to tell you about what to do with any of this."

He started yelling in response, but, just as suddenly, another voice cut through the din.

There was the detective, glaring at the landlord. "What is the meaning of this?" Eric snapped.

Frank glared at him and asked, "Who the fuck are you?"

Eric pulled out his official ID, and Frank's attitude improved right away. He was still red in the face, but his tone was modulated. "It's these people who don't pay their rent and who cancel their lease without notice, Detective. You should be taking care of them, not shouting at me."

At that, Eden snapped, "What you really mean is, people die and don't leave an empty, clean apartment."

"You're supposed to clean it."

"No, I'm not. That's not my job. From what I understand of Debbie's lease, she cleans it or she loses her deposit. And you've already told me that you would not be refunding her deposit," she declared, glaring at him. She turned to look at the detective.

The landlord, who realized that this wasn't the time or the place, swung past them both and disappeared down the hallway, muttering.

Eric quickly joined her as she stood in the living room, her back to the wall, trying hard not to start crying again. "Are you okay?"

She nodded wearily. "I'm exhausted. I've been going through her stuff all day, but Frank still thinks I'm responsible for cleaning the unit, for removing the furniture, for another month's rent." She stared around, barely functioning as it was.

"Frank can deal with that himself, I'm sure," Eric replied.

"Maybe, but you heard him."

"Does he know where you live or have your contact information?"

"Maybe," she said, with a shrug. "He won't care either way. I told him that he could keep the furniture, but I think he wants it out of here."

Just then a timid knock came at the open door, and there was the neighbor, Kali, again. "I don't know if you're getting rid of any of her furniture," she began, "but I could really use a couple pieces."

Eden considered that, not sure what to say.

Kali continued. "I don't want to sound greedy, and I know it's disrespectful to even bring it up when we're dealing with somebody who just passed away, but … I'm so sorry. I shouldn't have come. Never mind."

Eden stepped forward and said, "No, it's fine. Look around and see if anything interests you. I know that you were friends with her, and Debbie wouldn't mind in the least."

"I prefer to think she wouldn't mind," Kali added gratefully, "and I really could use them, even the bed." She shrugged. "I know it's creepy because she died in that bed, but I've been sleeping on the floor, so that doesn't bother me the least."

At that, Eric offered, "I can drag some of this over for you."

Eden added, "I can help. I can pick up one end." Then she looked over at Kali and swung an arm around the room. "What pieces would you like?"

Kali nodded, a sheen in her eyes. "I would take all of it. I hate to admit it, but I've been through some tough times recently."

With that, Eden and Eric each grabbed one end of the couch, and the two of them walked the couch into the apartment next door. Kali hadn't been kidding. She literally had a series of cushions on the floor. It didn't take long for them to move all of Debbie's furniture into Kali's place.

As Kali softly smiled in complete delight, she looked at Eden and nodded. "I'm so sorry Debbie is gone, but I so appreciate her furniture."

"I understand," Eden replied. "We are all sorry to hear about this, but, on the other hand, she would much rather you get this than have it all go to the dump. This way is much better. So, you enjoy it and don't even bother telling Frank that you got it. He wanted it all cleaned out anyway," she stated, with a laugh.

"No, no, I would never. He's already on the rampage over something," Kali shared. "So I would just as soon not speak to him anyway."

With the removal of Debbie's furniture, including her bed, Debbie's apartment was empty. Eden had kept the vacuum to do a quick cleanup, and that's what she did right now. When she was finally done, she pulled Debbie's keys off her keychain and placed them on the kitchen counter, holding back the tears. Sadly, with one last look, she turned to leave and realized that Eric still stood right here. "Do you still need me?" she asked.

"Did you go through her belongings from the seminar?"

"Debbie didn't seem to unpack them, so her bags are in my car," she noted. "I haven't even opened them. I figured it was something I could do at home, and I just wanted to get out of here."

He nodded. "Would you mind if I come take a look?"

She stared at him. "I thought you said there was no case."

"Technically there isn't a case, but I realized that I

hadn't done that, so I want to at least check to confirm that's all as expected."

She shrugged and nodded. "Sure, that's fine. My car is loaded up, and I'm heading over to my place right now. I do want to get out of here before the building super comes back."

"Debbie's place has been cleaned out, and you vacuumed," he pointed out, with a smile. "Anything else that Frank wants done, he can do himself. He's already keeping the deposit, and, from the looks of it, there is no damage, so he's coming out okay." With that, he motioned at her and said, "Let's head over to your place, and you can relax a little bit."

She had a prompt retort ready, but it never left her lips. She was just too tired. Nodding, she replied, "Fine, but I hope you're not planning on staying long. I'm way too tired."

"Have you eaten today?"

"No. I figured coming over here would make my stomach sick, so I didn't want to make it worse by eating."

"Of course not," he agreed. "Head on home. I'll be there in a few minutes." With that, they locked and closed the door to Debbie's apartment behind them and walked out.

ERIC STOPPED BY the local Chinese food joint and picked up a selection of food. He hadn't eaten, and it was obvious Eden hadn't either. She was also at the end of her rope, from what he could see. Tired and stressed, plus emotionally she was all over the place as well. Nothing was easy about emptying the apartment of somebody you cared about, no matter the circumstances, but particularly when they had died and when you were looking for answers but there just weren't any.

He didn't even know why he came to Debbie's apartment. Just his instincts told him to come and take a look, not that there was an expectation of any wrongdoing. Still, he needed to dot that *I* and to cross that *T*, which in his world meant that he couldn't walk away in good conscience until he had made sure absolutely nothing else was going on here.

To have somebody go to bed and not wake up was already rough, but, given her age and overall health, which, according to the coroner, was much better than most, her death was troubling. She was young, in good shape, with good teeth, but somehow her heart had just stopped working. Drugs may have been in her system, yes, but he had no supporting evidence yet.

As he picked up the food and headed over to Eden's place, his phone rang.

He parked outside her house and answered the call. It was Captain Louis. "Captain, what's up?"

"Where are you?" he asked, his tone brisk.

"I am just outside of Eden's place."

"Why?" the captain asked sharply. "Anything breaking?"

"Nope, but she called earlier to confirm that she was okay to enter the apartment of the dead woman to clear it out. I realized that the luggage from the seminar trip was there, and I couldn't see where anybody had checked it for anything suspicious."

"And you think that's important?"

"I don't know if it's important or not, but I didn't check it. I wanted to take care of that so it can't bite me in the ass later."

"Do you know Stefan Kronos?"

"Yeah, a little. Why?"

"He just called."

Eric frowned, but what could he say to someone calling his captain?

"Stefan mentioned something, more of an offhand comment really, but I don't quite know what to make of it."

"What comment?" Eric perked up, still not sure where this was going.

"A strange request really. To link Debbie with other possibly connected dead women."

"I'm sorry, what?"

"Yeah, I don't understand it either. I did try to get more of an explanation, but I wasn't successful. He did say that he would call me back later, and he would do more digging, repeating that we should be connecting the dead women."

"Good God," Eric muttered. "By any chance did he mention how many dead women we have on our hands? I've heard that he has access to some ... interesting insights."

"Yeah, that's what I heard too. I tried to tell him no."

"How did that go?"

"He laughed at me and then told me that he had absolutely no confusion over which women. I have nothing on this guy. I have seen enough to know that he's withholding information. He ended the call, but I did get a promise. He did say he would get back to us."

Eric sat back in the front seat of his car, still parked in front of Eden's house. "Are we literally talking about Deborah Kingston and our three other serial killer rape-murder victims?"

"I don't know for sure. That's why I was hoping you had worked with him before. Do you know if he's always this, *uh*, curt?"

"I don't think he is," Eric replied. "I mean, I have heard about his craziness, but he's got a solid reputation. Still, we're just starting to look at a connection between cases."

"And yet there you are, heading over to look at Debbie's luggage."

"Sure, but that's just because I wanted to confirm we didn't miss anything."

"Guess what? You're now on task to confirm you didn't miss anything, and, if you did, to confirm that you don't miss anything now." With that, Captain Louis ended the call.

Not at all sure what the hell just happened, Eric exited his vehicle, picked up the Chinese food bags, and walked up to Eden's front door. It opened before he got there, and Eden frowned at him. However, when she saw the Chinese food, her face lit up. But the light died immediately.

Eric nodded. "I figured, since neither one of us had eaten, this might not be a bad idea."

She hesitated and then opened the door wider. "Thank you. I haven't been eating very much, to be honest." When he frowned at that, she just shrugged. "What am I supposed to say? Somebody I cared about is dead, and we have no answers, yet it feels very much like we should." He didn't say anything to that for a long moment. She stared at him and added, "I appreciate the fact that you haven't called me crazy."

He smiled. "Do you know anybody by the name of Stefan Kronos?"

She thought about it, then shook her head. "Not really. I've never met him. Debbie mentioned him, but I don't know in what capacity."

He stared at her. "Interesting."

"Maybe, but, … as I said, I don't know how she knew him."

"Interesting," he murmured.

"You keep saying that, but you're not explaining what's interesting about it," she noted sharply.

"Can you remember anything about the conversation?"

"Just the name. Debbie was always into the paranormal and all that stuff. That's one of the reasons she wanted to meditate more, so she could reconnect"—Eric kept his gaze on her, and she shifted uneasily—"with her parents."

"Her parents?"

"Yeah, they died about ten years ago, maybe. At the time, she went to multiple mediums to try and contact them, until I finally managed to get her to stop. It just seemed there was never any contact when she went. She would get so depressed, and I felt it wasn't healthy for her."

"Interesting," he murmured.

"Again with the *interesting*. You say that a lot, yet it doesn't mean anything."

"Stefan Kronos contacted my precinct. He talked to Captain Louis about—" He hesitated, not sure if he wanted to let on too much, and diverted, "about a case."

"About Debbie's case?" she asked, turning to him.

"Maybe," he turned away to put the containers on the counter.

"What did Stefan say?"

"It was a very cryptic message."

"If he's a psychic, that's what they seem to do," she said, with an offhand swing of her arm. "A part of me was thinking about contacting a psychic just because I want to know what happened to Debbie. I can't get that thought out of my mind. Now, for the first time, … I understand why Debbie was so heavily invested in getting answers about her parents."

"What do you mean, getting answers?"

"They both died many years ago, together, while on vacation in Mexico. Their case was never solved," she shared, "and Debbie was very upset at the prospect of not getting answers. Now I feel as if I'm fighting to get answers for her and that she would be cheering me on."

Eric stared at her for a long moment.

She sighed. "I know. … I'm certifiable, right?" She turned and walked into her kitchen. She tossed him a backward glance and added, "But you have to understand, when you lose somebody—"

"I do understand. I lost my younger brother quite a few years ago," he said, with a sad smile, "and there isn't anything quite like it."

"Right, there isn't, and you do everything you can to deal with it. Yet, at the end of the day, you can just do nothing at times." She pulled out plates and chopsticks. He quickly dished out food on both plates while she watched. They ate quickly, both hungry. "Did you ever get answers on your brother?"

"Yeah, he was killed by a drunk driver," he replied. "A young life, tossed away, all because of too much booze."

"Did it feel better knowing? Did it help?"

"Time helps—at least dulls the sting. I was so angry for so long, but, at some point, you must let it go because it poisons you."

"It does, and I think that's what I was most concerned about with Debbie—that she was getting way too involved in trying to get answers. That, and I was really doubting the information she was getting from these psychics," she added, frowning. "I didn't know any of them and never had anything to do with them, but I just felt it was not good for her to get so heavily invested in them. After that she seemed to be okay for a while, and that helped a lot. At least I thought that she was doing better about it. I don't know now," she admitted, raising her hands in frustration. "Sometimes I think maybe she was still contacting people and just keeping it from me."

"Which is one of the reasons why I was looking for her cell phone and any other information that might be available."

"Right," she muttered. "I didn't even think about her cell phone when I packed up her things because it's always with her."

"Yet it wasn't."

She stared at him for a moment, ate the last few bites on her plate, then got up, and he followed her. She walked into the living room where she had dumped Debbie's stuff, pointed at two bags, and said, "Those are hers from the seminar."

When she reached for one, a phone in the outside pocket buzzed. She quickly pulled it out and held it up for him to see. "This is her phone, but I don't know who's calling."

He quickly reached for the phone and answered it, and, when nobody spoke on the other end, he explained who he was and added, "I need you to identify yourself. Who are you?" The phone call went dead.

She stared at the phone, then over at him, and asked, "You still think absolutely nothing is going on here?"

He frowned as he faced her. "I have no idea what's going on. All I know is that we have somebody with no visible means of foul play—but now something else may have changed."

"Could it be the guy you mentioned—Stefan?"

"Do you mind if I go through the rest of her bags?"

"No, go right ahead."

"And I'll be taking her phone with me."

"Yeah, I figured, and, if it helps, you're more than welcome to it."

"And if it doesn't?" he asked, glancing at her, and she just shrugged. "I have her phone now, so I'll look at her contacts, confirming that I have spoken to everybody who she has in her phone and that we haven't missed any of her friends somewhere along the line."

Eden nodded. "If you find something, I would just ask that you keep me in the loop."

He didn't say anything, just nodded. As he continued to go through her bags, all he saw was just dirty laundry that Debbie had apparently set aside to wash but hadn't put in the washer just yet.

"Would she normally have not unpacked?" Eric asked.

"Oh, God, yes," Eden confirmed, with the wave of her hand. "For the most part, she was a slob." He gave a bark of laughter, and she smiled and nodded. "Debbie didn't really understand why she should have to do any of that. She thought that maids were assigned for everything in life."

"If you want to pay the money," he replied, "there is. You don't even have to do laundry. You just take it to a dry cleaner, if that's what you want to do. I've known plenty of older men who did that."

"Maybe," she noted, without rancor, even though he stared at her sharply. She shrugged and explained, "I don't know why her phone would even still be in her bag, unless she came in and was so tired that she just collapsed on the bed. She called me twice, but I wasn't ready to talk to her." She stared off in the distance. "That's a guilt I'll have to find a way to deal with somehow." She looked over at him. "As for her phone, … I can only imagine she was exhausted and didn't unpack. Then again her bedroom was a disaster so …"

"I saw her bedroom and searched through it, as did forensics, but they missed finding her phone."

Eden asked, "You don't think someone left it there after you all were through with her apartment?"

Eric frowned. "It is possible, I suppose. Yet we try to stay with the more normal explanations, at least at first. Maybe she didn't want somebody to contact her," he suggested. "That would be another reason not to take your cell phone with you to bed."

"Maybe. I don't know. None of this makes any sense to me."

"It will make sense eventually," he noted. "It's just that we don't always get the answers that we need to make sense of it right away."

Having gone through both bags but finding nothing suspicious, he sat down in the kitchen again, finished eating, and then stood up. "I'll go back to the office and see what I can do with her phone."

As he walked to the door, he stopped and looked at her, and she just waved her hand. "Go on, Detective. I'll be fine. But if you want more of the Chinese food," she said playfully, "you'll have to come back later."

He laughed. "I'll keep that in mind." Within seconds, he was gone.

CHAPTER 6

ONCE ERIC LEFT, Eden sat down to look up Stefan Kronos. He had quite a reputation, and she was pretty sure that Debbie had contacted him about her parents. Not giving herself a chance to think, Eden quickly dialed the number she found online, realizing that it was probably not even close to being valid anymore, as this was provided in a very old forum.

But then somebody answered the phone. "Hello, Eden." She froze with a squawk, then a warm chuckle filled the air. "I've been expecting you."

"What do you mean, you've been expecting me?" she cried out in horror.

"Easy," he said, "it's all right. I figured that, once you had a chance to calm down, you would call me."

"Why would I call you?" she asked, about to hyperventilate.

He sighed. "I gather Debbie didn't tell you very much."

"No, she didn't tell me anything," she cried out. "When did you last talk with her?"

"Before she left for the weekend retreat," he stated. "I had a message for her and tried to reach her, but she wasn't picking up."

"No, well, I had that experience with her too," she muttered. "Why did you have a message for her?"

"She contacted me about her parents," he shared comfortably. "I don't do those kinds of calls, and I explained that to her, but then, over the weekend, I did end up speaking with her mother. I wanted to pass on the message to Debbie, but I missed her."

Such deep regret filled his tone that Eden wanted to know what the message was, yet she was too petrified to ask.

"Yes," Stefan continued. "It was a warning. The message would have been very helpful to her."

"And what exactly was that message?" she asked carefully. "Because to tell me that it would have been a warning when I know she was struggling so much just makes it even harder."

"Of course it does," he replied, "and I'm not trying to make your life any more difficult. I have contacted the police about her as well. It was too much, too fast. I'm sorry."

"What does that mean?"

He hesitated and then finally spoke. "I don't think her death was natural."

Eden closed her eyes, feeling the tears welling up. "I don't think it was either," she whispered, "but I can't convince the police otherwise."

"I spoke to Captain Louis, so that may or may not make a difference, but I hope it will."

"Will you tell me what the message was?"

"Her mother wanted to tell Debbie that she shouldn't trust somebody who she was about to meet. I understand Debbie went off to a weekend retreat."

"Yes, she did. The two of us went."

"And what happened? Would you mind telling me?"

"I'll tell you, but it's pretty crazy." She snorted. "She fell head over heels in love with the man running the meditation workshop. I told her to take things slow, and we argued. Later she told me that she was quitting her job, which she did by text. She had also terminated her lease, effective immediately. And she was planning on moving across-country to be with Richard, the love of her life. It was just bizarre. I mean, she went from being somebody I've known for decades to someone I didn't recognize anymore. She completely went off on me and became someone I didn't recognize."

He sighed softly. "Sometimes we do things that affect life in a good way, and sometimes there's just nothing I can do at all to stop people from doing things the bad way."

"And yet, if you had gotten a hold of her, would she still be alive?"

"No, not at all. Just because I had a message for her doesn't mean she would have changed anything. And, if you think about who she was as a person, and how she was behaving at that time, you would easily understand that too."

Eden didn't want to understand. She really didn't, but he was right. "True, and, if you interrupted her at the wrong time, she would have been really angry at you for having spoiled what she considered to be something very special."

"Exactly. However, we are left with the remnants of her life, which isn't very much."

She heard the concern in his tone as he spoke to her. "No, it isn't," Eden agreed, tearing up, "and it's wrong. All of it is just so wrong."

He didn't say anything for a long moment. "Did you talk with a detective?" he asked casually.

"Yes, Detective Eric Kent," she shared.

"Right, so that's who I need to speak with next," he said, a smile in his tone.

"Feel free to contact him. I don't know that he'll talk to you any more than he's talked to me," she noted, "because I'm the crazy one who thinks Debbie didn't die from her own hand."

"Is that what they think happened?" he asked curiously.

"That's one of the things that they're batting around. They are waiting for the tox screen. There was no visible sign of a struggle, no suspects who may have been seen or heard her that evening. There was nothing at all, except that her heart stopped."

"That's energy," he noted thoughtfully.

"What do you mean, that's energy?"

He explained, "Depending on a lot of issues, sometimes—when people do a lot of energy work—they can impact another person in such a way that their hearts can stop."

She stared down at her phone, not even sure what she just heard, yet it was the only explanation she could even begin to come to terms with. Still, she didn't even understand how that was possible.

"I know that you want some answers," he told her, "but I'm not sure that there'll be much in the way of answers, at least not for a little while." A contemplative tone filled his voice.

"Look. I'm really not sure—"

"Yes, I know," he interrupted. "You're not sure about any of this, and of course you're not sure about me. I get that. I respect that." A gentle understanding resonated from his voice. "But what I need you to understand is that, just because we want things to happen, they don't always, and, just because we want to understand what is going on in the world, we don't always get that option either."

"You talk in riddles. Has anyone told you that before?"

"So I have been told. What exactly was your relationship with her?"

"Best friends, for more than a decade, yet we first met about twenty years ago. She had had several rough romantic relationships, and she would call me. Then I would be the one to bail her out. We had other mutual friends too. I don't want to make it sound as if she and I were an item. We were not. We were very close friends. Thus, when she told me that she didn't need me anymore and that she would be with this guy who absolutely loved her, I didn't even know what to say."

She stared off into the room, without looking. She needed to vent, and she had the feeling that Stefan of all people would understand that. "It was so foreign—and yet in many ways not—because she had done this stuff before, but not as abruptly, not as cruelly, never shutting me out permanently."

It seemed as if Stefan still waited for more of an explanation, and she tried. She floundered through several more attempts and then just gave it up. "I don't even know what to say," she declared, frustration in her tone. "Obviously this whole thing has been extremely difficult, and I am working very hard at getting through it. Yet I'm just so, I want to say *angry*, and yet angry isn't quite the correct word."

"No, of course not," Stefan agreed. "You're feeling guilty. Was this something you could have somehow stopped? Would she have listened to you? Would anything you have said made a difference?"

"You are the psychic," she quipped, trying for a bit of humor and failing.

"And the answer is no because of free will. We're all here, and we're doing the best we can in the circumstances we're faced with. Debbie definitely had …"

"She definitely had what?" Eden asked, trying to calm her racing mind. "You can't just stop like that."

"Energy issues. At one point in time, she was also quite sick," he shared. "Or did you not realize that?"

"I know that she was complaining about not feeling great and wanting to go off and do stuff, but I don't really know that she was actually sick, outside of the longstanding heart issue that she told me was a nonissue, but what do I know?" she snapped. "It seems as if everything I thought I knew, I didn't know at all."

He made a small sound she could only describe as stifled laughter. "I won't say that either, but did she feel better when she was with you?"

"Sure." Eden sighed. "She was often very draining for me, but that was just because … I don't know. I don't want to say anything. Never mind. Just forget I mentioned that."

"It's not that I need to forget that, but I already under-stand a lot of what's going on here. More to the point, the question is this. The person she fell in love with and was completely changing her life for, did you ever meet him?"

"Not formally. Not directly. He led the retreat so, yes, I knew who he was. I'm thinking about doing the same retreat again because I need to retrace Debbie's steps and see if any clues of foul play were there," she noted. "I can't imagine that there would have been, but I also don't know, and it's that not knowing that's killing me."

He didn't say much more after that, and, once he rung off, Eden sat back and stared, wondering how he even knew who she was and then expected her to call him. She felt a weariness creeping in, so she phoned Eric before she crashed for the evening.

"What's up?" he asked, his voice distracted.

"That man, the psychic—"

"Stefan?"

"Yeah. I spoke to him a little bit."

"What did he say?"

"That he had been trying to get a hold of Debbie, and she didn't answer, but that she had come to him a while ago, looking for a connection to her parents. I thought she had stopped doing that, but I guess she never really did."

"So, this Stefan guy, what did he say?"

"That he doesn't really connect to the dead these days, but then afterward Debbie's mother managed to connect with him. So he was trying to contact Debbie with the message that he had gotten. It was a warning, but he didn't get through to her. So now I'm left wondering if Debbie could have survived, had he gotten through to her."

"Crap," Eric muttered. "What was the warning?"

"That she shouldn't trust someone she would soon meet."

"That's ominous."

"Yes, thank you for that deep analysis," she muttered, "and that's how I feel. Anyway, he asked if I was talking to a detective, and I gave him your name. He'll be calling you. It was a very strange encounter, but he seemed to know an awful lot about Debbie, and, in a way, he made me feel both better and worse."

"I get that. I don't suppose you told him you'd heard from Debbie yourself."

She stared down at her phone, a little embarrassed because she hadn't thought to ask. "Oh my God, no, I didn't. Should I have?" she cried out. "I mean I've been talking to her but it's not like a normal question and answer conversation."

"I don't know," he conceded. "You do whatever you want to do. But if he could …"

"Oh my God, oh my God," she muttered, "how could I have been so foolish?"

"Look. I have to talk to Stefan anyway, so let me do that, and then we can talk about it afterward."

She went to hang up but added quickly, "Get back to me soon. I'm leaving in a few minutes to go to the same retreat seminar as before." With that, she ended the call.

She had lied. She wouldn't leave in a few minutes. In fact, she wasn't leaving until tomorrow, but, for whatever reason, this seemed to be urgent, and she had no freaking idea why.

Feeling more than a little foolish over all this, she waited and waited for his call but got nothing. Just her sense of urgency remained.

ERIC HAD BEEN shocked by what she just told him. Surely she didn't mean to return to the retreat. Yet, considering how upset and distressed she was about everything, it was probably exactly what she meant. That just gave rise to more of his panic.

He had no reason to suspect that either of the two men who ran the seminar had anything to do with the death of one of the attendees of the retreat. However, Eric had absolutely no way to rule it out either. He made the umpteenth phone call to get through to Stefan. When somebody finally answered this time, he didn't even know what to say.

"Hello," a man answered. "Ah, hello, Detective."

Eric sighed. "How did you know it was me? Psychic

much?"

"For one thing, you've left numerous messages," Stefan pointed out, with a chuckle.

"That's true. I have. I heard that you spoke to Debbie recently and that you've just now talked to Eden Landon."

"I spoke with Debbie last week, and unfortunately I did not connect with her again before her death, and, yes, I have spoken to Eden today."

"Okay. She seems quite concerned that you may have had a message for her friend that would have saved her life."

"I don't think it would have, given the circumstances," he admitted, "but I can see how she might be thinking that, and, for that, I'm sorry."

Eric added, "My captain has also spoken to me regarding the message that you appear to have."

"Yes, and, Detective, I really don't care if you listen to me or not. I can only tell you what the message is, and you will do what you will with it."

"And yet you wanted to connect Debbie with other murdered women."

"Yes, that's the most recent message that I have received, and, no, before you bombard me with questions, psychic messages are never clear. They're never meant to tie up a case in a neat and tidy bow," he explained and then chuckled, as if he had sensed Eric's skepticism. "I can see that, for you, this would be beyond frustrating. However, … or maybe not, Detective. I'm sorry."

"About what?"

"I thought you were naïve, intolerant of the gift, but you have and utilize similar energy, don't you?"

He stared down at the phone. "Sorry?"

Stefan laughed again. "You can hide that stuff from a lot

of people, but you cannot hide it from me."

Eric raised his eyebrows and pressed his fingers to his brows. Yet he couldn't help but want to trust that voice, his silky tone. "That's very disconcerting."

"Of course it is," Stefan stated. "You thought you were well and truly hidden, and you were, … until you spoke to me. Now we'll have a completely different conversation, Detective."

CHAPTER 7

T HE NEXT MORNING Eden had everything packed and ready to go. Just as she carried her bag to her car, a vehicle drove up. She instinctively knew it would be Eric, and, sure enough, he stepped out and walked toward her. "Now what?" she muttered.

"I don't want you going alone."

"That's nice," she muttered, trying hard to suppress her annoyance, "but I'll figure out what happened to my friend."

He nodded. "That's what I presumed you were doing."

"Look. She went off to this *wonderful* retreat," she began, "and became a very different person. Not only a different person but someone I barely recognized at all."

"And that may well be true," he conceded, "but going off on your own isn't exactly the answer."

"It might not be the answer, but it's the only course of action I have right now," she stated, "so don't try to stop me."

He smiled and nodded. "I won't stop you."

"What?" She did a double take, sensing a *but* was coming.

"I'm coming with you."

She stopped and stared. "What?"

He nodded. "I checked out the place, and your single room is now a suite booked for two."

"What do you … no, no, no," she snapped, staring at him. "You can't do that. You don't have the right to do that."

"Yet I can do that," he declared. "Either that or you're staying here."

She blinked several times at the audacity and the heavy-handedness, but she couldn't even figure out what to say.

"So, my vehicle or yours?" Eric asked.

"What?" she cried out.

"I am already over the barrage of questions, so please, let it go. Which vehicle are we driving? Mine or yours? Those are the only options you have," he explained. "By the way, the captain did agree."

"Why would the captain agree, and how did you know I wasn't leaving until this morning?"

"I know it may sound stupid that we would listen to anything that came from a psychic, but this one in particular has a long history of working with detectives. I have some limited experience with him myself. As for you leaving today? I knew you were lying about something, and, after I checked that the retreat began midmorning today, I decided to come and see if you had left. If you did, I would have found you at the retreat."

She sat down on her front steps, her bags in hand. "Seriously?"

"Yes, seriously. So, I am coming no matter what you say. Since this Monday is a holiday, the retreat this weekend is a four-day event." She just stared at him, and he repeated, "So your choice. My car or yours?"

She blinked, looking at his car, which was in decent condition as opposed to hers.

"Good, my car then. I prefer to drive anyway."

Giving her no time to protest at all, he grabbed a bag out of her lifeless hands and carried it to his car. As soon as he had it stowed, he looked back at her and added, "Now you need to lock up."

She blinked at him several times, not at all sure.

"Hey, Earth to Eden."

She shook her head. "That wasn't the plan."

"No, it's not, but we're not at all sure exactly what you were planning. Therefore, we want to confirm that whatever you're planning doesn't end up causing another death."

She didn't know what to say about that. He was right, since it was a possibility.

"Come on. Lock up. Have you heard from Debbie's landlord at all?"

"No," she replied, staring up at him but still not moving. "I suspect he'll just clean out the place and not bother me. I don't have time for that, but I was able to arrange for cremation. Plus, I was trying to get her body released."

"Good. You arranged for cremation," he noted. "Beyond that, you don't have to do anything right now."

She raised her hands in frustration. "Right, just because you say so?"

"No, not because I say so but because you need to be operating with your head in the game, not just hell-bent on trying to solve this," he declared, his tone stern, his eyes squinting. "Do you really think I didn't have a clue what you were planning?"

"Yeah, I really did think you didn't have a clue," she snapped, glaring at him. "I don't even know how you figured it out."

"You did tell me that you were headed to the retreat again."

"Yeah, true," she muttered. "I regretted that as soon as I got off the phone."

He smirked. "It doesn't matter at this point because, at the end of the day, you're not going alone."

"So, you think the brothers in charge are dangerous?"

"I don't know that at all," he clarified, "and we can't go in there with that expectation." She considered that, and he nodded. "I get it. You want them to be guilty of some heinous crime and for me to arrest them and to put them in jail for twenty years, where they can suffer horribly."

She winced as she listened to that. For all intents and purposes, he was right.

He nodded. "You're not the first person to have somebody die who they cared about. You're not the first person to have somebody die under somewhat suspicious circumstances," he added. "I get it, and I am sorry, but just because Debbie died under strange circumstances doesn't mean a crime has been committed."

"And yet here you are."

"Yes, here I am to confirm you don't die by some odd circumstance either." He grinned. "And I want to see the brothers in action."

"But they'll know who you are because you talked to them. Did you not?"

"I did, but by phone. So who knows. Things are never what they seem to be. So, maybe nothing will happen," he cheerfully suggested. "Still, you're not going alone, so you're either staying here or you'll go *with me*."

"What do you mean, with me?" she asked suspiciously.

He sighed. "Meaning that we go as a couple, or you don't go at all."

"You can't stop me," she declared.

He turned to face her, and the look he shot her was hard and implacable. He snorted. "I can make your life very, very difficult. I can cancel your reservation. I can contact them and say that you're really struggling with your medications after the loss of your friend and that you're likely coming to cause trouble, and they would never let you in."

She closed her eyes, absolutely stunned at this turn of events.

"Or you can come with me." The smile he gave her was wicked. "Then we'll just see if anything is suspicious about it all."

"And yet you don't think there is."

"I don't *know* that there is or that there isn't," he clarified, "but what I do know is that I can't let you go off half-cocked into this and either get yourself into trouble or get into a situation that you cannot handle and end up in the same boat as Debbie."

She turned and glared at him, but he never looked away.

"Yes, I mean *dead*."

Without another word, she got up, handed him the last of her bags, and walked back to her front door, locked up, then turned to look one last time around her small place. Finally she headed to his car with him. As soon as she got inside, she pointed out, "I don't even know why I'm agreeing to this. I just know—and I get that this sounds very strange. I know that I must go, whether I want to or not."

"Doesn't sound strange at all," he replied, a knowing smile on his face. "I also have the feeling that I must go too. So, let's just both decide that we're following our instincts and that whatever is going on is something we need to get to the bottom of. Yet you also need to realize that it could be very dangerous, and, in this instance, I am in charge." He remained in the driver's seat, staring at her. "And I'm not turning on this vehicle until you agree."

She stared at him for a long moment, then nodded. "What made you think that this was getting serious?"

He pondered it for a long moment and then shared, "Partly Stefan, partly you and the commitment you had to making sure that I understand how bad this was. And then partly my own instincts."

She raised her eyebrows at that.

"I know something's going on. I just don't know what, and, as much as I love puzzles," he said, "I hate it when I can't get answers."

With a bark of laughter, she put on her seat belt and nodded. "Let's go."

CHAPTER 8

FTER DRIVING TO the retreat, largely in silence, Eric and Eden finally pulled up at the hotel and parked. Walking into the reception area with their things, Eric noted the soothing music playing in the background. Except for that and the hushed welcomes and polite greetings, silence reigned. After a brief discussion and an extra fee, since it was quite a bit earlier than the normal check-in time, they were able to sign in and headed up to their rooms.

Stepping into the elevator, Eric suggested, "How about leaving our bags upstairs, then grabbing some breakfast?"

"Sure," she agreed. A few minutes later, she dropped her bags in her bedroom, then headed back to the front door of their suite. She stopped when she saw something on the floor near the door stopper. She bent down and picked up a small locket, then gasped.

"What is that?" Eric asked.

"It is a locket, and I swear to God it's one that Debbie used to wear."

He looked at the locket, then back to her, and asked, "These are probably sold everywhere, bought by many. Can you confirm that this one is Debbie's?"

"It's not engraved, if that's what you mean. I'm quite stunned to see it in the first place, especially since this wasn't Debbie's room. Still, I do recognize it and think it was hers.

It was a gift from a boyfriend. But then," she added, with a chuckle, "everything was from a boyfriend."

He nodded and smiled. "She liked getting gifts, I presume."

"She loved getting gifts, and she particularly loved gifts—"

"What?" he asked, turning to her.

"I was about to say something terribly mean, and I can't believe it was about to come out of my mouth," she admitted, "and it's not me. I don't like this thought."

"You should tell me what it was anyway."

"I'll just say, she liked to get gifts from men," she replied reluctantly.

"Lots of women do," he stated.

She looked at him briefly and then smiled, nodding. "I guess it's a fairly common thing, isn't it?"

"Yes, it's a very common thing."

"Fine," she muttered. "Debbie liked to get gifts. In fact, all her boyfriends were *required* to get her gifts. We used to sit and joke about it sometimes because it was such a thing for her."

"Power trips?"

"*Nah*, not that. I think it was more that she felt, if she didn't get the gifts, she wasn't loved, so it was validation for her."

"And you felt sorry for her, didn't you?" When she frowned at him, he nodded. "That was a big part of your relationship. You felt sorry for her. It's not that you were there for your own reasons so much, though that would have been part of it, but perhaps a big part of your relationship was the fact that you felt sorry for her."

"I did in a way, I guess," she acknowledged. "She didn't

really have many friends and not any long-term boyfriends."

"Interesting. Now, let's go get breakfast." When she rolled her eyes, he added, "And remember that we're friends."

"We are friends, although I don't know how that came to be," she muttered. "I hardly know you. You just seem to be … you're not the normal friend."

"And there's a very good reason for that, but I don't want to try to explain it anytime soon," he noted, with a laugh. She stared at him, and he shrugged, a twinkle in his eyes and an amused look on his face. "I know it sounds cryptic."

"That sounds more than cryptic. I'm not sure I like that." And the conversation was left at that.

Eric added, "It's fine. I'll explain later."

When they went to breakfast, their waitress was a lovely young woman. Her name tag read *Loraine*. She wore a turban on her head, and she was bright, positive, and gave them a steady stream of welcoming chatter as she went through their ordering process and bringing them coffee. As she was about to leave, Eden shared, "I love your headpiece."

The woman looked up and smiled. "Thank you. I borrowed it from a friend. I'm not religious, but … I'm having chemo, so I needed something."

"Oh my gosh," Eden muttered, "I am so sorry." She couldn't help but squeeze Loraine's hand in empathy.

Loraine smiled at her. "I'm … getting by at the moment. I'm certainly not expecting miracles, but I am working my way through this. It just takes more time than you think. … And then you always just feel so tired."

"Of course." Eden patted her hand, and the waitress smiled and left. Eden turned to Eric and whispered, "Oh my, isn't that so sad?"

Eric stared at her, wordless.

"What?" she asked, staring back at him. "What's that look for?"

He shrugged. "You're very empathetic."

"Yet your tone is off, as if you're swearing at me again." He burst out laughing, and Eden continued. "It's not hard to be empathetic to a young woman facing the battles that Loraine is up against."

"I suspect she'll be just fine now," Eric replied.

"I hope so. I mean, you would prefer to think that, if healing was going on at this place. So, it would be something that would benefit the staff too."

"That would be good, wouldn't it?" he asked, with a nod. "Let's hope that's happening here."

As they waited for their breakfast, Eden yawned.

"Maybe we should go back to the suite for a nap afterward," he suggested.

"Maybe," she conceded, as she yawned again.

Their food came a few minutes later, she smiled up at the same waitress, who reached out a hand instinctively and whispered, "Thank you so much for your kind words."

Eden nodded. "Hey, anything that you need for support, I'm happy to help," she offered. "It's not an easy road ahead of you, but I know you'll do just fine."

"Thank you," Loraine said, with a big smile, and then her smile waned. "I've got to work in the back, so I won't be out here for the next little bit. Enjoy your breakfast. If you need something, you just might have to holler a little louder than normal."

Eden looked around and realized no other waitresses were nearby. "Not a problem," she said. "We're adults, and we can look after ourselves."

Loraine rolled her eyes at that. "I appreciate that, but you would be surprised at how many people can't." And, with that, she was gone, leaving the two of them smiling as she disappeared.

When they finished up their meal, they walked back to their suite. He watched as she yawned several times. "Nap time, maybe?"

She shrugged. "Maybe."

"Is there something you want to tell me?"

"I was doing great until we stopped. Then, once we got to the restaurant, it just seemed like … all the stuffing came out of me," she shared, with half a laugh. "Given a chance to unwind, my body jumped at it."

He studied her to see if she really was completely unaware of what had just happened, and that was certainly how it appeared. He filed that away in the back of his brain as something to bring up with Stefan. If Eden really had no clue about energy work, to what extent did she have any involvement in this?

Did she have any idea that she *was* involved in this? And what was Debbie's involvement in any of this? Or was it all just Eric's imagination?

He couldn't even begin to think about everything that was going on right now. As they walked inside their suite, he urged her inside her bedroom. "Go lie down. You'll feel better." She nodded, yawned yet again, and slipped into her room. He watched her door close.

His bedroom was right next to hers, and, as he walked inside, his phone buzzed. He checked his Caller ID and noted it was Stefan. "Right on time," he said into the phone.

"You just get there?"

"We did, just returned from having breakfast. Eden has gone to lie down."

"How does it feel?"

"Odd," he replied, releasing his pent-up breath.

"What's odd?" Curiosity filled his tone, along with a hint of amusement.

"The whole place feels … *off* in a way. I'm not sure exactly why. And," he added, looking out the window, "the thing is, I don't really feel it's off in a negative way. There's a unique, positive vibration here."

"And that would make sense."

"Does it?"

"I mean, they're selling a good-vibration package," Stefan noted, with a small laugh. "And people must feel good to have a successful retreat, with repeat guests. … What else is on your mind? I can tell there is something."

"Yes." Eric was unsure if he even wanted to broach the topic. "Maybe I just need to observe a little bit more and get a better understanding. It's not necessarily odd as much as unique maybe."

"Her abilities, you mean?"

"Yeah. Wait. … You knew that already?"

"No, but I had my suspicions." Stefan sighed. "She doesn't know she has any."

"That's the other thing I don't quite get."

"That's not unheard of," Stefan stated cautiously. "A lot of people don't necessarily know they have abilities. They do things instinctively and don't realize the full extent of what they're doing, and I would say that's exactly what's happening here with Eden."

"It is special—watching her, I mean. She has so much compassion for people, which is probably why Debbie took advantage of her … constantly. And the more I think about it, the more I believe Debbie was getting something out of that relationship with Eden."

"Of course. That's always the case, isn't it?"

Eric hated to admit that, but Stefan was right, nonetheless. People tended to gravitate to others out of curiosity, comfort, and ultimately need.

"Don't worry about it. Let's just see what comes from this and if you can spot any other abilities Eden might have."

"Is there anything in particular you're thinking of?" Eric asked cautiously. "I would love to get to know her better, but I don't know if she's up for that or not."

"Right, but—"

"I'm a little too far out of the norm for her at this point." Eric chuckled. "She would probably be pretty quick to come back to whatever *normal* is."

Stefan laughed. "You might be surprised. Anyway, take care." An odd note filled his tone, as he added, "You need to take care, for the both of you."

"Oh, *good*," Eric muttered. "I always love it when the psychic says to be careful but can't tell you why."

Stephan laughed. "I understand. More cryptic than anything, and unfortunately that is true with so much of the work that I do and see. I know it sounds corny, but it's darn irritating," he added, still chuckling.

Eric ended the call. Deciding to get the lay of the land, he went downstairs, grabbed a coffee to-go, and went outside to walk the grounds.

It truly was a beautiful location, and, if people were coming here to get away and to enjoy some stress-free downtime, an awful lot could be said for this site. As a matter of fact, everything about it had a special sensuous feeling.

He wandered about with a smile on his face as he enjoyed the area. When he came to a gardener standing over a large bed of roses, Eric stopped to talk. "It's truly beautiful here," he shared, with a friendly smile on his face. "You've done a heck of a job."

The gardener turned to him and smiled. "Thank you. I'm Samuel."

Eric nodded. "I'm Eric. How long have you been here?"

He shrugged. "I've been working for the hotel for a very long time. Though, at one point, it looked as if they would have to sell the place,"

"They almost sold the hotel? That must have been ominous."

"Yeah, it was a while ago. We were in a situation that almost guaranteed I would lose my job," he shared. "But somehow they managed to pull it back from the brink, and here I am, still working with my beloved plants. Most that I planted myself," he added, with a proud smile.

Samuel started talking about a couple specific plants in front of them, using names that Eric didn't recognize, then adding the Latin names to boot. They walked and talked, as the gardener showed him some of the different areas he was working on and some of the plants he was putting into place.

"You really love your job here."

"I do," he stated instantly, "and it would break my heart if I ever had to leave, but there'll always come that time when you must put down your tools. You can't just continue to work forever," he noted, with a smile. "I'll just be happy when that time comes for me, as I'll know that I've done as much as I can for this place. It's really been great."

"Do you have any idea what the owners did to avoid having to sell?"

Samuel nodded. "Bringing in all these retreats and seminars over the weekends. It's really been something to see, knowing how close they came to not being able to meet payroll. It was a very stressful time for everyone."

"So, what do you think of these weekend seminars?"

He smiled. "I love the fact that people come here to appreciate the beauty, and, although they aren't necessarily here for us, we're here for them, and they end up going home feeling so much better about everything in their life," he shared. "So, from that perspective, I absolutely love that they come here."

"Any downside to it?" he asked, as he turned to look around. "I presume there's no drama, danger, or anything getting damaged here."

"Oh no, that behavior would never wash with us," he stated, with a smile. "Besides, these people, they come here looking for peace. They come looking for joy, for hope, and all the good things in life," he added, his smile widening. "Are you a first-timer?"

"Yeah, so you figured that out already, did you?" Eric asked, with a wry smile.

"Yes, that's also quite typical," the gardener noted.

"What?"

"The grilling. I am used to it. After you've been here once or twice, you'll realize that you just want to keep coming back more and more."

"Maybe so," Eric conceded, with a nod, "and, if I get to enjoy your beautiful gardens, I would consider coming back," he admitted.

Samuel beamed. "Thank you for that. Gardeners are often very overlooked in terms of the work that we do. And it's okay. I get it, but sometimes it's nice to be appreciated."

"It's always nice to be appreciated," Eric confirmed, with a smile.

The gardener nodded. "As much as I would love to talk more, I need to get back to work." He pointed over to somebody standing off to the side. "Oh, that's the guy who's doing your seminar this weekend."

"Ah, maybe I should go over and talk to him."

"You've never met him?"

"No, I sure haven't."

"Here, come on. Let me introduce you to Richard Santino," he said. "I see him on a semiregular basis, just because he's here so often." Together, the two of them walked over, and the gardener quickly made the introductions. Then he waved. "Now I'm off. Enjoy the gardens." And, with that, he returned to where he'd been working, picked up his rake, and headed off in a different direction.

Eric casually studied the man standing here, deciding not to mention their phone interview. "Hey, I'm in one of your seminars this weekend. Sorry for the interruption. The gardener decided I should come meet you."

"Ah." Richard's face broke into a beaming smile.

For the life of him, Eric couldn't find anything obnoxious or dark about his aura. Something was genuinely nice about the energy around him. It was a little disturbing, in fact, because Eric wanted to pinpoint something as being wrong or negative about Richard. Instead he came across as someone quite lovely.

Richard spent a few minutes talking with him, and then he looked down at his watch and excused himself, saying, "I've got to deal with some of the paperwork."

"Of course, of course." Eric stepped back, giving him space to leave.

Richard headed to some small cabins off to the side.

Of course there were some cabins set aside for other people, and that would give them a little bit more privacy during the entire seminar too. A space to step back away from the attendees and to not be pestered and questioned by everybody. Eric didn't know if that was a challenge here or not, but it was conceivable.

As it was, Eric was perfectly happy to continue walking the gorgeous grounds and enjoying everything they had to offer. When his phone buzzed, he looked down at Eden's text. She was awake. He picked up the pace and headed back in her direction.

When he neared the front entrance to the hotel, he watched her slowly walking down the front steps, looking around at the surroundings. When he waved at her, she smiled and hurried toward him.

"Hey," she greeted him. "I must have been really tired. I don't know what happened," she muttered, shrugging. "I really crashed."

He nodded. "You seemed to need it."

"I don't know why," she murmured. She looked outside and smiled. "It's beautiful out there."

"Not only is this beautiful but they have absolutely stunning flower gardens too," he shared. "Do you want to get a coffee and then take a walk outside?"

She beamed at him. "I would love that."

And that's what they did. Picking up coffee first, they headed outside. It was a relaxing, peaceful walk through the gardens as he explained a little bit about what he had just been told.

But it felt natural. It felt right. And he was a little put off by that. Generally he would keep up his walls to maintain any general conversation with somebody, just because he always had challenges in his world for his energy. But Eden didn't appear to cause him any stress energetically.

He thought that was interesting and probably something else to discuss with Stefan.

Putting all thoughts of that and Stefan off to the side, Eric could get used to being at a place like this, just for stress relief himself.

As Eden wandered around beside him, she said, "It really is gorgeous, isn't it?"

"It is," he murmured. "I'm quite struck at how unusually beautiful and peaceful it is."

"I was just thinking that. It's almost as if there's a certain energy all over the place." He paused and looked at her. "What?" she asked, staring back at him. "What did I say?"

"Just your comment," he murmured. "I thought it was an interesting way to put it."

"You mean, about energy? Yeah, well, if anybody could learn to package it, that would be one heck of a selling point."

"It would, indeed," he murmured, his mind churning now, wondering if that could be what was going on here. Thoughts ran wild in his head. Could something nefarious be in all this wonderful and positive energy? Was *false* positive energy a thing?

For the first time, he looked around the place with a more distrustful gaze, wondering if something specifically odd was underneath it all.

She laughed. "You don't have to look at everything as if it's poisonous now."

He frowned and then relaxed, as he realized his reaction was probably over-the-top, and, if nothing else, was over-the-top in terms of other people seeing it. He smiled at her. "I don't know. I hadn't even considered that until you mentioned it."

"I didn't mention it in order to cause *that* kind of a reaction," she replied, smiling at him. "I was thinking more along the lines of, if anybody could package all this energy, they would make a killing."

"And they probably would," he muttered, thinking it over, considering the idea, "because, of all the things you would want to package and to sell, what people here want and are looking for is peace, quiet, and a chance to de-stress from their lives. If they could bottle that, they would have something the world would want, and honestly, it's something the world needs."

CHAPTER 9

S INCE EDEN HAD first mentioned it, the subject of bottling this feel-good energy remained on her mind throughout the day, popping in and out as they went through the registration process, which was identical to the one she had experienced with Debbie. The *getting to know each other* icebreakers were simple enough, and then they settled in for an introductory meditation to help everybody relax and get ready for a wonderful weekend.

Having not been great at meditating and always finding it a struggle—what with all the thoughts in her head—Eden really hoped tips and tricks would be shared to give her a little better technique in terms of shutting down her busy mind. Her mind always ran amok, her thoughts rampant. Plus, this time, hopefully her focus was more on the actual retreat and less about her fight with Debbie, like their last time here.

As Eden worked her way through this intro meditation, she felt Eric right beside her, dropping deeper and deeper, seemingly without effort or any struggle, and that was enough to drive her crazy.

When they had their first break, Eric looked over at her, and she frowned at him. "You are frowning. What is the problem?" he asked.

"You," she muttered in frustration. "I mean, you just

come out of the blue, sit down, and it's like you've meditated forever."

His eyes opened wide. "Did I ever tell you that I hadn't meditated?"

She frowned and then shook her head reluctantly. "I guess I assumed that you didn't."

"Don't assume," he said, with a laugh, "because it's not true. I may not have a ton of experience, but I'm certainly not totally green at it." She scoffed and he chuckled. "Any creative, deep-thinking work can be a meditative state," he explained. "It's not that it's right or wrong or good or bad. It's just the experience you want. So, I find that I do much better at work when I'm in that state."

"Right," she muttered, and then she sighed. "I was just getting so frustrated because I can't shut down my mind. It's a maze in there."

"And what is it that circles through your mind when doing this?" he asked curiously. "I mean, it could be a lot of things. I'm just wondering where your mind is at."

"Usually it's problems, like work, other people, and those sort of things, but right now it's Debbie," she shared. "And that just makes it even more frustrating because I don't want her to be part of this."

"Of course," he noted.

"I had always wanted to come here and had intended to do this solo. Yet she made a big point of coming along, then ended up ditching me. It was my plan to do all this—the retreat, I mean, to take a break myself." Eden sighed. "I wasn't even quite ready to come. I wanted to save up a little more, but Debbie insisted. So I ended up with half of it on my credit card, and now here I am doing it again. I always had to watch every penny, but Debbie spent money as if she had it, as if she always had more than I did."

"I thought she was broke, especially after that last boy-friend cleaned her out."

"Yeah, she was, but she worked a lot of overtime after that. Come to think of it, lately she had a lot more money than I did."

"Right. So, now we're back to that interesting friendship you had with her."

"I don't know that calling it that is even fair," she replied, shaking her head. "Maybe I'm the one who was not a good friend."

"And, as an empath, you would think that immediately too," he noted, shaking his head. She glared at him, and he just smiled, tucked her hand into his arm, and, although reluctant, she let him. "Let's enjoy the fresh air." Ignoring her protests, he dragged her along.

Almost immediately the fresh air hit and sent calming waves down around her. "Oh, this is nice," she whispered. "I don't know how you knew this was what I needed, but, boy, you're right. It is exactly what I needed."

"Sometimes all it takes is a chance to settle back and to let the frustration go. Sometimes we are our own worst enemy when it comes to this. Just calm down and let your mind drift. Watch the thoughts come and go, but don't get hung up on them. That's really all you need to do."

"You make it sound easy."

"I know, and, of course, it isn't. It's never that easy, and, if it were, everybody could do it and wouldn't need these retreats."

"It seems as if everybody is always doing it," she shared, "and I'm always the one *not* doing it properly."

He grinned at her. "It's really not always about you."

She looked at him for a moment, blinked, and then burst out laughing. "Thanks for that. That definitely put me back in my place."

"I'm not trying to put you into any place," he declared, with a dry laugh. "I'm just trying to give you the freedom to be you."

She smiled and nodded. "By the way, it worked. And you're right. I find it far too easy to trash myself."

"And that comes from a lifetime of not feeling as if you have any value," he shared.

"It seems you've been there."

"I have been there," he confirmed, "and that's okay too. We all must get to the same place on our own pathway."

"Is that right?" she questioned. "Because plenty of people believe they can get there first, and then they don't have to wait for anyone else."

"Of course they do. There will always be people in this world who think they don't have to do anything for anybody else. Those people don't want to help you. They just want to compete with you and win. That's because their egos are so damaged and so small that they only feel better if they're knocking down other people."

She winced at that but nodded. "I've seen more than a few people like that." He didn't say anything. "And you're right, to a certain extent. That's exactly who Debbie was too."

He smiled and nodded.

Eden added, "Yet Debbie would say, *It just never really mattered to me.*"

He just nodded again.

Eden frowned. "I don't know how an outsider gets a better perspective on my relationship with Debbie than I do."

"It's literally because I'm an outsider," he pointed out, turning to her. "I'm not caught up in all the drama of your relationship with Debbie. So I can get a much better perspective and can see it for what it is."

"If you say so," she muttered, frowning.

The second round of meditation went better, and then they attended some lectures and had a lunch break. Through it all, everything seemed normal, and Eden was caught up in the enjoyment of the seminar. As she walked toward the restaurant for lunch, about one hundred people came along too, all from this weekend's retreat.

She glanced around, looking for Eric, but saw no sign of him. She frowned, waited off to the side, when Richard walked over and asked, "You're not having lunch?"

She smiled at him and explained, "Absolutely I am. I was just waiting for Eric."

"Ah." He smiled and added, "I'm sure he'll find you."

Feeling a little foolish for waiting for him, and yet not knowing why, she walked toward the restaurant with Richard.

As they reached the one area where people were sectioning off into two sides of a buffet, he motioned at her and offered, "We have a free chair at our table, if you would like to join us. I'll be sitting there with my brother and some of the others. You are welcome to join me."

She flushed and mumbled something odd, not even sure what she said, then hurried over to the buffet section to get her food. The thought of Richard making a pass at her didn't make her feel special. It made her feel off.

And it somewhat dimmed the enjoyment she had felt so far this morning. When she looked up again, Eric was walking toward her.

Seeing her smile with relief, his eyebrows shot up. As he got closer, he asked, "Problems?"

She shrugged. "Richard invited me to sit over at the main table with them."

He didn't say anything, just kept his head down and glanced off to the side, then back at her. "Do you want to go?"

She looked over at him and rolled her eyes. "Pretty sure the invitation was for me only."

He chuckled. "I'm sure it was. When you look in the mirror, you don't see the beautiful young woman looking back at you." He winked at her, and a blush came on.

She stared at him and then shook her head. "I'm in my early thirties, and I think it's been at least ten years since anybody said anything like that to me."

He looked at her in surprise. "That's too bad."

"Whatever," she muttered. "Anyway, I don't want to go over there unless you come with me."

"If you're not sure the invitation was for both of us—"

She grimaced because, no matter how lightly he was taking it, joking and all, he was right. "I'll pass," she stated firmly.

"Okay."

He seemed agreeable to it, but she noted that he kept an eye on Richard's table during lunch. Then she realized that maybe something was off about the whole thing. "You don't think he knows, do you?"

Eric popped a bite of French bread into his mouth and asked casually, "Knows what? Did he seem to recognize you?"

"That's the problem," she noted, shaking her head. "I'm not sure he did."

He smiled. "Don't worry about it." And his tone was just firm enough that she wanted to believe him.

"But he was crazy over Debbie, so why is he scoping out the women here?"

"Hard to say, but, in case you hadn't noticed, quite a few women are looking at you a little enviously."

"Yeah, that's because you're with me," she replied. He frowned at that, but she nodded. "You think I can't tell when other women are scoping out the men in the room? That's just something women do."

"It's a male thing too," he admitted, "and, yeah, there's definitely a little bit of that going on, but there's way more women here than men."

Surprised, Eden looked around and then agreed. "I hadn't really noticed."

"It's probably at least a 70 to 30 percent mix on this."

"And is that because most men don't come to these things?"

"I don't think they come alone," he pointed out. "Maybe they come with a girlfriend or a wife, but I'm not sure how many guys would come here without a partner."

Eden laughed. "Or to find a partner."

"There's that too," he agreed, nodding, "and I have no clue what the percentage for that would be. It would make more sense if it was maybe a work thing or, you know, a girlfriend thing."

"Maybe." She wasn't sure what to think about it, but, ever since the lunch invitation, she felt a little uncomfortable, and all the ease that she had felt here before was dampened.

He smiled, clearly noticing her discomfort. "Just relax."

She'd been staring over at the main table. "I guess it's bad when I'm so obviously staring at him, *huh*?" she asked, chuckling.

"I don't know about bad, but it shows you're interested, which may get you a second invitation. Or you are curious, in which case, you'll probably still get another invitation."

She winced. "Not sure I like the connotation behind either of those."

"And maybe it's all good," he suggested. "I wouldn't worry about it either way."

She sighed as she looked over at him. "You make it sound so easy."

"It is easy."

"But what if he had something to do with her death?"

He faced her and then replied, "If that's the case, then we obviously don't want you to have anything to do with him. However, we don't know that's the case, and, considering that we have no evidence of any wrongdoing on his part, that would be something of a miscarriage of justice to blame him for it."

"But …" she began, noting the look on Eric's face.

"Was Debbie the kind of person—" Then he frowned and answered his own question. "Of course she was."

"What do you mean?"

"She was the kind of person who would immediately take him up on his lunch invite, wasn't she?"

Eden considered his question, then slowly nodded. "Yes, absolutely. And they were smitten." She glanced in Richard's direction. "At least I thought he was."

Later that night Eric knocked on her bedroom door, and, when she opened it up, he asked, "Feel like going for a walk?"

She frowned. "I'm feeling more tired than I would have thought, and it just seems a little harder to stay awake."

"That's okay," he replied. "I just wanted to go out and

maybe take a lap around the grounds again. You can stay in, if you aren't feeling up to it."

"*Nah*, I'll join you." She fell into step beside him, and, when they got outside to the beautiful grounds, the evening light was settling in around them. She whispered, "It really is magical."

"It is," he agreed.

"If only he could bottle this, right?"

They heard voices up ahead, so they turned to a different corner, so they didn't have to deal with people. "You won't exactly get your investigation going this way, will you?" she asked, half joking.

He smiled at that but nodded. "That's very true. Do you want to go back around?"

"No, I really don't," she muttered. "I would much rather have nothing to do with this whole thing."

"I'm not sure I can promise you that," he stated, "but we can certainly avoid some of it right now."

They walked down to a little rise with a big bench. They sat down, and she gasped as she took in the valley view in front of them. "Wow. I didn't see this earlier."

"I didn't either," he said, as he looked all around the area. "It truly is spectacular, isn't it?"

That was one word for it. She was still searching for the right words, when they heard a raised voice somewhat in the distance behind them.

Eric stood up and looked around.

She frowned as she asked, "Do we need to do something about that?"

"I don't know," he admitted. "They don't seem that an- gry, and nobody's calling for help. I'm not exactly sure what we're looking at but—" His attention appeared to be completely directed at whatever was going on. Still, he turned and sat back down again.

She smiled at him. "It's really hard for you to turn it off, isn't it?"

"Particularly when I'm here specifically *not* turning it off," he stated pointedly.

She frowned and responded, "Good point."

"And I'm not trying to remind you," he muttered, with a groan. "I was just, in a way, trying to excuse the behavior, which is so ingrained in me by now that I'm not sure I could turn it off if I wanted to."

"I think that's part of the point I was trying to make. Turning it off is probably an unreasonable expectation."

"I'm not sure it's something you should be worrying about either," he added, turning to her.

She smiled. "It's obvious that is who you are, and this is a huge part of what makes your world function. If so, then that's just fine."

He just smiled at that and didn't say anything but tried to relax again. After a while of peaceful silence, he asked, "You ready to go up to bed?"

"I think I can sleep now, yeah." She yawned several times as they walked back.

He pointed off to the side and said, "A little shortcut path is over here, if you want to take it back?"

She nodded, and, since it was a little bit darker, he looped her arm through his so she could keep a better footing. As they came out on the other side, he stopped. She looked down, not sure what the problem was, only to see something in the distance. Just then, he let go of her arm and bolted into a run. She followed, close on his heels, and, when she caught up, she found him bent down beside someone.

He turned to Eden, frowning. "She's ill, seriously ill." He quickly pulled out his phone and called for an ambulance. After that, some serious chaos ensued, as everybody came running at the calls for help. When she saw Richard running too, she pointed to where Eric was still beside the woman and explained, "We found this woman in the shrubs. She collapsed."

"Oh dear," he muttered, as he bent down at her side and checked her over.

One of the observers asked, "Is she one of the attendees from the meditations?"

Eden looked over at him and replied, "I have no idea." She looked back at Richard and asked, "Do you know?"

"She is," he confirmed, as he continued to check her over. "She's breathing, but it also looks as if her condition has worsened." He looked over at them and shared, "It's not public knowledge, but she's dealing with stage four cancer. I believe it involves the liver, but I could be wrong."

The ambulance arrived, and it took a few minutes for her to be assessed, to be loaded onto the gurney, then taken away. After they left, Eden looked around and saw that everyone was staring at Richard, questions in their eyes.

"Obviously this is not the energy we want here," Richard announced to the crowd, with a sad smile, "but it can't be helped in this instance. I suggest you all head back to your rooms, meditate tonight to help ease some of this energy that we've now been exposed to, and try to relax. In the morning, we'll do a special ceremony to help clear away this energy again." And, with that, he motioned for everyone to return to their hotel rooms.

As Eden looked around, expecting to find Eric, she saw no sign of him. She took several quick glances around, but

Richard was ushering her along with the others, away from all the *negative energy*, as he put it. Sure enough, as they got closer to the hotel itself, the energy felt a little bit better, a little bit calmer, though there was still a buzz in the air, and people continued talking excitedly.

Richard was trying to shut that down, and he quickly got people heading off to their rooms. As soon as Eden made it to her suite, she texted to see where Eric had gone. She tried a few times but got no answer from him.

Frowning, she checked the hallway, waiting until Richard had disappeared after trying to send the other women back to their rooms. It seemed to her that several of them were clinging to him, as if he were a lifeline in a shocking scenario. He wasn't trying to disengage himself, but it was obvious that he was also looking for a bit of space himself. After they had finally all disappeared, Eden picked up the phone and tried calling Eric again.

With no answer, she sent him a flurry of texts, getting no response. So she sent one last message. **You better respond, or I'm coming back outside.** That did the trick.

He responded almost immediately, with a single phrase. **Stay there.** That was it, and, not sure what to make of it, she sat here in their suite and waited for him to show up.

It took an hour, and, when she got one look at him, she pulled him into her room. "Oh my God, what happened to you?" He was covered head to toe in dirt, as if he had tumbled down a hill.

He looked at her and groaned. "One answer is that I fell."

She raised an eyebrow. "What's the other one?"

"The other answer is that I was pushed."

ERIC SAT GINGERLY on the small chair in Eden's bedroom, knowing that he was probably spreading dirt everywhere.

She just stared at him as she came out of her bathroom with a towel and handed it to him. "Are you sure you shouldn't see a doctor?" she asked for the umpteenth time.

He brushed off her concerns. "No, I'm fine."

"Are you sure?" she asked again.

He looked over at her and smiled. "Thank you for being concerned, but, right now, I think that's the last thing I need."

She just nodded and sat down beside him. "You seriously think you were pushed?"

"Yes, I seriously think I was pushed," he declared. "The problem is, I didn't see anybody, so I can't tell anybody who it was."

"Of course, and if somebody pushed you—"

"Not *if*," he declared. "I was pushed, no doubt."

"Right." She grimaced. "I'm not trying to suggest otherwise. I'm just trying to figure out what may have happened."

"When you figure it out, let me know," he replied grumpily.

In fact, he was mostly just pissed that it had happened and that he didn't see it coming. He wasn't expecting that kind of attack.

"Tell me where you were and how this came about."

As it was, at least the events were something he should clear up in his own mind, so he walked her through the chain of events after the scenario involving the woman. He added, "I wanted to go look in the direction where we heard the yelling and see if there was any chance that it involved this woman. However, no cameras were anywhere around this area that I could see, and that alone makes me suspicious."

She rolled her eyes at that. "Of course. Once a detective, always a detective, right?"

He snorted. "I didn't find very much in the way of pathways in that area. Not very much in the way of anything, to be honest."

"So that's not a bad thing, is it?" Eden asked.

"No, not if you want a corner of the world to keep to yourself, so that's the corner you'll make mischief in," he suggested. "The fact of the matter is, that is the corner where the woman collapsed. It's also the corner where there's that little bit of a drop-off. Remember when we sat on the bench, and it was on a hill?"

She nodded.

"That's where I went over. I came up around that same area but approached it from the other side, still looking for any sign of what may have gone on. Then I felt a hard push between my shoulder blades and went over. The thing that gets me is that I didn't hear footsteps."

She thought about it. "And we did hear footsteps of those other people when we were walking," she noted softly.

"Exactly, given the trees, I didn't hear even the crunch of the leaves underfoot. Not the squeak of shoes. Not the rustle of clothes. I heard nothing. Now, I won't suggest that I couldn't have been too embroiled, and maybe I was just too busy and missed something. I mean, obviously something happened, and, if I missed it, I missed it," he conceded, waving a hand around, "but I also saw no sign that someone waited around to see if I was okay."

She winced at that and then slowly nodded. "If it had been accidental, somebody would have come looking or would have called out for help."

"Exactly," he agreed, "and you can bet that nobody did."

He looked down at his clothes in disgust. "I didn't bring all that many clothes with me, and this will all need to hit the laundry."

"You can probably brush some of it off," she suggested, yet doubt surfaced as she studied his clothing, "but you would definitely feel better if you changed clothes."

"I have another change," he noted. "I just don't have many of them."

"Ah, so in other words, if this happens again, we're going home early."

"No," he declared. "I'll just have to wear the same damn clothes a second time. Now, if something suspicious wasn't going on, I would have peacefully made my way through the night. Right now, however—"

"You're pissed," she said, with a nod.

"I am pissed, and I have a reason to be," he stated, "and the fact that this happened here is just making me even angrier."

"Is there another place for it to happen?" she asked, frowning at him. Then she held out a bottle of water for him.

He accepted the water, had a big drink, and handed it back to her. "Thanks. I forget just how thirsty this work makes me."

She smiled. "I don't know that it's work necessarily," she pointed out. "I was looking for you out there, but you didn't show up, and Richard kept trying to get us back into the hotel and to calm down. Some people were a little more excited over this turn of events than maybe was good for them."

Eric nodded. "When something like this happens, a lot of people get excited. Life is simple, and, if they don't have a lot going on in their world, this is exciting stuff."

She winced. "That poor woman though."

"I know, and it was easy for Richard to say that she had cancer, but that's nobody's business but hers, if it was even true," he noted, shaking his head. "Anyway, I have sent off a request for information on her from one of my cohorts, and, depending on when they get back to me, we may or may not get a little more information on her condition."

"Do you really think something nefarious happened?"

He frowned as he faced her. "What I can't get out of my head is the fact that we did hear somebody having an argument right before we found her," he reminded her.

"We don't know who it was though."

"That's what I was trying to find out, and, no, I didn't manage to do so."

"Of course not," she muttered. "If it were that easy to find out, that wouldn't have made sense either."

He stared at her and eventually nodded. "To a certain extent, yes, but most criminals don't know how to clean up after themselves."

"Or to even care to," she added, nodding. "So, you're thinking that maybe it was deliberate?"

"I don't have a clue," he admitted. "All I know is that the evening didn't turn out the way we expected it to."

"No," she replied. "And I don't think it ended up the way he expected either."

CHAPTER 10

EDEN WOKE THE next morning, a little more tired than she expected, but it had been an exciting evening, and not in any good way. She had helped brush off Eric's clothing after his sudden fall and sent him off to bed, leaving his jacket behind. She put it in the shower this morning to get some steam while she showered, and it was looking better, but it wasn't back to the condition it had been in before.

It would probably need to be dry-cleaned when he got home, but she accomplished something with it, and hopefully he could still use it here on their trip. As she opened her bedroom door, she found him standing there, just getting ready to knock.

She smiled as she stepped forward. "Hey. How are you feeling?"

"I'm fine," he muttered, brushing off her concerns.

She rolled her eyes at him. "And, even if you weren't, you would say you were anyway."

He just half nodded, obviously something else on his mind, as he ushered her out of their suite and toward the elevators.

Eden's gaze sharpened. "Did you hear anything?" She glanced around, in case anybody else was listening in.

He nodded. "She died overnight."

She gasped. "Seriously?"

He nodded once more. "They're not sure what happened, and, of course, it'll take time for an autopsy, but she did have cancer. More details are still to come, but I don't have much so far."

"Cancer or not, that's still pretty awful."

"It is."

As they quickly finished up breakfast and coffee, they headed into the meditation lounge for the seminar events today. As soon as everybody was seated, Richard stepped out. In a voice full of compassion and sorrow, he explained the outcome of the previous night's misadventures, explaining that she had, indeed, passed away overnight and that his heart went out to the family.

Lots of murmurs followed, even a couple of cries. Several women were obviously distraught about the whole thing, and it didn't sound or feel fake. Yet it added such a pall to the entire atmosphere that Eden wondered how Richard could overcome that, considering that everybody was here to reduce their stress, not to increase it.

Richard led the group first into a meditation for releasing grief and shock and trauma, which was very smart.

Eden certainly appreciated it because she definitely felt better by the time she was done.

As Richard brought it to a close, he led them right into more lectures about the science of grief and how to overcome unexpected loss.

The lecture felt insignificant compared to the meditation, in Eden's opinion.

As they quickly went through the morning, she felt others starting to settle in and relax, releasing whatever had been bothering them about the entire scenario, which must have been traumatic for the woman's family. They were all here, hoping she would find some solace and healing. Instead she ended up dying.

During the coffee break, Eden heard lots of murmuring about it all, and she asked one gentleman, "What was she even doing out there at night?"

He shook his head, as he glanced around. "I wanted to ask about that myself. However, it doesn't really feel appropriate."

"Right. I understand," she agreed, then moved on, as he didn't want to talk anymore. Eden caught sight of Eric wandering through several of the groups, looking for answers himself. When they were called back into session again, they were all admonished, saying that it was natural to question these things when they happen, but, for the family's sake, if the others would keep their questions to something much less intrusive, it would be helpful.

Eden wasn't sure what precipitated the call for that, but, during lunch, Richard approached her and asked if she needed help dealing with the trauma. She looked at him, not sure where this was coming from—and specifically why here. "No, I don't think so."

He frowned, then nodded. "I understand you've been asking a lot of questions, and that usually happens when somebody is struggling."

"Ah, well, it certainly was upsetting because we were outside that night, and I really didn't expect to deal with that."

"Of course not. You were out there?"

"Yes, we'd been sitting outside," she recalled, with a sad smile, "enjoying the evening air, just looking at the views."

Richard nodded. "It's truly beautiful here, isn't it?"

She had to agree. "Indeed, and that just compounded the whole thing," she shared. "We didn't see what happened, so we feel that element of guilt that maybe we missed something. What if we had seen her earlier? She might be fine now."

Richard gave her a gentle hug. "It's very nice for you to be so worried, but she was dealing with a very difficult prognosis already. She was at the end by then. I probably shouldn't have let her come, but she was so insistent that she would make it through and how it would bring her so much peace that I gave in. I didn't feel as if I could deny her the opportunity to do something positive for herself."

"Of course," Eden replied.

"Hopefully you will just let it go now." With that, Richard smiled genially at her and then headed off to talk to somebody else.

Almost immediately Eric was at her side. "What did Richard say?" he asked.

"Let's just say it was noted that I've been asking too many questions," she summarized, "and he was hoping that I would let it go. I explained that we had been outside at the time, so we felt a certain amount of guilt that, if we had found her earlier, she might have been okay."

"I'm sure he thought that was something that you really couldn't have done, right?"

"No, he didn't seem to think it was anything we could have helped with."

Eric just nodded and didn't say anything more.

"He more or less asked me to stop raising the issue and to stop asking questions."

"Of course. It's probably very disruptive *to the energy*," he noted in a half-mocking tone.

She winced and then nodded. "It *is* very disruptive to the energy, which I can even feel myself. So, I guess I can't really blame him for that."

Just then, they were called back in for the afternoon session, which ended up going very, very quickly. By the time they were done with their first full day, Eden once again felt pretty wiped out.

Eric found her soon afterward and asked, "Do you want to eat now or maybe go for a walk first?"

"I would love to go for a walk," she replied, and they headed for the doors. They were called back by one of the organizers to share that dinner would be served soon.

She replied, "No problem. I just want a few minutes of fresh air."

The man watched them as they left.

As Eden stepped outside, she whispered, "Does that gaze feel a little too directed our way?"

"Absolutely," Eric confirmed, "but that's okay. Let's just see what they do with it."

She stayed close to him, and he wrapped an arm around her shoulders. They walked slowly out to where they had been the previous night, just wanting a few minutes of peace and quiet.

The man probably wondered if he should follow them.

As Eden and Eric reached the space, she pointed out a barrier, apparently to warn people away. She frowned at it. "Is it really dangerous, do you think?"

"I don't know," he muttered in a steady tone, as he studied it.

Eden continued. "It does appear they are trying to stop people from going there, and that could be just a safety consideration for the people here. Also maybe just to keep out people who are potentially looking to investigate."

Eric nodded. "Don't look now, but we're being watched."

She tried not to stiffen up, but it was hard. As they sat down, and a breeze came up, she jerked around as she thought she heard something. Something way too recognizable.

"What's the matter?" Eric asked.

"I swear to God"—Eden tilted her head, as another mocking laugh came her way again—"I swear to God, Debbie said something to me, which I didn't understand. She's here with us." Eden's voice was breathless. "How is that possible?" she muttered.

"I don't know that it is," Eric pointed out. "Are you sure it's Debbie?"

"No, I'm never sure it's Debbie. I always assume it's her because once it was her—or so I thought—but there's always that chance it's not her at all." She groaned, then glanced back in the direction where the woman had died. "You don't think the deceased woman is speaking to me, do you?"

Startled, he shook his head. "No, I don't think so at all. I don't think that's anything to worry about. Not sure we want to do hauntings as a weekend experience either."

"Yeah, well, you say that, but—"

He again wrapped his arm around her, hugged her close, and added, "I'm sorry this is turning out to be a little more than we expected."

"You're not kidding," she grumbled.

Just then her name was called across the wind. She stiffened and looked around.

Eric frowned and asked, "What's the matter?"

"Somebody just called my name," she replied, twisting

to look behind her again. "Somebody literally just called my name."

"I didn't hear anything. Are you sure?"

"Yes, I'm sure."

Frowning, he faced her and asked, "And was it earthly?"

She winced. "I don't know." She slumped back beside him and clarified, "I would have thought so, but I really don't know."

Just then, it came again.

Eden.

She stiffened. Eric eyed her, questions in his expression, and she asked, "You heard that too? It's not just me, right?" But, when they both turned, nothing was there. No one was there.

She cried out, "I feel as if I'm going crazy." Then she frowned. "You know, Debbie did mention something about that."

"What do you mean?"

"She told me once about feeling as if she were going crazy."

"When?"

"Recently," she replied. "I never even thought about it until just now."

He stared at her. "Want to give me some context to go with that?"

"I don't know that I can," she conceded. "I'll have to think about it and see if I can remember more about that. It was during our joint seminar weekend."

"Did Debbie ever take drugs?"

Eden grimaced. "I don't know. I would have initially thought no, but, after some of her choices in men, now I'm not so sure."

"Right," he muttered.

Just then, the voice—hard and angry—ripped across the air behind them. *Eden.*

She stood up, staring around. The sun was already setting, and she saw nothing ahead of her or around her, but there was absolutely no mistaking the sound of somebody calling out to her.

Beside her, Eric stood up too. He studied the garden, the areas around her, and whispered, "Seems to be time to go."

She turned to him and nodded. "Yeah, let's go. I just heard my name again, and the voice sounded … angry."

He nodded. "I know—"

"No, I swear I heard—Wait. You're agreeing with me?" She was shocked. "How did you know?"

"Because I heard it too."

"You did?"

"Yes, but the problem is, I'm not sure it was human."

AT ABOUT MIDNIGHT, Eric slipped out of their suite. As he got downstairs, somebody was at the front desk.

The clerk looked at him and asked, "Can't sleep?"

"No, I'll just go outside and get a breath of fresh air."

The front desk clerk frowned and suggested, "After last night, we're not really happy with the concept of anybody going outside at this hour."

"I get that," Eric noted, with a smile, "but no reason for me not to, unless you're telling me it's dangerous out there."

"No, it's not dangerous," he stated. Then he winced. "But if you come back dead—"

He laughed. "If I come back dead, I won't care."

"Yeah, I know what you mean," he muttered, groaning,

"but it's always been a peaceful place here. We've never had a death in all these years that the resort has been here, so this has got us in a bit of a tizzy."

"But it was under natural circumstances, right?"

"Yeah, and that's the only thing that makes it somewhat better," he added, shaking his head. "Otherwise this whole thing would be shocking and would stop me from sleeping at night. Yet I'm just sitting here, doing the books, trying to take care of all the lovely paperwork I get to deal with as the accountant for the hotel," he explained. "So go ahead for your walk, but I'll stay out here until you come back in. Be safe out there, and please come back as soon as you can."

"Good enough." Eric smiled, then stepped outside into the fresh air and headed back to the bench where he had been sitting with Eden earlier. As he sat down again, he waited, waited for some energy sensation to hit. When nothing came, he slowly opened his senses.

Massive waves of energy hit him. He was buffeted by the strong pull, wondering what the hell was going on, when suddenly he heard Stefan's voice in his head, bearing a warning.

Be careful.

"Yeah, I'm trying to be careful," he muttered. "What the hell is this?"

That, Stefan began, *is the opening of a pressure valve. We don't see very many of these,* he murmured, *but it's unmistakable.*

"And what am I supposed to do with it?"

For the moment, now that you've opened it, you'll need to sit there and try to assimilate some of the energies that are swirling around you. Try not to take on too many at a time, without letting them go, he explained, his tone sharp. *Let them in but send them right back out again. You don't want to mess with them, not ever.*

"And if I don't?"

They'll grab hold, and they won't want to let go.

Without thinking anything about that, Eric tried to close the energy, but it was too much, too strong for him. He struggled against the heavy winds battering him from left to right, when Stefan stepped in.

Hold tight. I'll see if I can help you shut this down a bit.

And it took both of them several long minutes working together before it was safe to relax ever-so-slightly.

I don't know what you just landed yourself in, Stefan noted, his voice breathless as he spoke, *but that was a training program I would love to have available, but I want it under my control, not something that can go wild like that.*

"Yeah, you're not kidding," Eric muttered, as he straightened up his clothes. "That was a little more than what I expected."

Are you okay?

"Yeah, I am," he replied cautiously, "but I still don't know what that was."

Yeah, we'll have to talk about that. Is she with you?

"No, she's not. I left her back in her hotel room."

Smart.

"Why? Do you think she's part of this?"

No, she's not a part of this, he snapped, *but she's part of whatever this overall problem is. And that is starting to sound as if it may be a much bigger issue than I thought.*

"I wasn't thinking that at all," Eric admitted. "I came to investigate the center and to help her sort out the fact that Debbie may or may not have been involved in something here."

Does Eden think Debbie was involved?

"I don't think Eden has any clue. She's still trying to reevaluate what her friend was to her and whether they were even friends at all."

That's always fun, Stefan noted in a dry tone. *Not exactly the thing anybody wants to do.*

"Especially when they were friends for a very long time, so anything I say doesn't hit quite right. Eden's got all these memories of how her friend was, but, after a little bit of time, Eden will finally see and feel the reality and will then discover that what I'm suggesting is quite likely the truth."

I hope you can get to the bottom of things sooner rather than later.

"Me too. What did you think about Eden's abilities?"

I don't think she has any clue. She's just instinctive …

"Powerful?"

Yes, but I'm not exactly sure in what way, he admitted. *I really want to spend some more time sorting her out, but I don't think she'll be interested in that for quite a while.*

"It depends on this weekend," Eric replied, "and it depends on how bad things go south."

You need to watch out because, based on what was going on just now, things could go south in a big way. Stefan muttered, *I also want to talk to Dr. Maddy about it.*

"Dr. Maddy? Who's that?"

Someone who's been doing this for a long time.

"Great. Any help you've got to give, I am here to listen."

Stefan snorted. *You might be there to listen, but something is happening at that place, and it's happening in a big way. I'm just not sure that it's contained to that place, or if it's much bigger, like …* an Origin.

CHAPTER 11

EDEN WOKE TO a warm sense of well-being and a curious happiness inside. The feeling was so unfamiliar that she considered it for a long moment—until everything came rushing back again as to where she was and why she was here. Her sense of belonging and her joy all disappeared, as if snapped away. "Shit."

Of course the whole point of meditating was to find that center of balance, that space where she could just let go, could relax, and wouldn't be stressed out by everything going on around her. However, that was easier said than done, particularly in these circumstances. Yet not impossible, since she had just woken up in the perfect zone, only to have something kill the mood.

She groaned as she shifted on the bed. Right now, as opposed to mere minutes before, her bed felt nowhere near as comfortable as it had when she first awoke. She wasn't sure how that trick worked, but it had happened to her enough times to realize it was all about mind-set.

And the mind-set angle was fine and dandy if everything in your world was going well. But the mind-set, as soon as anything shifted, was much less than ideal. She was all about mind over matter, but there were always limitations to what you could will into your life. It's what she had to work with, so that was all there was to it.

When her phone buzzed, her screen confirmed Eric was contacting her. She answered in a sleepy tone, still struggling to get the rest of her worries out of her mind.

"Good morning."

She smiled. "Good morning to you too, Detective." She tried for a neutral tone, but the playfulness in her tone was unmistakable. "Did you get any sleep last night?"

He hesitated, then replied, "I got some."

"Which probably means you got none," she suggested, surprised.

"I'll explain later, but definitely not something I want to do over the phone."

She bolted upright. "What happened?" she snapped. "You can't just leave that hanging."

"I won't. Are you up for an early morning walk?"

"Yes, particularly if I get an explanation for what you just said."

His reply was half laughter and half bark. "Fine. I'll meet you downstairs in about, what, … ten minutes?"

"Make that fifteen. I'm not out of bed yet."

An obvious smile filled his tone as he spoke. "Fine. And then we'll get breakfast afterward."

"Do we have time?" she asked.

"Yes, we're fine. The seminar doesn't start quite so early this morning."

"Good." She yawned again. "Can't say I'm quite ready for that yet."

"I'll meet you downstairs." With that, he ended the call.

She didn't know him well enough to really understand all his moods, but he seemed a little curt, or at least more so than usual, based on what she knew.

If something else was going on, obviously he needed to

fill her in. She pulled herself out of bed and quickly dressed in leggings and a long T-shirt. She pulled her hair back into a ponytail and laughed at her image in the mirror. She looked like a teenager. Ready to start the day, she walked downstairs to the lobby, not sure if she would see Eric there or if he would already be outside. But, sure enough, there he was, waiting for her at the bottom of the stairs. He smiled, and real humor was in his gaze as he took in her outfit.

She shrugged. "I know. I look like I'm about sixteen. It was the best I could do this morning."

He burst out laughing. "I would give you a few more years than that but not many for sure."

She smiled. "Sometimes it's just nice to be carefree. I woke up in an absolutely great mood this morning, and then somehow that feeling just died almost as quickly."

He nodded somberly. "As soon as you woke up and remembered, right?"

"Yeah," she muttered. "That's exactly what happened."

He reached out with an open hand, and instinctively she placed hers in it.

As they walked outside, the receptionist called out, "Good morning." She smiled at them. "Enjoy your walk."

"Will do," Eden called back.

Together, the two of them walked out into the morning sun.

They kept walking until they got to the place where they had sat before. "If we plan to sit here for a while, we should have brought coffee," she suggested.

"I thought about it," he replied in a low tone, "and then realized that it might be nice to just enjoy being outside for a bit, then go in for coffee when we're ready."

She didn't say anything but nodded. An obvious silence

followed for a long moment, and then she finally asked, "Okay, so what's going on?" She turned to him and waited.

He sighed and then began, "I came out here around midnight, just to clear my head. I wanted to be in this spot and to rethink this whole thing."

She stared at him. "You could have called me. I would have come out with you."

He gave her a lopsided grin. "Part of that was I just needed to be alone to try and … maybe assess the whole scenario."

She sank back and looked at him. "Why do I feel a whole lot more is involved in *assessing the scenario*?"

"Remember when I mentioned Stefan?"

"Yes, I do remember that, and I did look him up," she stated.

"I talked to him."

"What about?"

"I don't know if I mentioned it before, but I've worked with him a little bit," he said, with a snort, "in a purely professional capacity."

"I get that."

"But what you don't know is that I am also working with him personally, trying to increase my own skills and abilities. I didn't tell Captain Louis that. I haven't told anybody. I had seen and heard of some of Stefan's work through other cases, and he contacted me. He recognized what skills I had, and I asked him if he knew of any way to build upon, you know, a cop's intuition or whatever you want to call it, and, if so, would he help me," he shared, with a smirk.

She stared at him and could see that this clearly wasn't an easy thing for him to share.

Eric continued. "He confirmed that I had a lot of abilities, but I wasn't the best at opening up about them."

She continued to stare at him.

Though she didn't shift back, he almost felt her recoiling, even though she didn't mean to. "That reaction is exactly why I don't tell people."

She blinked at him several times and then added, "I guess I can see what a challenge that would be."

"It would be a challenge, but I'm really not too bothered about how people view me," he replied, yet his tone was a little harsher.

She winced. "I'm sorry. I'm not judging you. I don't want you to think that. It's just a lot to take in."

"Look. The only reason I'm even thinking along those lines is because, having talked with Stefan, I now understand that it's possible to connect with the deceased, and I guess I'm wondering about trying to connect with Debbie myself." He studied her for a moment, waiting for her reaction.

She frowned. "Through Stefan?"

"He doesn't do that, not that I know of anyway," he noted, "but that does go along with what I was about to say."

She grimaced. "And I keep interrupting, so I'm sorry for that."

He snorted. "It's not about interrupting at all," he clarified. "It's more about keeping an open mind."

"Which you're already afraid I don't have, right?"

"Not necessarily," he conceded. "I'm not looking for anyone's approval, but I do need information. Have you ever felt as if Debbie was at your house?"

Eden winced because she would rather not answer that. "I have spent some time yelling and screaming and calling out to her to tell me what the hell was going on, what she got herself into, and whether or not Richard had anything to do with her death."

"And did you ever hear a response?"

She stared at him, carefully considering whether she wanted him to know the truth. The answer was not an easy one, but who knows what he would think of the windows shutting, doors banging, and papers swirling. "I really didn't hear anything," she hedged, her tone sharp, "but then I wasn't expecting to hear anything either."

The look on his face revealed a lot of what he was thinking.

"Other than her calling out my name the other night."

"You're serious, aren't you?"

"Yes, I'm damn serious," she snapped. "And I get that I sound like I'm off my rocker now." She thought about it and then chuckled. "To a certain extent, you're right. I do," she agreed, "but I can't stop wondering if you contacted her. Did you get any answers?"

"I didn't come out here to contact Debbie, and, no, I didn't have more contact with her," he explained. "However, something did happen, and it was a fairly bizarre scenario."

"Scenario?" she repeated. "That sounds—"

He sat back. "I opened my senses, and a maelstrom hit me, strong, buffeting me from side to side."

She stared at him, not even sure if she wanted to know more. It was pretty far-fetched, yet he was a really down-to-earth guy. "So, what did you do?"

"I didn't have a clue what was going on, so I did nothing, though I ended up hearing from Stefan. He has a unique way of contacting you when you're in trouble, and he stepped in and gave me a hand to control whatever that was."

She stared at him. "This is starting to sound pretty scary."

"He called it potentially something like an *Origin*, but I don't really know what that means."

"I don't know what it means either," she replied. She wanted to refute what he was saying and to just flat-out not believe him, but so such sincerity filled his tone that she knew she couldn't easily walk away from it. Plus, she did feel Debbie was around, and lately that became more of a norm than anything else. Eden's sense of normalcy was gone, and she was always expecting things to fly around her, but that had happened only once, and she was pretty sure she imagined it all.

But if Eric felt something too … "When you say, *maelstrom, energies buffeting—*"

"Yeah, all swirling around me, like I was in the center of a storm," Eric confirmed, confused as hell, "and yet I was the only one there."

"I would have been terrified."

"Let's just say that I wasn't as comfortable as I would have liked. Stefan mentioned something about loving to have some training available for these things, but he would want to have control so that students wouldn't have any unpleasant surprises."

"Students? Does he really train people?"

"I think to some degree. I got the impression that it's not so much that he trains people but that people come to him looking for help, and he feels an obligation to help them. I also got the impression that it has come at a personal cost, which he may not have expected."

She shook her head as she studied the space around them. "Do you think it was Debbie?" she asked, both hope and worry in her tone. "Because, if it was her, wouldn't that mean she was stuck here? Even though she didn't die here. Or did she?"

Eden was worried, but, in the back of her mind, there was also fear. "I don't really understand ghost lore," she shared, glancing around, "and I can't believe I'm even saying that. But, if that's a thing, do you think it's something I should be worried about for Debbie?"

"I have no idea," he admitted, facing her. "That is something we would have to ask Stefan. Most people think that ghosts are intended to head off and to do their own thing as soon as they're dead, but I'm not sure that's the case here right now."

"How can you say that?" she asked curiously. "Do you think Debbie's here though? How do you explain that?"

"I can't, and I'm not sure that she was here. I just know that, when I sat here and opened up my senses—something I almost always do at a crime scene when I'm puzzled over something—all hell broke loose. Stefan says I should do a hell of a lot more of that sort of thing, but last night was nothing I've ever experienced before." He took a deep breath and added, "I wasn't even sure I should mention it to you."

"I'm glad you did," she said. "I mean, it's disconcerting to even think that that was possible, but I would rather know it's possible and have an idea of what is going on, especially in terms of where Debbie may be." *Not to mention not feel so crazy when I see that in the future,* she thought to herself, as her mind was off and running one hundred miles an hour again.

"God help me, that sounds absolutely ridiculous in this context," he shared.

She nodded. "What could *Origin* mean?"

He winced. "I'm not sure I have an answer for you. Stefan didn't really give me an answer either, but he mentioned something about not having ever seen one, or maybe it was not having seen one in a very long time. But said that there were places on earth that were more otherworldly than others. Places that opened doors…"

"So, they're rare and—"

"Say what you mean to say," Eric urged her.

"It could be a portal of sorts," she suggested.

"That's why I don't want to say it either, since it brings up all kinds of horror-movie symbolism that I'm not sure we really need or should be expressing at this point."

She scrubbed her face, her mind racing. "Good God," she murmured out loud. "This is not what I expected you to say this morning."

He laughed out loud. "No, I'm sure it isn't," he agreed, "but, regardless, one of the things I want to do is try to open that up again."

"Oh, hell no!" She stared at him, incredulous. "Why in God's name would you want to do that?"

"Because we need to know."

His tone was calm, adamant, and she knew for a fact that, despite her feelings on the matter, he was right. "When do you want to do that?"

"Tonight. This is Sunday, and the seminar ends today, remember? But we can stay on for a couple more nights, if I can convince my captain. My options are limited."

She stared at him, surprised, then nodded. "That's true. Not exactly what we came for though, is it?"

His jaw worked, as if struggling to get the words out. "Or it's exactly what we came for."

AFTER BREAKFAST, ERIC and Eden walked back into the main part of the hotel, heading to their assigned rooms for the meditation seminar.

Having a few minutes to spare, Eric stopped at the front desk and chatted with the woman there, talking about Debbie's death after attending last week's seminar, even going so far as to explain he was a detective.

Turns out she was the hotel manager, mentioning how sad it was that she died, but the manager knew nothing further about it apparently.

Eric didn't know if he believed her or not. But then, nobody really considered Debbie's death suspicious, since she'd died at home, so most people here at the hotel felt it didn't involve them.

The hotel manager had obviously been quite upset when he continued to speak about Debbie, but more so about any potential negativity of her death being associated with the hotel.

He assured her that he didn't see anything out of the ordinary. Still, he was wondering if the hotel manager had seen or had spoken to Debbie while she was here. So he asked her about that.

Shrugging, she replied, "I'm not even sure I know which one she was." When Eric pulled out her picture, the manager's response was unmistakable.

She winced, and then she sighed. "Yes, I remember her. I mean, it was hard to miss her as she and Richard appeared to be an item."

"When did they become an item?"

"Here, as far as I know," she said cautiously, as if trying to not say anything wrong.

"So, they didn't know each other beforehand?"

"I don't think so, but that's really just an assumption," she stated.

He nodded. "I suppose it could have just been a weekend fling. I mean, that must happen here a lot, *huh*?"

"Absolutely, and, chances are, that's exactly what it was," she noted. "You know how it is. You get a chance to get away, and you let your hair down a bit, and sometimes the clothing comes off too," she added, with a tentative smile. "However, it wouldn't have had anything to do with us."

"What about Richard? How often does he arrange a retreat here in this location?"

"He does these, oh, twelve, sometimes fourteen times a year, mostly during the spring and summertime," she shared. "But all we do is provide the space, and, for the most part, we get a lot of positive feedback, and it's good for business. He's apparently an excellent trainer."

"And, of course, you don't want anything to affect that."

"No," she declared. "I really don't. As I said, it's been very good for business."

He nodded. "I'm not here to cause any trouble."

She looked at him warily, as if not quite sure she believed him.

He smiled. "And I get it. Hospitality is not the easiest of industries, and anything with a potential for a negative impact could reverberate and could cost you valuable business."

The hotel manager grimaced. "It can be brutal, you know? Nobody says anything, yet they say everything. So, from our perspective, if there is any problem, we would want to hear about it early, so we could stop it before it lands someone in serious trouble."

"Has anything landed someone in trouble?"

"To the best of my knowledge, there hasn't been any trouble. I'm sorry to hear about Debbie, but I will admit it's a relief that she didn't pass away here."

"Yes, of course," Eric replied, trying hard not to express his opinion, "particularly after the death of the other young woman recently here on the grounds."

She blanched and nodded. "That isn't a good thing either," she agreed, "and she's been here multiple times. I know she really loved being here."

"And maybe that was a good thing for her, in that her passing was at a place she loved," he suggested.

She nodded. "I want to think so." She wrapped her arms around her chest. "It is a little disconcerting that you're now talking about somebody I spoke to several times and won't see again."

He considered that and nodded. "And again I'm not trying to cause you any trouble." She looked at him in disbelief, and he sighed. "I do have a job to do. We're just crossing the *T*s, dotting the *I*s, and making sure nothing here needs to be investigated."

"There isn't," she stated crossly. "I don't know anything about what happened to the poor woman, and I certainly don't know anything about what happened to Deborah Kingston." She looked down at the picture again. "I'm just very sorry that two beautiful young women were here, and both of them are now dead, but it's also the nature of the work Richard does."

"In what way?" Eric asked, surprised. "I thought it was meditation."

"Sure. But along with meditation comes self-healing, sometimes hands-on healing. It frequently comes with people who have high expectations that nobody in their right mind could ever possibly meet, but some people are determined that they should get some miracle."

"And?"

She sighed. "Hey, I'm not against miracles. I would absolutely love for everybody to have a miracle in their life. I'm just not sure how often that happens, but, if it does happen, good for them. We all could use a few more miracles in life."

He smiled. "I'm with you there. Life is hard enough without anything causing distress and derailing any progress."

"Exactly," she muttered, her tone softer now. "So, enjoy your time here, but be aware that the hotel is not involved in anything related to these two women."

"I'll keep that in mind," he said.

"I must admit that you've depressed me over these deaths," she shared. "I think I'll step outside and take a walk in the gardens for a bit." And, with that, she excused herself, called one of the other women to take her place, and slowly moved outside, where he watched her taking several large, deep breaths, trying to recenter herself.

Eric headed to his assigned meditation room, where everything was set up. Everybody was gathered around, and he seemed to be the last one to arrive. That didn't particularly bother him, but he was checking out where Eden had ended up.

Not seeing her, he frowned, and he widened his efforts to confirm she was nearby. He had to admit that his experience with the Origin last night had unnerved him in a way he had never expected. He wasn't sure what was going on, and the fact that Stefan saw something that half made sense to him, yet was not necessarily smooth sailing, unnerved Eric even more.

The last thing they wanted was to get into energetic psychic crap with a difficulty level off the charts, especially when Eric had no clear answers on how to proceed. He took his spot in the meditation room, just a little farther back than he had been the previous day. He wanted to be close to the exit so he could sneak out.

He had seen multiple people do the same thing throughout the day and knew that nobody would cause him any issue if he wasn't here. Yet he also didn't want to bring Eden into this if he didn't have to. She was here to find answers to Debbie's death, if any were to be had. So, if he found answers for both deaths, that would solve a lot of their problems.

At least it would solve some of them.

Eric sent Cody a quick text, asking for an update on the death of the woman from the other night.

He got a text back saying he would follow up with the coroner, asking Eric if he thought they were connected.

No. Maybe. No idea whatsoever.

But the fact that two deaths were associated with the same seminar program, at the same hotel, with the same people involved was one thing. The other thing was Stefan talking about this Origin thing—which made Eric's skin crawl but also brought his intuition online in a big way.

He just didn't have any clue in which direction this was going.

And, because of that, it felt as if he were throwing out feelers in all directions, hoping that something would land properly and would give them the answers that they needed. He just hoped it would be soon because, with two women dead, the last thing he wanted was to see a third.

Seeing that the lecture would go on for a while, he

slipped outside and headed around to the back of the gardens and up to the same place where he had been sitting with Eden.

He wasn't sure how long it would take, or if he could even go to the same place or could elicit the same response he had had earlier. But he sat down in the same place as before and tried to slowly open his senses a little crack. Much to his dismay, the energies crackled, as if a sliver of light were enough to coax out whomever or whatever was hiding just behind the curtain.

Almost immediately the forces rent that opening wider and wider. He struggled to hold on, feeling his own abilities quickly maxed out.

Suddenly Stefan was there again. *You should have told me,* he muttered, as he joined forces to close the curtain again.

"I just thought I would see what was going on," Eric explained, just as the door was slammed shut. He sat here for a moment, stunned at the speed at which *something* had taken over. "I didn't think it would be that bad."

No? Stefan snapped. *You need to be careful with this, Eric. And I'm not sure* that bad *will be measurable. A crazy amount of raw power sits there, and we need to take another look at that before you go barging in again. Give me a heads-up next time, and I'll get reinforcements.*

Stefan was right, but, then again, Eric was too stubborn to admit anything. "Is there a map of these places around the world?"

Wouldn't that be nice? Stefan muttered, with half a laugh. *It would certainly make life easier if there was. But nobody will travel around the world and try to map them. We already know of a lot of these, but we have no clue where they are until we stumble across one. Only as they come up can we figure out where it's located and what kind it is.*

"There are different kinds?"

Stefan laughed at Eric's question. *If you are stepping into this world, you need to be aware of the risks. People like to close their eyes and ignore what they don't understand, but you are not most people because you can throw back the curtain and let loose all kinds of shit.*

"Yes. Of course," he muttered. "I just thought—"

The thought was correct, and you're right in your own way. That's how we figure this out, in steps. And you were close, but you let fear get in there. That can be a powerful thing because it gives these places something to feed on, and they only get stronger, then ravage the other energies.

"It just opened so fast," he tried to explain. "I opened it just a tiny bit, thinking maybe I could figure out what was there, if somebody … needed *out*, needed to say something. Although that feels right too."

A moment of silence came from Stefan. *That is a pretty interesting thought, and we can certainly try again. Now that the two of us are here, if you want to give it a go, this is as good a time as any.*

"Are you sure?" Eric asked.

Yes. Now I want you to focus. Remember some of the things we've been working on. In this case, we also need protection because I don't know what's on the other side of this. As soon as Eric had done the few things that Stefan had asked of him, Stefan began, *Now we'll open this, and we'll only let out just a little bit of the energy. Hold it steady, and don't panic.*

"Out or in?" he asked.

In this case, probably both, Stefan noted. *We're letting something out, but we're also potentially letting something in.*

"That makes no sense."

No, to you, it probably doesn't, Stefan corrected, *but let's just take it one step at a time and see what we can come up with.*

As soon as they opened it, just that little bit, the forces were screaming to rip wide open that tiny slice of a door.

As the energies stood at the entranceway, Eric noted, "It's almost like I can see in here."

Stefan pondered that for a moment and said, *Good because it's just total blackness for me.*

"Seriously? I'm seeing faces," Eric stated.

What kind of faces?

Eric frowned. "I don't understand that question. Plain and simple faces, Stefan, like people."

When you say you see faces, are they clear? Can you see features? Or are they indistinct? As in maybe, you know, people who have been gone a long time ago?

Almost understanding what Stefan was asking, Eric tried to search a little bit deeper, a little bit closer, and then realized that, as soon as he tried to lock on to something, it would disappear. When he explained it, Stefan chuckled.

That makes a lot of sense.

"I'm glad it does to you," Eric muttered, "because it doesn't make a lick of sense to me."

That's because you're trying to work with something that's old and doesn't necessarily have the same rules as what you're used to.

"Rules? I wasn't aware any rules were at play here," he stated, with a snort. "Anytime you want to give me a copy of the rule book, I would sure be happy to have it."

Most people can't even begin to do what you're doing. So, just the fact that you're even in here with me and holding your own is fabulous. The fact that you're doing better than that is even more surprising, but I'm thrilled because having these abilities can go a long way in your work.

"I don't really want to be dealing with the dead."

Stefan laughed. *Maybe, but think of the advantages. Something is always happening in your line of work, where the dead are speaking up and looking for answers. You may have just opened yourself up to that.*

"And if I don't want that?" he asked, his voice gaining in strength.

A calm, almost contemplative moment passed before Stefan replied, *I don't think you have a choice.* And, with that, he announced, *That's enough for now. I need to step out and deal with something else. Don't open this any further, but keep it as it is.*

"What? You sure I can do this alone?"

You can, Stefan shared. *I want you to just hold it right here. If you see something weird, don't let go, don't panic. Just hold on. Don't let it get to you, and I'll be back in a minute.*

And, with that, Stefan disappeared, leaving Eric alone and shocked, stuck in whatever this portal was that he had somehow decided was a good idea to open.

CHAPTER 12

SITTING IN YET another meditation session, Eden kept looking around for Eric but couldn't find him. She couldn't shake the feeling that something was wrong. And yet she couldn't tell if it was just her growing anger or a valid concern that he had headed off to do something without her.

Either way, it felt wrong to just sit here and to ignore the sensation. She sidled toward the back exit and then made a dash out of the room, hoping it would look as if she needed to go to the bathroom and would soon return. As she went around the corner, she saw Richard's brother talking to the receptionist.

He raised an eyebrow. "Problems?"

She shook her head and then blushed. She had the perfect excuse. "Just have to run to the bathroom." And, with that, she made good her escape, as if heading toward the bathrooms, which thankfully were right around the corner. But around that corner was also a set of stairs.

And that's where she headed. She didn't know what the hell was going on with Eric, but his continued absence was something she couldn't ignore. So, she quickly slipped out the side door, hoping it didn't set off any alarms.

She bolted up to the green area where Eric had been sitting before. And, sure enough, there he was, sitting with a strange expression on his face, completely motionless, yet almost as if he were fighting a battle, … just not physically.

She knew how insane that sounded. She noted movement, but it wasn't outside of him. It appeared to be inside his body. Everything in her wanted to touch him, but she somehow knew that even the slightest touch could be catastrophic.

Why had he chosen to do this once more? Particularly when he had encountered a problem before. And yet here he was, out here trying to do it all over again and all alone. Angry, perturbed, and feeling so helpless, Eden sat protectively beside him as the fear built up inside her.

She was afraid he needed to do this, but he didn't know how to do any of this safely. Yet her instincts had brought her here, even now clamoring at her to do something, … anything.

She bounced up, walked around him, sat down again, bounced up, walked around, raising her hands in frustration as she sat back down again. "What am I supposed to do?" she asked out loud because it felt as if she was supposed to do something.

A crystal-clear voice announced, "And you need to do it now."

She looked around and asked, "Who said that?" Eden knew it wasn't Debbie, as the voice was masculine. Scared, she watched Eric's expressions twist, as something built up inside him, as if fighting something, and she didn't know what.

"Eric, come back to me, please. Get back here." Her voice rose, until she realized that she would cause a scene and could attract attention, which was the last thing she needed. When another voice sounded so close to her, she twisted around, looking for the speaker.

She finally called out, "Who is that, and what do you want?" But no clear-cut answer came, and now she was starting to freak out even worse. Who was here? Who was talking to her? And what the hell was Eric doing?

That same voice spoke again, "Inside."

"Inside what?" she whispered angrily.

"You need to go inside you."

What the hell?

She sat down, took some deep breaths, closed her eyes, and tried to step into a meditative state. As she started to calm, she grasped Eric's hand.

He gripped her hand almost like a lifeline, as if fighting some force that only he could see. When he released a heavy sigh beside her, she watched as his shoulders sagged, and he took several deep, calming breaths.

When he finally opened his eyes, his gaze was dark, deeper, with depths that she couldn't explain. He squeezed her hand but didn't let go, and she knew that had to mean something.

"Thank you."

"You're welcome. What were you doing?"

"I wanted to open that portal again."

"Why?" she asked bluntly. "You didn't think you had enough problems with it already?"

"I was afraid that," he explained, "whatever was going on, might get people stuck in there." He added a headshake, followed by a laugh, and then he went on. "Maybe I don't mean *people*, but it felt as if maybe something—some entity, for want of a better word—might be capturing those people."

She stared at him in shock and then, in a low voice, she asked, "Do you think Debbie is there?"

His gaze opened wide as he stared at her. "I don't know," he whispered. "I really don't. I don't know her, but I also didn't get the sensation that anybody named Debbie was there, but again I don't know for sure." She just nodded, and he added, "I'm sorry."

"No, it's okay. You tried."

He laughed. "I'm the one who should apologize. You were heading into a meditation, so I just thought I would take a moment of privacy."

"But, when I realized something was wrong, I ran up here to find you."

"Did anybody see you?"

She nodded. "Richard's brother saw me in the hotel lobby. I told him that I had to go to the bathroom. I was hoping he would just take that at face value and wouldn't question it. And then, of course, as soon as I got around the corner, I ran out here. I don't know if he figured it out and saw me or not," she added, showing her palms. "By the time I got here, you were the only one I was concerned about."

He smiled and squeezed her hand. And this time, almost reluctantly, he let her hand go and shared, "I think I'm okay now."

"You might be okay," she conceded, staring at him, "but I am not."

He faced her and then nodded. "All of this has turned out to be much more of a surprise than I anticipated."

"I don't know that I anticipated anything like this," Eden admitted, narrowing her gaze at him, "but I can tell you that, whatever this is, it's a far cry from anything I thought would happen today."

When he burst out laughing, she hushed him and whispered, "What will they say if they find us up here?"

He smiled, but a fierceness had been added to it. "They'll just think we've stolen a few hours to be by ourselves."

"Maybe, but, in that case, why did we need to come for this meditation retreat?"

"Good point," he noted, but he was still chuckling. He got up and stretched high to the sky and then bent over, dropping his arms and hands to the ground, letting his arms rest on the ground below as he struck a plank pose.

She sighed happily at the prime male in front of her. "You must do yoga."

He turned to her and laughed. "I do enjoy yoga."

"Never pegged you for the type."

"I don't know about *the type*, but I find certain things help me to de-stress at the end of the day, and yoga is definitely one of them."

She nodded. "I had been doing more and more of it myself, … until Debbie's death. Then it seemed as if I let everything go because of it."

He nodded. "And you don't need to blame yourself for that either."

She winced and then shrugged. "You read me so well."

He smiled. "It's not so much that I can read you," he clarified, "but I do seem to understand you better."

She wasn't sure what to even say to that. He was a detective after all, an intuitive one at that. She believed him when he told her that he had some insight into what was driving her, and yet it scared her at the same time. She stood up and asked, "Are you ready to go back?"

"Maybe," he muttered. They took several steps forward, and he fell to his knees, as if a force hit him from behind.

"Whoa, whoa, whoa," she said, checking on him. "Are you okay?"

He frowned. "I *was* okay. … I'm not sure what just happened." As he got up to take another step, something slammed into him again.

She stared, not understanding what was happening here. "I don't like anything about this," she stated, turning and twisting around. "Something out here is terrifying."

He didn't say anything, slowly got up once more, and almost immediately was sent to the ground again. He took several deep breaths and then just sat down.

She looked at him and asked, "Do you want to try again?"

"I'll just sit here for a moment," he murmured. "I'm not sure what this is, why this is here, but it does appear to be something that might require my attention."

"Meaning?"

"Meaning, something *or someone* doesn't want me to leave," he offered.

"Oh." She frowned. "Can we go sit on the bench again? It might be a little more comfortable for you. Can you walk back?"

He thought about it and then nodded. "I'm not getting any resistance to that idea."

"Yeah, but wait until you stand up again."

He gave her a droll look, rose, but faced in the direction they had come. As soon as he did that, the pressure seemed to ease. He nodded. "I can do that much."

Frowning, she watched as he returned to the bench and sat back down again. "*Okay*," he began, "this is weird."

"This is scary—and beyond weird."

He frowned and nodded. "I think I might know someone who I can get to help with this."

"Good," she muttered. "Why can't things just be simple?" she snapped.

Just then she watched as his eyes almost defocused.

"Whoa, whoa, whoa," she cried out. "What's going on? What's the matter?"

He looked at her. "What?"

She stared at him, peered deeper into his eyes, and shared, "Your eyes just went inward. Do you feel okay?"

He frowned and then nodded. In a calm voice, almost acting as if it were completely normal, he announced, "Stefan, we might have to do this out loud."

Immediately an odd sprinkling of a form appeared, standing before her. Just enough light was here that she could see it, yet, at the same time, it was so bright that she couldn't really see anything. "What the hell is happening?" she asked, stepping back, holding her hands in a prayer position.

"This is Stefan," Eric explained. "He can't maintain this state for long, but I need his help right now. So I'll talk to him internally."

"What the hell do you mean, *internally*?" she cried out.

"Telepathically."

That one-word bomb was all she needed to sit down with a *thud*, dumbfounded, staring at Eric in disbelief. Just then a booming voice filled her head, and she clapped her hands over her ears and cried out.

Eric covered her hands with his and shared, "That's Stefan. And it's a whole lot easier if you don't fight it."

She just stared at him in shock, as suddenly the volume was reduced to something almost bearable. She took several deep breaths and asked, "Stefan?"

Yes, the man replied softly in her ears. *Sorry about that, but we really don't have time for niceties.*

She stared at Eric, who nodded. "Oh my God. I can hear him."

You can figure it out later, Stefan suggested. *Right now Eric has a problem, and we need your help.*

ERIC LISTENED AS Stefan explained what was going on. It was a little confusing to Eric, and, from the look on Eden's face, it was beyond shocking to her. However, she wasn't running away, and she appeared to at least be calm for the moment. For Eden's benefit, Stefan added, *I'm speaking telepathically to both of you, yet I do need to save the bulk of my energy to remain in this form before you.*

"So, what have I done?" Eric calmly asked Stefan. "Apparently I've done something."

You did something, all right. Stefan groaned. *Whatever contact you made with somebody, with something, doesn't want you to leave now. Maybe they can't leave themselves, so they want you to stay, or maybe they need to leave and need your help to do so. I just don't know which.*

"How do we figure out which it is?" Eric asked him.

I don't know what the answer is. I'm just telling you that's what's going on.

"If I can't leave, I can't help them," Eric pointed out, "unless they want me to join them in eternity."

Eden snorted.

You can use all the logic you want, Stefan replied, with a note of humor, *but that doesn't mean they understand or care.*

"Ah, I can totally see that," Eric noted. "So, what are our options right now?"

Either we communicate with them and find out what they want or overpower them so that you can detach from whatever energy they have attached to you. That's something you'll need to do regardless because you can't have anybody else yanking your chain like this.

"I agree with that," Eden interjected.

Eric nodded. Just then they heard voices of people nearby, and he stiffened. "This will get awkward," he noted, trying for some calm. Sensing panic in Eden, he quickly reached out a hand and whispered, "It's okay."

"Sure, sure, it's okay," she quipped in disbelief. "I mean, do you hear yourself?"

"It needs to be okay," Eric stated, "because, if I can't leave right now, I'll have to just sit here and look pretty, and that won't last for long." She snorted at that, and he gave a half a laugh. "Okay. So maybe not the best phrase."

"No, you are most definitely not okay. I just watched you forced to your knees by little green men or whatever that no one can see. Nothing about this is okay."

You are right, but you need to let that go, Stefan pointed out. *We need to focus on things right here, right now, and we will find a way through this. Meanwhile, you also need to get rid of everybody.*

She stared at him. "And I'm supposed to do that … how?"

Not only is this now a danger for Eric, but, if anybody else comes around, this entity, whoever it is, could latch on to them as well.

She stared back at the blinking image of Stefan, only nothing was there. "Do you hear yourself?" she whispered.

I do hear myself, he confirmed, *and very quickly other people will hear you as well.*

She blinked, looked over at Eric, and admitted, "I don't know what I'm supposed to do."

He winced. "I have an idea, but chances are you won't like it."

She snorted. "I haven't liked anything about this yet."

It's not the issue at hand, Stefan interrupted. *We obviously have bigger more-pressing priorities to deal with.*

Just as the people were about to crest the hill, Eric offered, "This is the only idea I have, but don't take it personally." And, with that, just as the people were coming around the bend, Eric grabbed Eden's face in his hands, then pulled her toward him and kissed her with as much heartfelt passion as he could muster.

Eden returned the kiss with equal force.

In the background, she heard the people twittering to each other as they laughed and retraced their steps. By then she wasn't aware of anything except Eric's arms, as they wrapped around her and crushed her tightly to him.

She got sucked in immediately to the incredible power of whatever had them in a grip such as she had never, ever experienced before. When she finally let go, she was gasping for air, and she stared at him. "I think they're gone."

His gaze, dark, and his face, unreadable, he nodded, his breathing barely in control. "Yeah, and that's a good thing."

She didn't say anything, still gasping for breath herself. She got up and walked over several paces, trying to shake off whatever the hell had just happened.

When she came back to him, he reached out a finger and gently rubbed her bottom lip. "I don't know what the hell that was, but we're picking that up again later."

ERIC FOUND IT hard to refocus, but he only had a small window to get Stefan's help with this. "Okay, Stefan, the coast is clear. Now what?"

Only silence came.

Stefan's form reappeared, shimmered once, and wisped out. *At least they're gone for the moment.*

"Yes, they're gone," Eric confirmed, "but we have a very small window before another group comes along, particularly if this is the lunch break."

Right. In that case, we need to contact whoever this entity is and find out what they want, Stefan suggested.

Suddenly a squawk registered just inside Eric's head. He looked over to Eden, who stared at him in shock. He frowned and asked, "Are you okay?" She just nodded. But her gaze was curious, not upset, more like unsure of something. He realized that she heard the squawk as well. He reached out a hand and squeezed hers again. She clung to it. Meanwhile he discussed things with Stefan.

Stefan replied, *We'll have to go back in and try to get that person back there.*

"And yet ..." Eden stopped.

Yet what? Stefan asked.

Eden continued. "If this person is a prisoner, how do we let them out? Maybe they shouldn't be let back out. Even if we can somehow free them, what's to say that will stick, and they won't be sucked right back in?"

Stefan paused for a long moment, before responding. *Later tonight we could possibly do that, but, right now, I'm not sure it'll be that easy.*

Eden frowned. "Right, I agree. However, if putting them back in means locking them up again, you know that we'll have a hell of a fight on our hands." She looked around to check if anyone else was coming their way. "If it were me, and I had been locked up—as it seems they have been—I would do anything to avoid that again." She snorted. "I would fight tooth and nail to ensure I didn't have to go back in there."

Eric agreed. "I just don't know that we have time, considering the amount of energy needed and the limited space we have here." He swung his arms around, noting the nearby drop-off by this very bench. "It's not as if this is a good place to do it."

She gave him a droll look. "*Right.* And yet you thought it was a good place to open this door." He glared at her, but her lips twitched.

You also have to consider, Stefan added, *that they may not be so much the victim as the hunter.*

Eric's gut clenched in that. "Seriously?"

Yes, seriously, Stefan stated. *We don't know anything about this situation. For you to continue to function without this person controlling you, we need to know more.*

Eric swallowed hard and then nodded. "Agreed. Suggestions?"

Yeah, we'll stuff them back in and will help them get out at another time, Stefan noted.

"Can we do it?" Eden asked.

Yes, I believe we can, and we must because, if that doesn't work, Stefan replied, *we've got a much bigger fight on our hands. So, before they gain any more ground, we need to move and fast.*

Eric nodded. "Let's start then."

Sure, but we need a different location where you aren't quite so … public.

Eric stood up, looked around, and then pointed. "There is that little hollow where I found the woman."

The dead woman? Stefan asked in a brash tone.

"Yes, the dead woman."

As they walked toward it, waiting to hear back from Stefan, Eden looked at Eric and asked, "Is there any chance that woman is dead because of this Origin portal?"

He froze on the spot, then turned to face her. "I don't think so, but I don't know." He looked around and asked, "Stefan, do you have any insight on that?"

Not at the moment, but obviously—Oh, yes, there is absolutely some connection. This is … interesting.

"What's interesting?" she cried out. "You can't just say it's interesting and then not fill in the blanks."

I hadn't really looked into her death, Stefan admitted, *because it didn't appear to be related in any way, but it absolutely is related. And that's an even bigger reason why we must deal with this Origin.*

"Damn," Eric muttered softly.

"Enough with the damns and all," Eden snapped. "None of what you just said, Stefan, makes me feel any better," she murmured. "And why are we walking over to the place where a woman lay dying, particularly if her death is connected to this Origin, to what's going on right now? Wouldn't that mean that she opened the portal herself?"

No, not at all, Stefan stated. *It doesn't mean that she opened the portal. It's likely that someone did, or, if somebody is controlling this portal, they had some way to open it, potentially to gain new inhabitants.*

She stopped and swallowed. "What do you mean?"

"He means they are harvesting more of them," Eric explained somberly.

"As in new people to lock up?" Eden asked.

Yes, Stefan confirmed.

An odd silence followed. Then finally, knowing that he

had to ask for Eden's sake, if nothing else, Eric spoke up. "Is that likely what happened to Debbie?"

I don't know, Stefan admitted. *Yet I don't think we can discount it. It might just be that this woman's death is connected to only Debbie's death. Regardless, this portal is open, and somebody is trying to get out. And now they seem to want new people to get in.*

"How do you want to do this?" Eric asked.

Carefully, Stefan replied. *We can't make a mistake here, nor can we assume anything. The last thing we want is to find out that whatever choice you make will be your last. We don't want you to end up being their next guest.*

"How old is something like this?" Eden asked into the dead silence that followed.

The portal? This one? Stefan asked. *I have no idea. I don't know if there's any way to even figure it out. All I can tell you is that it's far older than anything you have ever even imagined,"* he shared.

"Hundreds of years, thousands even?" she asked.

Yes, Stefan replied. *Yes, to all of it, and again there's no way to know.*

"So, why would they need new souls now?" she asked.

Eric felt her tension. Hell, he wasn't feeling very good about any of this either. And it seemed as if the entity was swirling around him faster and faster, almost as if the entity's own fear just funneled faster and drew Eric closer. "We have to do something fast," he finally said, sensing the urgency. "Whatever is going on, this energy is terrified and is not looking to get locked back up again. I can feel its terror. I can feel its pain. I can feel so much of it," he said, "that, believe me, they won't go back where they were."

Agreed, Stefan replied, *I can feel that too.*

Eden added, "Yet we need answers, and we need them now."

Stefan snorted. *That's fine. You might need answers,* he pointed out, *but making a mistake now could mean saying goodbye to Eric, and then there will be no answers, ... at least none that we'll like.*

"I get it," Eden muttered.

No, you don't, Stefan countered. *You're in a rush, but I can tell you that whatever is going on at that retreat is completely different from what's going on here at the Origin portal.*

"Are you sure?" she asked. "I mean, you're absolutely positive that the resort people have nothing to do with this Origin?" When Eric turned to her in surprise, she shrugged.

"Eden, look at me. This Origin *could* be why Debbie died the way she did. As for Richard and Rinaldo, I just can't be sure if they had something to do with her death or this most recent death or not. And I know it probably sounds as if I want them to be involved, but I really don't. I just want answers."

"That's all we ever want," Eden stated. "Whether it's in your field or mine, we just need to know what's happening."

And the way to do that, ... the only way to do that, Stefan interrupted, *is to contact the entity who's now controlling you and talk to them. Or open that damn portal, try to stuff them back in, and deal with it another time. Those are our only options now.*

CHAPTER 13

E DEN STOOD UP and suggested, "I probably need to go back and make it all look normal. I'll pick up a cup of coffee, tell people we might be late returning from lunch," she added, with an eyeroll. "And you know what kind of response that'll get. But at least it will stave off anybody coming in this direction."

"That's actually a good idea," Eric noted.

You two do what you need to do, but you need to do it fast. Stefan replied.

And, with that, she went to step away, only to have Stefan call out, *Stop.*

She froze, then turned back to look at him, and said, "It would be a hell of a lot easier if you weren't ... hidden," she muttered.

Maybe for you, but not for me, Stefan explained. *I stopped you because whatever is going on here affects you too.*

She froze. "What do you mean?"

Once you try to take a step away from this area, you will probably get hit with the exact same bulldozing effect and blockage that Eric did.

Staring in his direction, she headed toward the hotel. And she got smacked right up against an invisible wall. "I didn't have anything to do with this."

They don't care, Stefan noted. *Apparently, whatever is*

going on here is powerful enough that they're not against utilizing both of you for whatever they want right now.

"Un-*freaking*-believable," she muttered, as she turned to look at Eric.

Eric winced and muttered, "I am sorry."

She raised both hands and asked, "Now what? We have to deal with this now, and, since we apparently can't go anywhere else, we have to deal with this here."

Eric nodded. "I agree with you absolutely."

Come back and sit down, Stefan began. *We'll open the portal, and we'll do our best to put whoever this is back in the hole.*

"And I hate that," she muttered. "I absolutely hate the thought of putting this one back in again. I mean, if it were me, you know how hard I would be fighting you," she cried out softly.

We already know this won't be easy. Sit back down again and get ready. Stefan's tone was sharp.

She plunked her butt down right beside Eric, who immediately wrapped an arm around her and pulled her close. She leaned in, needing the comfort from whatever this nightmare was.

"It's all right," Eric muttered. "It'll be fine."

Stefan declared, *I might need to borrow some energy. I need you both to stay there and to not move, while I try to contact this entity and see if we can figure out what happened and how to free you two.*

"So, we just stay put and don't move?" Eden asked.

Yes, just sit still and look pretty. Then he barked, *Do you understand?*

"I understand," she snapped back.

This time humor filled his tone as Stefan spoke. *Good,*

do not leave. And, with that, he disappeared from her mind.

She looked over at Eric. "Did he just disappear from your mind?"

"Yes, he did, and you're amazingly calm about it."

"Yeah, well, … that's because I haven't really told you everything about Debbie." When he frowned at her, she shrugged. "I feel as if she's been talking to me, telling me that I had to come here, telling me that she'd been murdered, telling me that somebody needed to fix it. And that I was it."

"How long has that been going on?" he asked.

"The whole time." She blinked. "I didn't think anybody would believe me," she explained, "so I didn't say anything. I didn't believe it myself really, but it seems as if she's been getting—I don't want to say stronger because I don't know that *stronger* is the word. She slammed a door in my face when I tried to ignore her. However, with all this?" She waved her hand about. "I don't know what the hell's going on. I just know that, wherever she is, she's not happy about it. Whatever happened to her, she's … pissed off. More so, she's pissed at me."

"If she didn't have any say in what happened to her, then I can understand that she would be pretty irate," Eric replied, "but that's still not your problem nor your responsibility. And that's the thing she needs to understand."

She stared at him and asked, "Do you trust Stefan?"

"Yes, absolutely," he stated.

She sighed, relaxing slightly. "That's good to hear. … I don't even know who he is, and I don't understand what all of this is about. It's so far-fetched. I can't imagine anything worse than having your very soul imprisoned, without anybody knowing."

"This is just horrible," Eric agreed. "No question about that, but we can't do anything about it now. So, we'll just sit here, calm and quiet, as we let Stefan do his thing. And then we'll see what we're doing after that."

As she considered that, she added, "I know it's not as if I have any say here, but it feels wrong. Something is off, and I can't feel Stefan at all."

Eric nodded. "I agree with you. I'm just not sure what *wrong* means in this instance."

"I don't know." Then she bolted to her feet, but he grabbed her immediately and pulled her back down.

"Remember what we were told?" Eric asked.

"I know. I know, but something is wrong. Stefan's in trouble," she cried out. She looked all around them. "There has to be somebody who can help."

"Stefan *is* the one who can help," Eric pointed out. "And, if he can't help, I don't know that there is anybody else."

Just then another weird shimmer filled the air, and she gasped. "What's that?" she cried out.

Eric wrapped his arms around her and just held her tight for a few moments, and then his body relaxed. "Stefan does have somebody with whom he works sometimes. I suspect that we're seeing somebody he has called to help."

The shimmer was there, and then suddenly it was gone. Yet the air seemed calmer, quieter.

They sat for a moment, staring at each other.

Finally the knot in her stomach started to ease, and she gasped. "I feel as if a galactic war just happened. Something so far removed from our actual reality that it's almost impossible to explain."

Just then Eric's phone rang. He pulled it from his pocket, glanced at the screen, and shared, "It's Stefan." With an odd look in her direction, Eric put it on Speakerphone. "Stefan?"

"Yes," he replied, exhaustion in his voice. "We released that one person. A friend of mine will communicate with her. It was a woman, an older woman who died quite a few years ago."

"What does *quite a few years* mean?"

"Let's just say a lot of years ago," Stefan replied. "My friend will talk to her and will see if we can get any answers from her. Her soul, her energy is—well, I would like to say it's ready to go back to where it needs to be—but it's not."

"What do you mean?"

"I'm not exactly sure what has happened to her, but we need to get a better idea. So, I've got Dr. Maddy on it, and we'll get back to you as soon as possible."

"Is it safe to move now?" Eric asked.

After a moment of silence, Stefan replied, "Yes, it is safe for you guys to move. But what is not safe is for you to be separated. I need you two to stay together until we get to the bottom of this."

"Stay together?" Eden asked. "Like, *together*-together?"

"That's up to you but stay together, meaning stay in the same bedroom tonight. Absolutely do not let each other get out of your sight. Both of you. Do you hear me?" Stefan snapped. "It's important. The Origin, whatever it is, whoever is controlling it, is really pissed because they lost a round today. Not only were they looking to enhance their numbers with the acquisition of you two, they've now lost someone who they desperately needed. I have no doubt that they will be looking to regain that advantage."

Stefan sighed, with a weariness evident in his tone. "You

both need to be very careful. It's critically important that you stay safe." His apparent level of exhaustion was very disconcerting to Eric and Eden. "I'm done for the moment, and we will help this soul later," he added. "Whether we get answers or not remains to be seen. But the bottom line is that you guys are at risk and need to stay safe. A very pissed-off entity is out there. And it's not only looking to replenish its stock but now it'll also be looking for payback. And you guys are the likeliest targets."

"So we are it, aren't we?" Eden muttered.

ERIC STOOD UP and wandered a few feet away. Shaking out his arms and legs, he looked over at Eden, and she nodded. "Let's go," Eric said. "We need to get sustenance for whatever is coming. And, given that, we don't want anybody else to know what's going on," he pointed out. "Yet we must appear somewhat normal."

"*Great,*" she muttered, "as if that'll work out well for us."

He smiled. "It will work out. We just have to take it easy."

With that, they headed to the restaurant adjoining the hotel. Several people from the seminar looked up, some with smiles, some with disapproving frowns.

Eden basically ignored everybody and headed over to the food buffet.

Luckily they were just in time to get themselves a plate of food before the servers took everything away.

When they sat down, Richard walked over and sat down beside them. "Is everything okay?"

"Absolutely," she said, as she looked at him. "I wasn't feeling very well earlier, so I ended up going outside and found out Eric wasn't feeling great either. We just spent some time, you know, relaxing and taking care of each other."

"Good, good," he replied, but a wariness filled his gaze. "Did you see anything out there?"

She frowned at him. "See what?" she asked. "I mean, it's beautiful out there."

He just nodded and didn't say anything else right away. He stayed for a few more minutes, gently prying with a few more questions before he appeared to give it up. Then he just sat with them, as if not wanting to leave them alone.

It was a little disconcerting to Eden, yet she needed a chance to see if he had anything to do with this. She really didn't know who this man was.

The trouble was, so much strangeness had gone on by now that she wasn't even sure what Richard could possibly have had to do with any of this. According to Stefan, some connection existed between Debbie's death and this seminar, which may or may not include Origin. So, considering what Eden and Eric had just experienced, she no longer held any animosity toward Richard.

She smiled at him and added, "Sorry. We didn't mean to disrupt your sessions."

"No, but it's always a little upsetting when people pay to come and then don't show up. I'm always left wondering why."

"Of course," she agreed, "but I can assure you, in this case, it had nothing to do with your program."

He just nodded and didn't say a whole lot.

To Eden, he seemed a little on the morose side. "I'm sorry. It was inconsiderate of us."

He shrugged. "No, that's fine. It's all good."

Yet it was obvious to Eden that something wasn't all that good. She noted, "You seem a little sad."

He nodded. "Somebody I knew passed away not long ago, and, though I didn't get a chance to know her that well, sometimes things are a little hard to deal with. You remind me of her for some reason."

Realizing he probably meant Debbie, Eden nodded. "I lost somebody not very long ago too," she shared. "And that was really difficult. She had attended one of your seminars."

He looked at her in surprise. "Really?"

"Yes," Eden began. "She was a good friend of mine, and that's one of the reasons I came. I just … I feel so guilty because I didn't get to spend the last bit of time with her."

"What happened?" he asked.

Eden shrugged. "She just didn't wake up one morning."

He winced, went pale, and then nodded. "That must be very difficult," he muttered. Then he got to his feet far too quickly. "Thanks for letting me know. Enjoy your lunch."

"You can stay if you like," Eden offered.

"I have business to take care of, and we'll be resuming right afterward. I'll take a few minutes for myself before we begin the afternoon session." And, with that, he moved quickly away, heading out of the room.

She watched as his brother caught sight of him, frowned, then looked at her, picked up the pace, and followed Richard.

Beside her, Eric noted, "That was interesting. Had you never talked to Richard before? Surely he would have recognized you from the earlier weekend session."

"Not really, he had eyes only for Debbie," she pointed out. "I just now more or less decided that Richard had absolutely nothing to do with this mess. Stefan can't yet link the Origin portal to Debbie's death necessarily, and while he did say the seminar *was* connected to Debbie's death, he didn't say that Richard was involved. I guess the least I can do is let him off the hook." She added a wave of her hand. "He didn't acknowledge that he was speaking about Debbie, but it seemed as if he was definitely concerned that my friend might have been Debbie."

"I don't know if *concern* is the word," Eric noted, "but I'm sure he cared. If not Debbie, it's also a reminder that he lost somebody."

Eden winced. "Right, and I wasn't thinking about the aspect of his grief at all."

"No, of course not," Eric noted, with a gentle smile. "I think you've had enough to keep your mind busy for a very long time. Yet you are an empath, so would end up visiting that too."

She rolled her eyes at that. "I'm still really struggling. How is all this even possible? And what just happened?"

He didn't say anything, just smiled.

She sighed. "I don't even know what to say."

"I know. I get it. Yet, as Stefan said, we need to stay together to stay safe." Just then his phone buzzed, and he looked down, his eyes squinted. "That's work calling." He hopped up. "I'll be back in a minute."

She bolted to her feet. He stopped, looked at her, and she shrugged. "We were told to stay together."

He frowned at her, an odd expression on his face. "I don't think it matters for this. I'm just taking a phone call outside."

"It matters," she snapped. She had no idea why she was so upset, but, as far as she was concerned, it mattered.

He shrugged. "Then it's a good thing you finished eating. We can go outside to take my call."

With that, they walked back outside, Eric already on the phone, trying to call his partner.

When he couldn't get through, he frowned and tried it again and got nothing. Finally he sent texts in the hope that Cody would respond to one of them. When he still got no answer, he shrugged.

"What's wrong?" she asked.

"I can't seem to get through to anybody."

"Could it be a signal issue?"

"Could be. Why don't we grab a coffee and go sit in the lobby?"

Some comfy chairs were in the lobby, which for her was a boon. It didn't happen often enough in a lot of these hotels, particularly where conference events were held. You would think that would be an immediate consideration for their guests, but apparently it wasn't.

With coffee and dessert in hand, they sat in the lobby, where they could be seen in public, where they could be friendly, still together, and allay some of the laughter, suspicion, and curiosity about their absence earlier. Several people came over and sat down in the vicinity, although nobody struck up a conversation. And, since they were in such a public space, Eden and Eric also couldn't speak about all that had happened to them.

Frustrated, she just sat here on her phone as she waited for the bell to ring for the next set of sessions. Even as it rang, she watched as he got up beside her, then directed her attention to the entrance, where Richard Santino and his brother, Rinaldo, were arguing animatedly out on the front steps.

She winced as she watched obvious signs of strife between the two brothers. When they were done, clearly no meeting of minds had happened. Richard turned and walked back inside.

When he saw that multiple groups of people had been watching them, he just smiled and raised his hands. "Are you guys ready to head in for the afternoon?"

Several people bounced to their feet and walked toward him with a big smile. Others stayed where they were, a little disconcerted by the obvious strife between the brothers.

"Nothing like family to drive each other mad," Richard quipped, followed by a laugh, "but don't you worry. My brother and I are doing just fine."

Several people laughed and said they would expect nothing else.

Richard nodded. "That's it exactly, isn't it? I mean, life sometimes sends things a little sideways, and that's okay. The important thing is that we keep going forward."

And, with that, he led the way to start the afternoon sessions.

CHAPTER 14

THE GROUP WAS excused for a coffee break a couple hours later, and Eden walked over there to stretch her legs. She was all too aware that her last meditation had been deep but very disturbed.

It had been hard for her to let go of the thoughts in her mind. Just way too much was happening, and all of it was disturbing. As she stepped closer to the nearby coffee bar, someone called her name, and she turned to see Richard walking toward her.

He smiled. "Hey, I thought maybe we could visit during the break. It might be nice to get to know each other."

She slowly nodded. "Sure. Sounds good."

Not exactly sure why he'd picked her, she knew for a fact that Eric would not allow her to do so alone. As she walked over to the coffee bar with Richard, she saw Eric heading toward her. She smiled, calling him over. As he reached them, she motioned for him to join them. "Richard suggested we have coffee together."

Eric nodded. "Sure, sounds great."

Richard was obviously not expecting that, but he smiled, recovering quickly. "I wanted to ask if your friend who had passed on was Deborah Kingston."

Eden nodded. "Yeah, we called her Debbie. She died without any obvious signs of ... anything at all." Her voice choked at the memory.

He nodded, his voice gentle as he added, "She was a very special person."

"Indeed, and she is sorely missed. Unfortunately she tended to get into trouble sometimes, and it wasn't always easy to get herself out of it."

"What kind of trouble?" he asked. "She seemed to be someone who was trouble-free."

"No, not trouble-free at all," Eden corrected, with a shake of her head. "She had a habit of diving into relationships quickly, then, one way or another, she tended to dive right back out again." She sighed. "I've had to bail her out of the consequences of a couple of them, and it was always depressing and difficult for her."

"Define a couple," he asked, his face slightly pale.

"It happened a few times. She tended to jump in feet first," Eden explained, with a smile. "That was so Debbie."

He didn't say anything for a long moment and then added, "I guess that's quite true, isn't it? She was a very happy-go-lucky soul."

"Very," she agreed, looking at him. "She did say that she had fallen head over heels in love with somebody during the weekend workshop."

"Oh," he replied, looking at her sideways.

"Yeah, do you have any idea who it was?" she asked, staring at him directly.

He shrugged and shook his head. "No, sorry, I don't."

She nodded, not sure what she had expected him to say, but, in a way, she was disappointed that he didn't come clean about it. It just made his involvement even more suspicious. "I know that she enjoyed the weekend that she spent here very much," she shared. "It was a highlight for her, so I'm glad that her last few hours were filled with joy and happiness."

He nodded. "I'm really happy to know that. It makes it a lot easier on me."

"You didn't know her that well, since I'm sure she was just one of many students."

"No, of course not," he replied, almost in a lecturing tone of voice.

"However, for me, she was a very special friend," Eden added. "We'd known each for almost two decades."

He then lapsed into teacher mode, probably to tell her all about the facts of life, but she forestalled him with her next comment. "It would be nice if I knew who she had fallen so deeply in love with. I know the police want to talk to him too."

"Oh, why is that?" he asked, looking from one to the other, his frown instant, as if realizing that Eric hadn't spoken to him.

"That's simple enough. He was somebody she was interested in and was involved with in her last few hours," she explained. "I think it's pretty standard in most cases."

"That could be," Richard conceded. "I don't have any experience in that."

"No, neither do I, and unfortunately neither did my absolutely beautiful friend Debbie. She really had a lovely personality."

"She seemed to, indeed," he agreed. When his phone rang, a look of relief came over his face as he picked it up, answered, then looked over at her and said, "I'm sorry. I have to go."

She just nodded and watched as he scurried away.

Eric turned to her. "You were having way too much fun

with that. Was it wise?"

"I don't know," she admitted, "but it certainly felt good."

He snorted at that. "Do you still think he had nothing to do with Debbie's death?"

"I wouldn't say that, but then why not admit that he was the one she was involved with? It's not such a bad thing, but he's hiding it like a dirty secret."

"And, as you said, the police do want to talk to him, but he's not willing to offer that information. That's also interesting," he murmured. "I have spoken to him and his brother but over the phone, not face-to-face."

She shot him a look and then shrugged. "It does feel as if something odd is going on here that we can't see, at least not right now."

"Are you kidding?" He laughed as he stared at her. "Something odd? *Ya* think? Look at everything that's gone on since we arrived. I would say *more than something odd* is going on." He picked up her hand, patting it gently for all the world to see, showing everybody that they were together.

She knew why he was doing it, yet it brought back images of that kiss she'd shared with him. Any kiss would have done the trick in terms of getting rid of the people headed their way, but she had kissed him back with a fervor that had surprised them both.

Unfortunately for her, it continued to resurface in her memories as something that she wanted to try all over again.

ERIC WATCHED AS Richard scurried away, obviously relieved to let the phone call end his discussion with Eden and Eric, allowing Richard to escape.

And it was definitely an escape, no question about that at all, which was interesting, and a little disconcerting that it would be so easy to send him off running. He wasn't the same Richard whom Eric had spoken to on the phone. It made no sense to him. So, why did Richard want to talk to Eden on her own? Eric looked over at her and asked, "Did you get any sense of why he wanted to speak to you?"

"No." She shook her head. "I did wonder, which is why I said yes right off the bat. Then once he brought up Debbie, I thought maybe I could question him somewhat," she shared, with a wry look. "But that seems to have backfired, since he ran away at the very first opportunity."

Eric smiled and nodded. "He was definitely making his escape. I don't know what horrible punishment you had in mind, but he was clearly not willing to give you the truth. Maybe it was a case of differing perspectives," he suggested, "meaning that perhaps Debbie made more out of it than he did, which is definitely quite possible."

"I would hope not for her sake, but it is a definite possibility," she conceded. "Still, why wouldn't he at least say something?"

"Because he didn't want anybody to know, didn't want Debbie to be associated with his company," Eric offered. "Still, I'm not sure Richard had anything to do with her death."

"It wasn't like that though. He had her up front where everyone could see them. Still … I'm not sure either," she murmured, "but, when he runs away like that, it sure makes him look guilty."

"A part of you wants Richard to look guilty too," he pointed out.

"True. This whole thing today has been incredibly unnerving. I just want to go home with some answers as to Debbie's death, yet I don't want to leave anybody in Origin, or whatever it's called. Why does it even exist?" She looked around to confirm that no one was listening or paying them any attention. "How is it even a thing?" she asked softly.

He grasped her hand gently and whispered, "*Shh.*"

"I know. I need to keep it quiet, but that's not easy. Not when you've seen something so shocking, so horrifying, hearing about a concept that just leaves you cringing at the thought that it might be true," she whispered. "The last thing I want is to even think about that, yet now I can't get it out of my head." He squeezed her fingers again, then his thumb stroked the top of her hand, gently soothing her.

She stared down at their joined hands and asked, "How the hell did we even get to this place?"

"I don't know," he admitted. "I felt compelled to check out that corner," he murmured, "and apparently that was not the right thing to do."

"And yet how can we say that?" she asked. "We know somebody was suffering. Trapped, alone—"

He nodded. "I don't have an answer for you. I don't know what to say."

They sat here for a few more minutes, hands touching, almost as if the physical contact was helpful in a literal sense. Finally he suggested, "Maybe we should go upstairs for a few minutes and give ourselves a chance to regroup. Are you okay with that?"

"Sure," she murmured, "anything to get out of here for a while."

"Unless you want to go back outside?"

"No," she snapped. "I don't."

He nodded. "Okay, then let's go up to our rooms for a

rest. It'll be another twenty minutes before the next afternoon session begins, so we can assess them as to what we want to do."

"You know what everybody else will think we're doing, don't you?"

He looked over at her and shrugged. "It doesn't matter what they think," he stated, with a smile. "The only thing that matters is that we stay safe, right? Maybe also consider why you aren't panicked, why you're not all that bothered by this whole situation."

"But I am bothered," she said absentmindedly as they walked to the stairs.

"Yet not in a big way."

She pondered that and then nodded. "You're right. I'm not as bothered as I could be. I'm not sure why."

"Which just leads me to think that you've had more than a little experience with something like this."

She looked at him sideways for a moment. "I told you about feeling as if Debbie was talking to me, so there's that."

"Yes," he noted, his penetrating gaze locked on hers. "Are you sure it isn't more than that?"

She shrugged. "Maybe, I don't know. What if it's more than that?" He didn't say anything, just stared. "Maybe it's a little more than that," she conceded. "I've always been the curious sort, and I've always thought there was more to these things than anybody was ever willing to state. I just never really experienced it until Debbie."

She stepped onto the landing and walked to the window nearby. "I mean, this Origin," she added, as she waved to the space outside, to the side garden, "is not normal."

"I would say that Stefan would agree with you there," he agreed, as they continued up the stairs. Even if somebody was listening in on their conversation, it was too ambiguous for anybody to sort out. "I don't think he's ever seen anything like this."

"I think he's literally struggling to figure out how to handle this—recovering and sorting things out through his peers, whoever that ends up being. And who would have thought there were peers for something like this," she noted, with half a laugh. "Do you think he'll get back to us today?"

"I don't know. Today? Tomorrow? I just don't know."

She nodded. "And, of course, we can't expect him to spend all his time on this."

"I think he'll spend as much time as he possibly can, if for no other reason than the fact that this portal is—" He stopped.

"Oh, don't stop now," she said. "It's just getting interesting."

He hesitated. "I feel like it's *feeding*."

She stared at him, the color draining from her face.

He winced and then nodded. "It's hungry. It's opened the portal to feed. And, in the process, it managed to lose one soul because of me, which has likely made its situation worse."

"And now it's not only hungry, but also angry as well," she pointed out. "Right?"

"Yes, and either one of us," he noted, "would make a great next meal."

CHAPTER 15

ERIC'S WORDS REVERBERATED in Eden's mind throughout the afternoon sessions. She tried hard to sink into the meditations and to find a center of peace, but it was hard. She had just so many questions now, and Eric's suggestion had created a frisson of fear that wouldn't let go.

By the time they hit the afternoon coffee break, he looked over at her and asked, "Are you okay?"

She shook her head. "I haven't been able to pay attention at all. All those thoughts we shared beforehand just keep running over and over in my head."

He nodded. "Mine too. Sorry. I should have just kept my mouth shut."

"What good would that have done?" she asked, glancing around, making sure nobody was close enough to hear.

"The last thing we want is for you to be so upset and so triggered by all of this that you can't enjoy being here."

She frowned at him. "Enjoy being here? I'm not sure I will ever enjoy being here. I mean, look at the reason why I came."

He contemplated her for a moment and then nodded. "That's fair."

She smiled. "Look. If we can get answers about Debbie, great. About the other woman who died here? Even better. If we can solve a problem with Origin, that's a bonus. But expecting this to be an easy process? I'm not sure that is even in the equation." And she left it at that.

Just then another woman approached them and casually started a conversation, which gave Eden a chance to step away from the one crowding her mind.

When Richard announced that they would all head outside for forty minutes just to take a break and to clear their minds, she was completely overwhelmed with relief and, at the same time, fear.

Where were they going?

Was it safe for anyone to go outside?

Would they become food to feed whatever the hell this monstrosity was that lingered outside in Origin, lying in wait to snatch some poor sap?

It was on the tip of her tongue to say something, but, as she glanced over at Eric, he discretely shook his head. She frowned and kept her mouth shut because, really, what could she say? Yet, at the same time, if something happened, and she said nothing, that would be way worse for her.

She walked toward the exit, a cup of tea in her hand, as Eric stepped up beside her. "If we get there first, hopefully people won't disturb us."

She frowned at him. "They might though. They might want to come visit us."

His lips twitched. "Unless of course you're thinking of doing what we did the last time. If it worked then, it might work now."

She frowned. "We can't just stay here the entire time and make people think that everything is hunky-dory."

"No, we can't," he agreed. "I do understand that, and we do need to do something, but I think we have to give Stefan a chance to sort out what that something is."

She let out a soft sigh. "For a minute there, I forgot about Stefan."

"I'm guessing he wouldn't appreciate that," Eric quipped, with a smile.

"I know, right? He's hardly forgettable, and yet there's something about him," she muttered. "It's as if he's here, yet he's not, so I tend to forget him."

"I'll tell him that," Eric teased, with a laugh.

She shrugged. "There's also such a sense of peace when I think about him, and maybe that's what the difference is."

"I know he would definitely appreciate that sentiment," Eric shared, as he looped his arm through hers. "Come on. Let's head back up there."

She winced, dragging her feet. "What if the portal opens?"

He pondered that as he moved at a slow and steady pace, inexorably dragging her along with him. When they got to the bench, he looked around and muttered, "It is a beautiful place."

"How does something like this come about?" she asked. "For such a beautiful place, how is it that this becomes a scene of some horror film?"

"Maybe specifically because of that fake sense of serenity and beauty," he suggested, looking over at her. "Maybe literally that is the answer. It could be a very simple and almost elegant explanation."

"About what?"

"What if somebody died here, possibly violently, and so many years ago, which started all this?"

"How is it that one person could have that much power?" she asked. "That makes no sense."

"For all we know," he replied, eyeing her, "that could go

back centuries ago, where something once stood here that goes back millennia. We don't know, but Stefan says there's an Origin here, and I don't really know what that means, but I'm willing to go by his naming convention on it. In that case, it would make sense that whatever this is has been here for a very long time, and, chances are, we won't ever know the how and the why of it."

She sat down on the bench, glancing around to confirm that they were alone, and then she added, "If it's been here for a very long time, it won't budge very easily."

"I know," he admitted. "I was trying to think about that during the meditation."

She snorted. "I'm glad it wasn't just me who struggled to disappear into the unknown while doing the meditation. I found it almost impossible to follow his voice. Everything else was happening in my mind."

"Everything but what?" he asked, looking at her.

"Just the usual things we need for meditation—calm, peace, quiet, serenity, balance—all the things I was hoping to find here."

"Along with answers," he noted. "Don't you think the two of them could happen at the same time?"

"I was hoping so," she whispered softly. "I was really hoping for that. However, although I suspected Richard had something to do with Debbie's death, I was hoping to find proof that he hadn't. Maybe there would be some proof that she had died of natural causes, and nobody could have done anything to save her." She stared around and asked, "Do you think she's here?"

"I don't know," he replied. "That's the question we have to ask somebody who may have come out of the Origin portal."

"I wonder if Stefan had a chance to talk to the … spirit, entity, woman? What do we call her?"

"I don't know." He shook his head. "I'm also at a loss when it comes to the right wording of these things."

She stretched back out on the bench, sliding her hips forward so her head could drop along the back of the seat, allowing her to stare up at the sky. "It just goes to show you how little terminology we have to give us a way to communicate on this topic."

"I suppose a lot of words would work, but it's not the words that are the issue for us," he pointed out. "We're looking for something much more in-depth than just that."

"And yet communication is everything," she noted.

"Speaking of communicating, that is also something you mentioned, but you didn't go into details."

She winced.

"Right, I gather you were hoping I wouldn't bring it up again?"

"I guess I was hoping, yes," she acknowledged. "It's not as if I have any answers for you."

"You could at least clarify. Have you had other ghosts, for lack of a better word, speak to you before?"

She rolled her head sideways so she could see him, then whispered, "My grandmother. … My grandfather. … My mother." She rolled her head back to stare up at the sky. "Maybe a few others. But all the encounters, before all this, have been minimal."

"What does *minimal* mean to you?"

"A sighting, sometimes a *hi*, sometimes a *hello*. My mother told me, *I'm fine. Just relax and let go* because I was having such a hard time. After speaking with her, I felt a lot better," she shared. "So, I can understand the need to hear and to speak to somebody who's already gone past this world. But I wasn't looking for answers from them. I wasn't looking to speak with them, and maybe that's the difference here."

Eric frowned. "I don't know."

When she looked over at him, she asked, "Are you angry that I didn't tell you?"

"No, not at all," he said, with a wry laugh. "I understand why you didn't. I mean, it's not as if you know me very well."

"Right," she agreed, "and it's not as if you know me very well even now. We appear to have come together over something completely unexpected, even if I have seen a ghost or two in the past," she murmured.

"As an estimate, any idea how many you've seen?"

She frowned and asked, "Does it matter?"

"No," he replied carefully, "I guess it would just help me understand a little more where you stand on all this."

She shrugged. "Probably dozens, maybe twice that. I don't know. At some point in time, I just stopped seeing them."

"Any idea why?"

"Yeah, they were in my way. I sounded a little bit crazy, talking to people who were not here on this physical plane, so I just told them all to go away."

"And it worked?"

"It worked," she confirmed, turning her attention to the area around them. "I was thinking about what you said earlier, … wondering if some bad event happened here, something that might have started Origin."

"Like a natural disaster or something?"

"It could have been an earthquake. The *hungry* part is

what really got to me. It's the only thing I can think of for why it's open, or why the woman, that one spirit, escaped."

He sighed. "And I haven't had any contact with Stefan, so I don't know." Just then, his phone rang. He looked down and said, "And, of course, here's Stefan now." He answered it. "You're on Speaker, and I have Eden here with me."

"Good," Stefan replied, his voice brisk. "I have had several conversations over what is going on there. Nobody really has any answers, except for the fact that whatever has opened needs to be closed. We're not sure how it opened, or why it opened, but we are very united on one front."

"Which is?"

"Origin needs to be closed and fast."

"And how do you close something like this?" she asked.

"Hi, Eden," Stefan greeted her, his voice gentle. "I think the reason why you are there, in particular, is because you're instrumental in closing it."

She stopped, her gaze widening as she turned to stare at Eric. "I don't think so," she declared. "I don't have any experience with this."

"We weren't expecting you to have any. I don't think anybody really has experience with this," he shared, a note of laughter in his tone.

"You can laugh," she stated, "but we're sitting here on the spot and terrified."

"Of course you are," he said, his voice soothing. "I'm not trying to laugh at your predicament, but we rarely ever understand what we are capable of doing until we're called on to do it."

"Yes, but listen to yourself. We don't even know what this thing is. According to Eric's assessment, it's hungry and looking to feed, and I don't want to be its next meal. For all I know, that's exactly what happened to Debbie. Were you able to find out anything from the woman who you helped escape?"

"No, she disappeared into the light very quickly, with a huge sense of gratitude for having been saved from whatever that was. There was definitely the sense that she had been there a very long time, but it didn't seem as if whatever it is had taken her deliberately. It was more likely she fell into it and had been searching for a way out ever since."

"That almost sounds even worse," Eden whispered. "The thought that somebody can fall into this, then have no idea how to get out, is very disturbing."

"For a lot of souls, when they pass over, there's no thinking about it. They go directly to where they are intended to be," Stefan explained, "and their crossing over is simple and clean. And sometimes you get either people who are still caught in the middle or who don't even realize they have died because it happened so fast. You know, people happily having a conversation while driving in a car, and suddenly something falls on top of them mid-conversation, and they know nothing. Yet, in their mind, they're still sitting in that car, trying to figure out what happened, maybe even still talking to the person who may or may not be there beside them anymore."

She winced. "And you're saying that sometimes the one person stays and the other person has already crossed over?"

"Yes, it depends on what their perception of death was at the time. As in the case of a child, they generally don't come with all that baggage, and they move on very quickly. In some cases, the parents are still looking for that child, refusing to leave until they can take that child with them."

"Which would be horrific," she whispered.

"Absolutely. The depth of love often supersedes this transformation process in some situations, though not all of them. I mean, if we have a mother dying of cancer, she generally dies in a peaceful manner, heavily medicated, and she carries on. But, if she's murdered, while being kidnapped with her child, then she may be clinging to whatever that landscape was in the hope of finding that child and still being able to rescue it. And, if that child was murdered at the same time, which has certainly happened, the child quite often will have crossed over, but the mother may not have been cognizant of that happening, and she is stuck, still looking, whereas the child is long gone."

"I don't even want to contemplate any of that."

"Right, so we have a problem with that portal—"

Just then, while they were talking, a heavy rumble cane underneath their feet.

Eden jumped up, spinning around in a wild circle.

Stefan was still talking, until Eric said tersely, "Stefan, hang on a sec."

Stefan asked, "What happened?"

"An earthquake beneath our feet," she cried out.

Stefan paused for a moment, then replied, "It's listening to us. It's hearing us. Good God."

"Now you're saying it's alive, as if it has senses?" Eden asked.

"Everything is alive," Stefan noted. "Whether we want to think of it or not, everything has energy. And if there's energy, there is some semblance of cognition to go along with it, with different levels for each state."

She closed her eyes. "So, are you saying that this entity, this … whatever this is, knows we're talking about it?"

"Yes, that would be my presumption."

She took several deep breaths and kept backing up, farther and farther away from Eric on the phone.

"Easy," Eric muttered, as he stood up and walked closer to her.

"We need to get off this hill," she snapped. "We need to get out of here."

"Why?" he asked, his tone sharp, as he reached out a hand.

She grabbed his hand but turned to run, dragging him with her.

Eric spoke into his phone. "Stefan, I don't know what's going on, but she's freaking out right now."

"Freaking out?" Stefan repeated.

Eric asked Eden, "Are you trying to tell me that was an earthquake? Earthquakes do happen around here, not very often, but they certainly do happen."

"That wasn't the same thing," Eden yelled, turning to look at Eric. "You know it wasn't the same thing."

Stefan called out through the phone. "She's right. It wasn't the same thing, and it is interesting that it's hearing us, that it's listening in."

"It's not interesting," she cried out. "It's—I don't even know what to call it, but this is not good. We need to leave, and we need to leave now."

"And where will you go?" Stefan asked. "Will you take everybody with you?"

She froze, and Eric noted that she was hyperventilating.

"Easy, easy," he whispered, as he tugged her into his arms and just held her. "Stefan, I'll need to talk to her a little bit."

"Understood, and I will call you back because—"

"I know," Eric interrupted. "This isn't over."

"No, it can't be over," Stefan countered. "This cannot be left as is."

"She may not be the right person to help," Eric pointed out.

"She is," Stefan confirmed. "She has an awful lot more abilities than she has any idea of."

"But she's not interested in working with any of these abilities," Eric argued. "She's apparently told ghosts to buzz off before because they were in her space, in her face, or just generally irritating her."

Stefan snorted. "Yeah, a lot of them are irritating, but the fact that she can see and can communicate with the dead means a lot."

"But that's a different story with me," she cried out into the phone. "I communicated with somebody who I knew, my mother, my family, and my friends who had passed over, and I did ask some of them to move on because they were in my face all the time. It was so hard to concentrate at work. Every time I looked up, there they were."

Stefan didn't say anything for a moment. "That just means that your ability to communicate has been fine-tuned more and more. Have you ever had to try harder to talk to them?" Stefan asked.

"Yes, with Debbie, I tried. She just kept telling me that I needed to figure it out because she was murdered. Almost threatening me. She is so angry."

"And yet she didn't tell you where she was?"

"No, but she was talking to me normally, as if burped out of the world, like that other woman."

Eric asked, "Stefan, does that have any correlation to the two deaths and this Origin you're talking about?"

"I don't know," he replied, "and yet it is very interesting because a lot of seismic activity has happened around that area. So it's entirely possible that something has woken up from whatever sleep it was happy to rest into. This one woman is free, and I have no idea how many others could be in there."

"Please tell me that we don't have to open this up and deal with them too," Eden muttered. "That would be a little more than anyone can handle."

"No, I don't think it is more than you can handle," Stefan stated. "I find that people who end up in these situations tend to be precisely the ones most equipped for the job."

"That is *not* making me feel any better," she muttered.

"Of course not," Stefan agreed, "and I am sorry. I'm not trying to scare you, but I do feel as if we need to explore this a little more."

"Great, and when do you want to do that?" she asked, staring at Eric.

He noted the trembling and the fear in her gaze.

After a long moment of silence, Eden added, "Look. If I can do something, I'm willing to help, but when and how? We're only here overnight, before a short session on Sunday."

"And overnight might do it," Stefan noted.

"Plus, I'm due back to work in two days. I took an extra day off, but I'll have to get back to my life."

"I know, and we all want that," Stefan said. "But, if I am right, this thing can follow you to the ends of the earth to get what it wants regardless."

ERIC KEPT AN eye on Eden for the next few hours as they

tried to assimilate into the next meditation session. He wasn't even sure why they were bothering, considering they were both now looking at something completely different and wondering just how it was all supposed to fit together. Still, he had no answers.

It's certainly not what he expected when he got here, but, now that he was here, it wasn't something he would walk away from either, nor should he, not if this madness was going on and there was any way to stop it. He didn't know about Eden, but it felt very much like, even if she didn't stick around, *he* needed to. However, since they had come together in his car, it didn't give her much of a choice. Finally he gave up any pretense and slipped away from the meditation session and headed back up to the hill.

He had looked around for Eden first but, not seeing her, decided that it didn't really matter at this point. He needed to come out and see what he could do on his own, and maybe she would change her mind—or maybe not. He didn't know.

Right after Stefan told her that she may not have choice in the matter, she'd freaked out and ran like hell. It took some time to get her to calm down.

As he sat out here again in the bright sunshine, he thought he heard a rustling behind him. As he turned around, he saw the caretaker working away on one of the hedges off to the side. "Hey, Samuel." They had met the day he had arrived at the hotel.

Samuel was old, still fit, and in very good shape. The older man stopped when he saw him and nodded. "You gave up on the meditations, did you?"

"Let's just say that whatever was going on out here seemed to be much more fascinating."

The old man cackled and nodded. "You ain't seen nothing yet."

Not sure how to take that, particularly in view of what they had already seen, Eric continued. "I guess you've seen some pretty wild things over the years here."

"Yeah, I sure have," he replied, "and it's not going away anytime soon."

That appeared to be enough of a come-on that he looked at him, wondering just what the old man had seen. "Anything interesting, Samuel?"

He laughed again and shook his head. "Yeah, but you wouldn't believe it," he said, with a smile. "Nobody does. I've seen some shit over the years, I tell you. And there's days that I go home early. Although that hasn't happened in a long time. Days where you feel as if you need to go home early, otherwise—" He left it at that, and Eric had to wonder what it was.

"Yeah, you're not kidding," Eric agreed, with a head-shake.

"But don't you worry about me," Samuel noted. "You just keep yourself safe. Only be where you're sitting during the bright afternoon, *huh*?"

"Maybe," he replied coyly. "I wondered if I was seeing ghosts here at one point in time." He snorted. "That would be interesting."

Samuel eyed him and added, "If you ever feel like that, you're already too close. You need to run."

"What are you talking about?"

"It's not common knowledge, but, every once in a while," he explained, turning to look around, making sure that they were alone, "every ten, maybe fifteen years, this place gets spooky as fuck."

"But you are still here, aren't you?"

"Aye, but I don't even come into work when it's bad." And, with that, he lifted his digging fork and went to work on the soil, planting the pots scattered around him. "I don't bother asking questions and don't you bother asking me any because I sure as hell can't answer them."

He quickly tossed soil over the newly planted pots, picked up his things, then headed off on his own and was gone, long before Eric had a chance to even ask him what the heck he was talking about. But it sounded more like a warning than anything he had heard yet. Did Samuel know about Origin?

Eric sat down on the bench again, then looked around, wondering if, over time, Samuel had seen what was going on here. It appears the man had either ignored it or, as he said, disappeared until things got better.

Eric wanted to run after the man and see if he would say anything else. But, so far, it seemed as if he was determined to stick to whatever variation of the truth served him best and to not let anybody know too much. And it was an understandable position.

Depending on what he had seen over the years, that might have been the better answer all along. Hell, if Eric had known about this Origin ahead of time, would he have had anything to do with this? He wasn't so sure. It just seemed the further into this they went, the less they really understood, and that was disconcerting too.

Frowning, and hating that he had so many unanswered questions, he sat here, just letting his thoughts flow through him as much as he could. When he heard a voice beside him, he looked up to see Eden standing there, glaring at him.

CHAPTER 16

"YOU COULDN'T LEAVE it alone, could you?" Eden snapped.

He gave her a little smile. "It's hard to when you're afraid that other people will end up dead."

She sat down beside him with a heavy *thump* and nodded. "I know. That's why I'm here too." He reached out a hand, and she placed hers in it. "You know this is stupid, right?" she asked him.

"I know it is."

She added, "And it could end up with a really bad deal for both of us."

"Hopefully not," he replied, "but I can see how that would be a fairly major concern."

She rolled her eyes at that. After a moment, she asked, "What do you want to do?"

He hesitated and then spoke. "I was wondering about trying to contact whatever is in that portal and seeing if we could release more people."

She frowned. "Wasn't the first time enough to let this go? And the second time?"

"We have to do whatever it takes."

"While you were in the lecture hall earlier, did you get any weird sensations over it?"

"No. ... Why? Did you?"

"I don't know," she muttered. "It sounds creepy, but it felt as if I was being watched."

He studied her closely. "By Richard?"

"I don't know," she replied. "I don't think so, but I really don't quite know what the heck was going on there."

Eric shrugged. "I didn't feel it."

"I guess that's a good thing," she murmured.

"You're serious though, aren't you?"

"Yeah, I am," she stated. "I was being watched, and that's why I finally just got up and left, realizing that you weren't there, and I just didn't feel safe all alone." He frowned at that, and she shrugged. "I know I'm being silly."

"No, not at all," he said. "I think it's very important that we know exactly what's happening here, whether we can do anything to change it or just confirming that we can't interrupt this cycle. In which case, we're better off not even touching it at all."

"You already know how I feel about that," she pointed out, "because I would quite cheerfully disappear from here and never come back."

"And what about Debbie?"

She nodded. "That's the only reason I'm here, and it's scary as hell."

He smiled and squeezed her hand. "I'll try opening it just a sliver."

"And what if the wrong thing comes out of Origin?"

He shrugged. "I don't know, but, if it's Debbie, wouldn't you want to be the one to help her out?"

"I would," she stated, and seeing the look on his face, she raised her hands. "I know. I know." With a wave of her hand, she added, "You go do you."

He laughed. "I don't even know what *doing me* is," he

stated, with a shrug. "Apparently, according to Stefan, you're the one who has more experience with this."

She frowned and shook her head. "No experience with this, no, sir."

He studied her. "But you do have some experience, is that what I'm hearing?" She just stared at him, saying nothing. "I really want some clarity before I go into this. If you have experience to share, it would be great if you would tell me."

"I've just had experiences," she clarified, as she shook her head. "I don't know what they are because I didn't stick around long enough to find out. Some I already told you about, and then some I really don't want to talk about, … never ever, not at all."

He didn't say anything to that and just stared off into the distance for a long moment. Then he sighed. "I guess we're about to figure it out." And, with that, he closed his eyes and settled deeper into the energy around them.

He let Stefan know what he was doing, and Stefan hadn't really responded in any way, so Eric just took the initiative upon himself. As he opened the energy and probed Origin, that same maelstrom surged toward him.

He felt his hair lifting and all kinds of chaos swirling around him. He heard Eden gasp at his side, but he couldn't take his focus off what was in front of him.

Whatever this was, it was all about control.

Then she squeezed his hand and murmured, "Soften it." He didn't even know what that meant, but he immediately felt the energy around him soften.

So now it wasn't such a maelstrom. It was more of a gentle wind. As he softened it a little more, he sensed her approval as the wind turned to a breeze.

Somehow he had a sense of what she was feeling at the same time, and he squeezed her hand, needing that connection. He almost felt her laughter whisper through him as if she heard what he had just thought.

As he calmed the energy yet again, he heard a big whisper of something going past him. It came out, and yet it was still somewhat attached to the place they had left behind. He didn't understand the attached part, but, in some way, it made a weird kind of sense.

As he stood to take a step forward, Eden spoke, her voice calm but urgent. "It's trying to draw you in, and you can't go in there."

He hesitated, yet took another step, the temptation too much, the pull getting stronger. "I don't think I have a choice."

"You do have a choice, Eric," she stated, her tone firm. "You can't go in. If you go in, you can't come back out."

He sighed softly at that and whispered, "Entities are in there."

"Yes, I can feel them," she whispered.

Was she in his head, around his head, or somehow connected to him, a part of him, speaking through him?

He didn't understand what was happening, but they were all so very blended into this same experience that he knew that, no matter what it was, he had to do something with her, as she was an integral part of it. "I think I can return, if you go with me," he suggested.

After a moment of silence, she sighed heavily, almost regretfully. "But that doesn't mean I can save you," she whispered.

"You *can* save me," he declared. "I know you can."

"I don't know that," she snapped. "This place is not for

any of us to visit. It draws on your fears and insecurities."

And then he got it. "That's it. ... You've been here before."

"No. No, I haven't," she cried out. And, with that, she snapped back and dragged him right back out of wherever he had been, kicking and screaming, until he opened his eyes and saw her sitting there right beside him.

AS SOON AS he opened his eyes, she bolted to her feet and took off running. She couldn't stop the shaking. Even running was hard. She ran like the devil was on her heels because it just seemed as if she could do nothing to get away from it, to control it. She wasn't even sure what *it* was but felt as if it was right there after her, right on her heels.

When she was forced to a halt, jerked back around, and pulled tightly into warm, strong arms, she knew exactly who it was. As she burrowed deeper into Eric's chest, she still shook, her quivering overtaking her system.

When it finally slowed down, he whispered, "You know we need to talk about this." When she shook her head, he sighed and added, "Oh yes, we do." She shook her head again, and he murmured close against her ear, "I don't know what you're hiding or why you're hiding it, but what you did back there," he shared, "was amazing. It was incredible, and we need your help to do it again."

"Absolutely not," she snapped, stepping away from him, glaring at him. "In case you didn't get the memo, this is not what I want to do, and this is not where I want to be. In fact, if you won't take me home, I'll just grab a bus and go home. I'm not staying here and getting pulled into this nightmare, ... not again."

And then to her horror, she realized that the one thing she didn't want to say had slipped out and still hung in the silence between them, before landing into his awareness with a resounding crash.

"*Again*," he whispered in shock and amazement.

She shook her head. "No." She raised a hand. "I'm not talking about this, not now. I don't want anything to do with this mess." She pulled free and took several steps forward, only to hit an invisible wall, almost as if being slammed into it, and she froze. Trying to move was useless. Trying to change direction was useless.

She slowly sank onto the ground as everything inside her stilled, and her sense of alertness sharpened, waiting for everything to come crashing down, like it always did.

She had managed to forget about this and to put this away for so very long. Yet, right here and now, without any warning, she was right back in the same nightmare she'd fought so hard to escape.

Eden muttered, "I didn't mean to say that."

"Oh, I got that message," Eric stated. "I'm not sure what I'm supposed to say to that."

She shook her head. "I shouldn't have said anything."

"No, that's not true," he argued. "I would have preferred that you say something earlier, but I guess if it has anything to do with this nightmare, I can understand why you didn't."

"I don't think anybody can understand this nightmare," she muttered, with a wave of her hand. "I'm not sure I even know what this is."

Her voice was faint, and, even though she tried hard to bolster it with firm resolve, her words came out wavery, creaky even. "Look. It's not that I've seen this exact thing before," she clarified, "but I have experienced a couple very scary scenarios, and I just didn't want to ever deal with this again."

"And when you say *this*?"

She waved her hand out there into her surroundings. "Psychic stuff, weird stuff, energy stuff, ghosty stuff," she shared. "I don't know how to explain it any more than that," she snapped, sounding frustrated. "It started to get to me, ever since that opened, and I sensed them around me," she shared, "and that is the last thing I want."

"Sense *them*?"

"Yes," she snapped again, glaring at him. "I know. I'm crazy."

"You're not crazy, so stop saying that," he said, "but I do need to understand."

"I'm not trying to keep you from understanding," she yelled, turning to look at him. "I don't understand it myself, and, if I don't understand, I can hardly explain it to you."

He sat down beside her and suggested, "Let's try this then. Have you ever been to an Origin before this one?"

"No, I've never heard of such a thing before," she muttered, "and I'm damn glad because I don't even want to think about there being another one." She snorted, rubbing at her face in frustration. "This stuff gets into your psyche and makes a mess of your mind."

"Yeah, it absolutely does," he agreed, looking at her. "I can see how this is affecting you, but I'm just not sure how to help you."

"You can't help me," she declared, frowning at him. "And I don't know why you would even want to. You've been hell-bent on running to this place ever since you got that woman out."

"Whoa, whoa, whoa," he said. "I know I messed up that part, but whatever you have going on is something completely different, and it has nothing to do with me." She glared at him, and he leaned back, raising both hands. "I admit that I messed up opening this Origin, but we have a lot of other stuff on our plate, and apparently we're very short on time to deal with it."

She sighed. "That's what my grandmother told me too."

At that, he raised both eyebrows, waiting for her to continue.

Eden shook her head. "At the time, my mother was dying of breast cancer. She was in the hospital at the end stages, and the hospital staff could do nothing more for her. So my grandmother thought it would be a good idea for me to spend every waking moment with my mother before she was gone."

"And you didn't agree?" Eric asked.

"Let's just say, watching your mother fade away, agonizing breath by agonizing breath, was not a memory that I would ever put on *my* child."

"I can't imagine that was very easy."

"Not only was it not very easy," she stated, "it was terrifying. She was always in pain, and the machines around her made unbelievable noises."

"How old were you?"

"I was only six, almost seven, I guess," she shared, wiping her eyes, "and there was no getting away from the horror of what was happening. Yet, as far as my grandmother was concerned, I needed to spend every waking moment with her because I was about to lose her."

Eric watched Eden silently, letting her vent.

"While I now understand the basic philosophy of closure," she added, "it was not a memory that I hold dear. Though I absolutely adored my mother, the dying woman on that bed was not the mother I knew. Not in any way, shape, or form. And that made it even harder because I felt horribly guilty. Nothing about that time do I want to remember."

She took a deep breath and added, "I didn't want to be there, and everything about it tainted me, convinced me that I wasn't the person I should have been. On top of that, my grandmother told me to stop being foolish and to focus on spending the quality time that I could with her. Plus, I was being beset by …" She let out a long exhale.

"Just get it out and tell me," he said firmly.

She shrugged. "This is where you'll think I'm absolutely nuts," she began, "but it felt as if every dead or dying person in that hospital was swooping around me, coming to visit, trying to talk to me, trying to touch me, wanting something, screaming at me, yelling at the world around them, wanting help or to let them go or something. I didn't even know if they were dead or alive, if that was their spirits, their souls, or whatever."

"When did you figure that out?"

"Not soon enough," she stated curtly. "I ended up crying so loud, so hard, so heavily that my grandmother ended up pulling me away from the hospital. Everybody decided I was beset by grief, but it wasn't just grief. I mean, obviously I was horrified and paralyzed by grief over the impending loss of my mother, but it had far more to do with the fact that I was being tormented by every ghost-like thing out there. Honestly, I don't know what half of them were."

"Wow," he muttered, stunned.

"Believe me that I never wanted to know any more. Not

a one of them was saying, *Hey, little girl. How are you today?* They were all screaming and yelling at me, outraged over something, wanting something. To this day, I don't know exactly what the hell that was."

"How long were you there?"

She stared at him, a haunted look on her face. "Days and days. I was traumatized for a long time afterward, but my grandmother didn't believe me. She thought it was just, you know, foolishness, because I was trying to cope with the loss of my mother. And I *was* trying to cope with the loss of my mother, but I was also trying to cope with whatever madness had happened while I was there. Unfortunately that part didn't matter to my grandmother."

"Do you ever talk to her about it?"

"I tried to, but she was all about telling me exactly what I should and shouldn't do and how to do it. I was not very good to her either afterward. In the end, I checked out. I stopped speaking, stopped communicating. She put me in a special place because I was too traumatized over my mother's death to handle living, at least according to her. I don't even know how long I was there," she muttered.

"I don't know that anybody even knew why I was there, though I'm sure I was diagnosed with everything under the sun. Nothing they were treating me for was accurate because none of them understood my trauma, because I couldn't explain anything to them," she shared. "It just became one of those nightmares that I could never quite get free from."

"Good God," he murmured.

"Yeah, well, now that you mention it, for the longest time I didn't think there even was a God." She stared around her. "I may have been there a year, maybe two. I ended up in the foster system, as my grandmother had passed away by that point in time. She'd been beset with grief over my mother's death. Me being in a mental hospital didn't help either. And whether it was because of me or a lack of capacity to handle me, I don't know, but whatever her reasoning was, Grandmother never came back."

"So, what then? You never saw her after that?"

"Nope, I don't remember a time that I ever saw her after I was institutionalized," she stated. "I blocked out as much of that as I possibly could, and apparently I blocked it out just fine." She stared at the madness in the ethers around her, and something was stirring, brewing just on the brink of spilling over. "Until now."

He reached out a hand, massaged her shoulders, and then pulled her up close so she leaned against his chest. "It would have helped if I'd known all that."

"No, it wouldn't have," she snapped. "You couldn't have done a thing about it, and all this craziness still would have happened."

"Probably so, but regardless, I'm sure Stefan would say there's a time and a place for things to happen, and it happens in its own time. At least that's my understanding."

"I spent quite a bit of time researching and studying all this—not with any great success, mind you. And Debbie? Debbie was a very good friend who didn't really know much about what I did or what happened to me because I never told anybody. She had her own problems and kept searching for ways to contact her parents. I could have helped her but I didn't. I couldn't." She groaned. "I wasn't planning on telling anybody *ever*."

"Things have changed now," he noted. "And Stefan believes you are very important to whatever is going on here."

"Stefan is wrong," she declared.

Eric gave a bark of laughter. "I think there are probably times when Stefan is wrong, but somehow I don't think this is one of them."

She stared daggers at him. "You're wrong, and I know it because I can't have anything to do with this. It's just not possible."

He smiled and nodded. "I understand your perspective, but that doesn't mean I believe it."

"Yes, it's my perspective, and that is what I'm going with. I'm not letting this be twisted around into something."

"No, of course not," he said. "Yet it does explain a little bit why Stefan thinks you're involved somehow."

"No, it doesn't explain anything. There is absolutely no reason for Stefan to expect me to be part of anything." She stared at him. "Why would there be?"

He frowned, then shrugged. "I'm sure, if we brought him into this conversation, he would have answers. However, I don't have them myself."

She shrugged. "I don't know what is happening here today. I do know that I felt somebody watching me. I don't like that feeling, and I just want to go home."

"I understand that you want to go home, but what makes you think that particular feeling will just go away, won't just follow you home?"

She stared at him, swallowed hard, and closed her eyes, aware that he was right. Whatever this was, it's bigger and nastier. "Thanks for reminding me that this may never go away. I don't really have the energy, the tolerance, or the patience for that," she snapped. "I really just wanted to have a normal life, but apparently I won't ever get what I want."

CHAPTER 17

ERIC HAD HIS phone out and was already calling Stefan. Eden stared at him, shook her head, and grumbled, "I really don't think that's a good idea."

"Maybe not, but we can't let him go in blind either. That's just not fair," Eric explained. "So, we'll loop him in to our latest update, and then you can tell him that you don't want anything more to do with it."

She laughed at that. "You know he won't listen to me."

"Still, it's up to you to tell him and to not become another victim," Eric pointed out. "And, maybe when you explain, he'll understand you better."

When Stefan answered the phone, his voice was very gentle. "How is she doing?"

Eric looked over at Eden and replied, "She's been better, that's for sure."

"Of course," he agreed. "That scenario is never good."

"What scenario?" she asked into the phone, staring at Eric.

"I heard what you shared with Eric," Stefan began. "And I can understand what you're feeling and why. We have institutions full of people who never manage to control their abilities, who were exposed to something like you were and were never able to come back from that. I heard you managed to push aside your insecurities, and the fact that you have is amazing. I'm very proud of you."

She stared into the phone in shock. "Did you say you heard me?"

His tone carried a smile when he replied, "Yes. Pardon me if that's interfering, but I do hear things that aren't necessarily available to others."

"Yeah, you're not kidding," she muttered. Yet she felt a certain amount of relief that she wouldn't have to explain it all over again.

"And you're right there too," Stefan added. "I understand, and I can see what's happened. Finding a way forward for you is a whole different story. Particularly if you don't want anything to do with refining your abilities."

"I don't think you get the whole ability thing," she scoffed. "I don't have any abilities. I don't even know who and what those people were."

"Those were people who were looking to find answers and were reaching out to anybody who might see them, who might talk to them, who might help them. At the time, you were probably energetically wide open and not even understanding what that would mean, so they latched on and didn't let go."

"Nobody understood. I sure didn't," she stated. "I was screaming bloody murder and apparently acting crazy enough that I was led away and medicated. I didn't understand what happened and just had this horrible feeling of something latching on to me and trying to literally crawl inside my skin."

"That's not a bad description," Stefan acknowledged, his tone somber. "One that anybody who's been possessed to that degree would immediately recognize. And being possessed, particularly if it's against your will, is a horrible feeling. It does happen, and sometimes a little too often with people who are more susceptible. However, in this case, we will have safeguards in place to protect you."

Stefan continued. "Understanding what happened to you and why it happened would go a long way in helping you to deal with the fear. That's obviously beneficial, though I certainly understand the stance that you're taking in terms of not wanting to help. Yet the time has already passed for that."

"Whoa, whoa, whoa. What do you mean by that?" Eric asked, his tone sharp. "Surely she can't be forced into this."

"Not by me," Stefan confirmed. "But that feeling she's had of being watched? She's right. She absolutely is. *Something* is watching her, and whether it came from the Origin portal or from someplace else, I don't know. But some energy has been watching her for most of the day," Stefan stated. "In order to keep her safe, her awareness needs to be on max, which isn't possible all day long."

Eden and Eric exchanged confused glances.

Stefan explained, "Someone who is very sensitive to all these energies around you, like you, Eden, make it possible. So other energies around are sitting up and paying attention. I'm sure you've felt drained after being around certain people, right?" Eden didn't respond. "That's because you are giving away your energy with abandon because you have not been trained to properly handle your energy."

She stared at the phone as Eric put an arm around her shoulders, adding, "I'm obviously not leaving her alone."

"Good," Stefan said. "You shouldn't, not for a moment."

He swallowed hard and asked, "That bad?"

"Yes, it could be that bad. And again this isn't necessarily something unexpected. She's highly sensitive to the energies. I don't even know if she realizes how much she does for other people. I suspect she may not even be cognizant of it, but, because of what she is doing subconsciously, other energies are naturally attracted to it. It's making her light up like a neon light in the dark."

"So, being empathetic is bad now?" Eric asked, frowning.

"It can be if our energy worker is unaware of these skills. Her empathy is bringing all kinds of attention her way that I don't think she particularly wants."

"I don't want any attention," she declared, her tone harsh. "What do you mean when you said, *I don't even know what I'm doing?*"

He spent a long minute just breathing into the phone, as if carefully trying to formulate answers. "So, when your mother became severely ill, how long was she expected to live?"

"I don't remember exactly, but just a few weeks. Yet she lived a lot longer," she replied.

"That must have been a big surprise to the medical staff, wasn't it?"

"Yeah, the doctors and nurses were amazed."

"And your friend Debbie, whenever she came to you after a breakup, do you have any idea why?"

"I asked her one time, and she told me that it comforted her."

"Right. And, at work, wasn't somebody in the office dying at one point?"

"Oh yeah," she said, "when I used to work in the insurance office, a woman named Dolores was there. She had breast cancer. She was expected to die within months, yet lived for years—might still be alive but I lost touch with her. I liked her a lot."

"Were you ever close to her?"

"Yeah, she was a sweet woman. We used to hug every morning. She always told me how it made her feel better."

"That's because it did make her feel better," Stefan confirmed, "the same way it made your mother feel better and many of your friends. It didn't just make them feel better, because you were actually sending healing energy to them. And, whether you believe it or not, you were helping them heal. And not just one person, but every person around you. When you reach out and grasp someone's hand, you're giving them a shot of healing. That's why Debbie kept coming to you. And Dolores, your mother, and everyone else. … They all had something to gain from the interactions you had with them."

"Oh my gosh," Eric replied in astonishment, "the waitress at the restaurant too." When she looked at him and frowned, he reminded her. "We stopped there on the way to the seminar, and you were holding her hand. The two of you looked to be best friends."

"She was a sweet girl," Eden stated. "What's that got to do with anything?"

"She was also quite sick," Stefan added. "And, when I say *was*, I mean she really was."

Eden stared into the phone and shook her head. "No, that's too unbelievable."

"Of course it is. When your grandmother put you into the home, I bet your mother faded very quickly after that, didn't she?"

"Yes, she did."

"Of course."

"But that proves nothing, Stefan. She was already fading very quickly before I was taken out of her custody," Eden stated.

"And how did your grandmother feel about it?"

"She was angry at me in many ways. She went on about not doing my best for her or something. I mean, I was six, almost seven," she snapped. "I never understood half the things she said. And she kept telling me to keep trying, keep trying." And then she suddenly stopped, her realization dawning. "Are you suggesting that she thought I could heal my mother?" she asked, incredulous.

And, with that, Stefan appeared in his glittery wispy form, now swirling off to the side. Eden turned back to Eric. "Oh, God, could I have healed my mother? Did she die because I didn't try hard enough? And did my grandmother know all about this?"

CHAPTER 18

EDEN SAT HERE after the phone call with Stefan, just waiting for life to pass by, stuck in time, trying to glean something that would make sense of the craziness of her world. When she turned, Eric walked toward her, holding two cups of tea. She frowned as he sat back down again.

"You didn't even realize I was gone, did you?"

"I did and I didn't," she muttered, with a shrug. "I was just lost in my own world."

"You were also getting cold," he noted. "I had Stefan keep watch while I ran for some hot tea and your sweater." He now wrapped it around her shoulders.

She sighed. "I'm really not used to being taken care of, you know?"

"You also aren't used to what you've been through today."

"That's true," she agreed.

"Do you feel any better about it?"

She looked over at him and shrugged. "How much better could anybody feel?"

"Are you still being watched?"

"No," she replied in all honesty. "I haven't felt that since I came outside. It was inside and very creepy at the time, but it's not a problem now."

He didn't say anything, sat down beside her, and placed

the hot cup of tea in her hands.

She stared as the steam rose above the take-out cup. "This weekend has not been what I expected, you know?"

He laughed. "I don't think it's what any of us expected."

"Did you get a chance to phone your office earlier?"

"I did. We still have a very active case that I am working on," he shared, shaking his head. "It's kind of bizarre too."

"Something to do with the rapes and murders in town, right?" she asked, turning to him.

He stared at her and then nodded. "Yes, a woman was raped and murdered in her own home."

She just nodded.

"Why? Do you know anything about it?"

"No, I don't know anything about it," she replied, looking far off into the distance, "but I can tell you that it's not his first time." Her voice had shifted into a weird droning whisper.

"Okay, humor me. What else can you tell me?"

She shrugged. "He doesn't really like doing it, but he gets a sense of anticipation, a sense of excitement from it that he can't stop. He doesn't really want to stop." She let out a heavy sigh. "Not now."

"Did he ever want to stop?"

"There was a time when he wanted to stop, but now it's too good, too exciting. And he also knows that he can't get caught."

"Can't get caught? How is that?"

"He hasn't been caught, has he?" she asked, frowning. Then she looked around, and her voice dropped even lower, "He's connected to here."

Eric reared back ever-so-slightly and shifted so he could look closer into her eyes, finding them unfocused. "What did you just say?"

She frowned, then shook her head. "I'm not sure."

"Oh no, you don't get to say that," he snapped, frustration in his tone. "You just told me that this rapist and killer was connected to this place."

She tilted her head, staring at him, then nodded. "That seems right, but I don't really know what that means."

"I hope you do because we really need to catch this guy."

She gave a headshake, then frowned at him.

He raised an eyebrow. "Hello? Are you listening?"

She stared at him in surprise. "Yes, … but I was out of it there for a moment, wasn't I?"

"I'm not sure *out of it* is quite right," he corrected. "When Stefan shared how you could be affected by energies, I wasn't thinking he meant you were a medium."

She stared at him. "I'm not."

Eric stated, "Whoever I was just talking to—"

"It was me," she declared but with a quizzical expression. "But I *was* different, wasn't I? I was getting messages from someone."

Then he sat back, studied her, and asked, "From one of the energies around here, maybe?"

"From *an* energy and that's as much I know. I'm not sure it's from one around here," she replied, twisting to look around her. "Yet she had been murdered." Eden frowned.

"And you know the person who did it?"

"No, I don't."

"Do you remember her name?"

She stared at him, and the name flashed into her mind. "Valerie."

He stared back. "One of the victims is a Valerie," he confirmed.

"Yes, I think it was her." Then Eden groaned. "I really don't need this happening again."

"This *again?*" he asked, frowning at her.

She sighed but nodded. "Yes, like I told you about my grandmother, how she insisted I stay in the room with my mother, but it was horrible. And I had all those people talking to me."

"Right. And I get why you feel the way you do because they were all dead."

"Yes." She frowned, then shook her head. "No. … Some of them were dead. Some of them were not. Some of them seemed to be in a coma," she clarified. "I couldn't really tell who and what they were. Plus, I was really too young to understand. I can't believe my grandmother did that to me."

"Yes, but, if she sincerely thought you had any way to help your mother, her daughter, live, I can see why she did it."

"I guess," Eden muttered, as she stared off into the distance. "I had helped people before. My mother used to get me to help. There would always be somebody nearby who would need something, and she would say that I could help."

"But sometimes you couldn't—"

"Yes, and it was terrible," she exclaimed. "Absolutely terrible. I always felt I had failed her but never really understood how."

CHAPTER 19

EDEN AND ERIC slowly walked back to the hotel, just wanting to get away from where they were and yet not wanting to see anybody. Eden was still a bit dazed and surprised to find that very little time had passed and that everybody was still in the workshop.

As she peeked in through the doors, they all seemed completely oblivious to what had gone on. As she went around the corner to head up to her room, the old caretaker was there, talking with somebody. Eric had told her that his name was Samuel.

He caught sight of her, then frowned and noted, "You don't look too good, honey. Are you okay?"

She shrugged. "Can't say that I'm feeling all that great."

The receptionist stared at her in alarm.

Eden shrugged. "I'm sure it's nothing."

The other woman, not quite convinced, nodded and suggested, "Might be time to go lie down for a little bit?" Her tone was caring. "If you need me to, I can call a doctor."

"No need. I just need some rest, and I'm sure I'll be fine."

Samuel looked closer. "Maybe, but if you need someone to check you out, one good fella can come by."

"I don't know at the moment. I'm just feeling a little off." Worried, the two of them appeared to watch her as she headed up the stairs.

She didn't know where she had lost Eric. She knew he would be around somewhere. She needed some time to just assimilate a bit. She didn't really know what she needed, just a time out. He understood, or at least he told her that he understood, but, whether he really did or not, she wasn't sure.

She just needed that moment, that glimpse of normalcy, that might come from some downtime in her own room. As she walked upstairs, she felt eyes on her again. At the top of the stairs, she turned and looked down to see both the receptionist and the caretaker whispering together.

She wasn't sure if it meant anything or if they were just worried that she'd come down with something that could be contagious and could affect other people. As she got to her suite, she noted the door was open. She hesitated, then pushed it open. There she found the cleaning girl.

"Oh, sorry," the woman said, looking at her. "I was expecting you to be in the seminar."

"I was, but I'm not feeling well, so I've come to lie down."

"Oh gosh," she muttered, nonplussed as she stared at Eden for a moment and then nodded. "Let me just quickly finish up, and you can have your space to yourself."

Her name tag read Jillian. Eden waited and watched as the other woman quickly collected the dirty towels and did a last couple swipes in the bathroom before walking out to the hallway where she tossed everything into the linen bag sitting there, waiting. Jillian looked over at her and asked, "Do you need anything else?"

Eden shook her head. "No, I'm fine, thank you." She wasn't so sure that she would ever be fine again, but this young lady could do absolutely nothing for her.

There wasn't anything anybody could do; it was just way too bizarre. Everything that had gone on had stirred up horrible memories of her childhood that Eden had always kept locked down. She thought those bizarre events would never happen again. Yet here she was, looking at her life from the outside, and, for all intents and purposes, it was happening all over again.

As she closed the door behind the cleaning lady, Eden leaned against it and just closed her eyes.

Her phone rang just then. She looked down, not recognizing the number. As she went to refuse it, her instincts said, *Don't.*

She sighed. When she answered the phone, wondering at the hit and miss reception, it was Stefan. Maybe that's why her phone worked now? Something to ponder later…

"How are you doing?" he asked, his voice gentle.

"I'm sure you have a good idea how I'm doing," she replied, "so it is probably easier for you to answer than it is for me. As far as I'm concerned, this entire weekend was a huge mistake, and I want to turn back the clock and to not have opened that door again."

"And it's the *again* part that is the real issue here, isn't it?"

"Maybe. Once you've had those experiences," she explained, "no way you can ever continue living your life normally."

"And yet you did," he pointed out.

"Did I?" she asked. "I think I was a shadow of myself. If anything, I stomped it all down and carried on."

"Until now."

"Yeah, until now. And I very much want to go back and

shut it out all over again."

"Understood," he said, his tone light. "But if it does have something to do with your friend's death—"

She cut him off because she'd had enough. "If it does, I'm not sure that it has anything to do with me. I don't want to be the next victim, which sounds horrible, but I'm being honest. And I don't want to open that door and give it any ideas."

"Right," he agreed. "It wasn't much fun, *huh?*"

"Fun?" she snapped, her voice breaking. "It was horrific. I don't even know how I managed to get past it all, and the reality is that somehow I blocked it all out."

"You had help blocking it out," he noted casually.

That irritated the hell out of her.

Stefan continued. "Therapists are like that, at least the good ones. They find a way to help you move on."

"Get past it?" she repeated, her voice climbing with an edge. "Are you telling me *this* is getting past it? Because to do that, I need tools, but I don't know what those tools are because nobody taught me. My grandmother didn't teach me. My mother didn't teach me."

"You have the power here, Eden."

"You say that, but I'm sitting here, not at all sure how to get back to that same level of normalcy I had just a few weeks ago."

"I'm not sure you ever had it," he clarified. "And I get it. Right now you're in a state of shock, and everything is either pissing you off or upsetting you to the point that you don't even know if you're coming or going."

She stared down at her phone. "You make it sound so simplistic." It was impossible to keep the sarcasm out of her tone. Right now she just wanted him to go away. She wanted it all to go away.

"And I get that, but, having opened that door, I don't think you can close it again."

"If it was closed once before," she declared in a determined voice. "I will close it again." Dead silence came from the other end. She added, "I am not in the mood to talk to you or to deal with any of this. I'm going to lie down and try to get some sleep."

"Safety, *remember*? Are you alone?"

"Yes, I'm alone," she snapped. "What difference does it make?"

He hesitated and then replied, "I don't like the idea of you lying down alone."

She blew out her breath in a big gust and snapped, "That's where I'm at. I'm alone in my room, and I'll lie down alone here because I live alone. That's my world. What difference does it make if I'm alone or not?"

"The difference," Stefan explained, "is that you have opened the door to Origin, and opening that door and them getting your energy signature means that now you are susceptible to whatever they are up to." He took a deep breath. "So sleeping gives them access to your subconscious, if you don't have protection in place."

She pinched the bridge of her nose. "Damn. I vaguely remember my grandmother telling me stuff like that."

"But you were too young, and she probably moved through it far too quickly," he noted, "so you didn't get the proper training."

"Yeah, *ya* think?" she muttered. "I didn't get any damn training. Although I'm not sure what training there was to get. It was more a case of *go and sit there beside your mother because time is running out.*"

His voice gentled. "I know it's frustrating for you, but

your grandmother did what she had to do." When Eden started to protest, he manifested in front of her, as the shimmering wisp she recognized.

I'm not saying she was right, but nothing you can do about it now. She was running against the clock, hoping you could extend your mother's life. But, in this case, your mother didn't want it. Your mother wanted to pass with more peace than your grandmother would let her have.

"Sometimes it's hard to let go of the people we love, and Mother was incredibly upset that it was taking her so long to pass," Eden shared. "I didn't know what I was supposed to do for her." She looked up, expecting to see Stefan's glowing ethereal form, but he was gone.

"Sorry. Can't hold that image for long, so I'm back on the phone. Just remember that you did what was needed for your mother. Whether you recognize it or not, you did it."

"What did I do?" she asked, followed by a snort. "I mean, I did everything I could to avoid my grandmother's tantrums. But that's not exactly the way I wanted to see my own mother die."

"I don't think there's any way to see your own mother pass that's good," he murmured.

The soothing quality of his voice helped to calm something down within Eden.

"And I understand how trapped you're feeling."

"*Trapped* works," she grumbled. "Absolutely that fits. I am feeling trapped to the point that I don't even want to be around people anymore. Not you, not Eric. I went through this once, and I didn't think I would ever have to face it again. And yet here it is."

"Maybe there's a reason why you have to face it again," Stefan suggested, his voice raising ever-so-slightly.

Eden could almost sense him bracing for an argument. Her shoulders sagged. "Look. I'm too tired for this conversation. I'm exhausted on the inside from something I don't even know or understand."

"You're exhausted because of the mental blocks you've been using. You've been fighting the blocks, trying to keep them in place, even though the time for them has long passed. You're tired because you've been fighting against your nature, your energy-working nature, but it's already coming through at odd times. You must let go and move on."

"I don't want to get past anything—"

"You're tired and miserable because you're at war with yourself. Something that we never recommend. There will come a time when you will lose, so why not give in?"

She stared down at the phone and groaned. "It's just too much, and I don't need that right now."

He sighed and then said in a very soft voice, "Have a nap. I'll watch over you. You need to recharge emotionally, and then we'll talk again." And, with that, he ended the call, before she even had a chance to register what he said.

Stefan would watch over her.

She wasn't even sure how he would do that, yet for some reason it brought her a certain amount of peace. She just didn't know how or why.

She called out to the room around her, "Thank you for that." And damned if there wasn't a soft chuckle.

You're welcome. Now get some sleep.

She walked over to her bed and, without ceremony, collapsed onto it, pulling one of the blankets at the foot of the bed up and over her shoulders. Within minutes she was asleep.

ERIC WALKED OVER to her bedroom door and knocked but heard only silence on the other side. Even with his ear against the door, he wasn't sure if she was sleeping or if she was even in there. When he tested the doorknob, it opened easily. Frowning, he peered around the door, and there she was, crashed on the bed, sound asleep.

He smiled, but only briefly as he suddenly watched her fighting some unseen demons in her dreams. She shifted, almost in pain on the bed, caught in some agonizing nightmare. He hated to see her suffer like this.

She had so much going for her, yet had battled so many demons she wasn't even aware of. He tiptoed in and pulled the blankets back up across her shoulders, hoping it would help ease her panic. She calmed under his ministrations, only to rear up in anger, with some weird look in her eyes.

She turned, shifted on the bed, and stared at him.

He stepped up because clearly something was wrong. He just had no idea what or why. "Are you okay?" he asked cautiously, not sure if it was her or somebody else.

The person who stared back at him blinked several times, then sagged back into the bed, only to have a weird cackle come through, a noise that made the hair on the back of his head rise.

He pulled out his phone and tagged Stefan, who answered his call on the first ring. "Is she asleep?"

"She is, but I don't know what's going on."

"She came back with somebody," Stefan shared, his voice strained. "I'm trying to figure out who it is before we send them back because we don't want to leave them out there to torment other people. She doesn't have any training," he shared, "and she's too powerful. Her light, her innocence, is so strong that anything can latch on and is trying to do so."

"And they're all coming from that hellhole?" Eric asked, hating himself for having gone in there, for opening it up, when she had clearly asked him not to.

"From the hellhole, yes," Stefan confirmed, "but it also looks as if it's growing—expanding."

"Meaning, it's already caught more victims?"

"No, I think it's growing *because* it needs more victims. It's pulling in all the energies it can from around the place, to find what it needs to feed on."

"And you think it's pulling on her energy, or is it looking to feed on her?"

After a moment of silence, Stefan said, "Both. Once they find somebody as strong as her, I don't think they'll let her go, not without a fight."

"They can't have her," Eric declared hotly. "She told me not to go in there. It's my fault because I wouldn't listen."

"It's not your fault. With something like this, you can blame the energies that are twisting us all up in knots," he shared. "What we have to do is confirm that she doesn't become the next victim to this Origin."

"Agreed," Eric snapped. Then he stared down at the woman who was becoming way too important in his life. "Should I try to wake her?"

"No. I know it sounds harsh to you, but it would be good if we could learn something first."

He stared down at his phone. "I don't want to just let her suffer here as some learning experience. And that's not the Stefan I know either."

Stefan sighed. "It's not that I'm letting her be hurt, but she's caught up in some nightmare, and I don't want that nightmare to be something that hurts her as we try to bring her back. You know yourself that, if it can hurt, it will hurt."

He hesitated at that and then realized what Stefan was saying. "Fine, but I want her back, safe and sound."

"Oh, I know you do. Believe me that I know. We need to also see that she doesn't have to go back in there again."

"Yes," Eric muttered. "She was open for the longest time. I'm not sure how she managed to close herself down or whether her grandmother did."

"I don't think it would have been her," Stefan replied, "because it sounds as if the grandmother insisted Eden stay and keep working to keep her mother alive, even though her mother wanted to leave. … People like that often can't let go. So, in this case, she used her granddaughter and everything she had available to force Eden to keep the healing going, even though her own daughter was ready to leave."

"I just can't imagine doing that to a child."

"Desperation brings desperate times," Stefan noted. "You can't judge her grandmother for it."

"I can," he snapped. "Absolutely I can."

A moment of silence came from Stefan, and then he added, "We will help Eden, and we will free her from this, but first we need to free her from the Origin portal, which is sensing her. I'm afraid it might have sensed her a while ago."

"Meaning?"

He sighed. "I have this absolutely horrible feeling that Debbie was killed in order to bring Eden back here."

CHAPTER 20

EDEN WOKE UP slowly and stared around her, somewhat surprised but not completely, to see Eric sitting on the chair, staring at her. She blinked several times, glanced around, then settled back into the bed. "Hey."

"Hey. How are you feeling?"

"Maybe a little better." She motioned toward the door and asked, "How's the meditation seminar going?"

He stared at her blankly and then snorted. "I have no idea. Do you really think we're going down there?"

"I don't know, but I came here because of him."

"You came here because of your friend," he corrected.

"Debbie." She frowned and then slowly nodded. "You're right. I did. And obviously I'm not getting very far on that."

"That's because you also came here with a bit of a closed mind, looking to prove that Richard was guilty."

She didn't have anything to say to that because he was right. She'd been so sure that he'd had something to do with it that she wanted proof that would secure some vindication for her friend. "But, if he didn't have anything to do with it," she whispered, "who did?"

"I hate to say it," Eric began, shaking his head, "but maybe nobody."

She looked at him strangely.

He shrugged. "With this whole Origin thing, it's hard

for me to even think that somebody could have hurt Debbie, unless it was the Origin itself."

She stared at him with narrowed eyes.

"And I don't know if that's a thing or not," he admitted. "We need to talk to Stefan as to whether that's an option or not."

"I'm not sure Stefan even wants to talk to me," she noted, with a choked laugh. "I may have been a bit harsh on him."

"That's not so hard to understand. I mean, you're feeling out of your depths to begin with, and you're caught up in something inherently frightening, something triggering past traumas," he explained. "So, that makes sense."

"It doesn't matter if it makes sense or not," she declared. "This just feels like my childhood all over again."

He stared at her and nodded. "This could be your chance to put all that to rest … permanently."

"You say that, and I know you mean it," she clarified, "but it's not that simple."

He shuffled over to sit down beside her. "I just want you to know that, whatever it was, however it works out, I'm not leaving you alone."

Instantly tears filled her eyes, as she realized she hadn't really known quite how alone she'd been feeling. She muttered, "But you have to go back to work. You have a job to do."

"So do you, and I do have a job to do," he noted, "and I'm not sure if you have anything to tell me about that job because you're the one who mentioned that the rapist is connected to here."

"Maybe," she muttered. "I don't really understand what I said either."

"Right, and that's the frustrating part for me because it would be nice if you could say, *Hey, he's over here.* However, if you can't, I certainly won't hold it against you."

She stared at him, feeling slightly better for the first time in several hours, and a quirky smile twisted her lips. "Maybe that will happen," she noted, "but, for the moment, I do not have any insight as to that situation."

"That's good to know," he replied, "because I need to stay around, just in case you find out exactly what's going on. And that would certainly give my boss more incentive for letting me stay here."

"You do know that staying here is the last thing on my list."

"I do," he confirmed, with a smile. "It is also one of the last places I want to be. However, that doesn't change the fact that I feel the Origin needs to be closed."

She sank back into her bed, her eyes closing as she thought about what he was saying. "I'm not against it being closed," she clarified, "but I am against having anything to do with the closing of it. I think it's dangerous—very, very dangerous."

"You're right. I just don't know very many people who can close it," he pointed out.

Her eyes flew open, and she stared at him. Then she narrowed her gaze suspiciously. "You think I'm part of it, don't you?"

"I think you are part of the process, yes," he clarified.

She closed her eyes again and just drifted, letting the thoughts about everything that had happened go on. "It almost seems as if it's calling me," she shared.

"Yes, I think it probably is."

Her eyes flew open again, and she stared at him.

Eric nodded. "Stefan was wondering if part of the reason why Debbie is dead is because this thing was calling for you."

She bolted up out of her bed, even as he tried to calm her down, and she stared at him in horror. "Please don't say that."

"I'm sorry."

"No, no, no, no," she wailed. "I can't have somebody killing my friend in order to drag my sorry ass over here."

"But you're very strong," Eric told her. "Not only strong but powerful and untapped, full of energy, and that would probably feed the Origin for a very long time."

Her eyes welled with tears. "No, no, no, and no."

He sighed. "I hear you."

"No, you're not hearing me," she snapped. "No, absolutely not." And then she threw herself back down onto the bed and burst into tears.

ERIC WASN'T SURE how to help Eden get past this. When she finally stopped crying, she got up, went into her bathroom, and he heard water running. Eden presumably was washing her face or prepping for a shower, he wasn't sure.

When she opened her bathroom door a few minutes later, she looked over at him, her face red and puffy from the tears, and she announced, "We need to deal with it. We have to deal with it. Tonight."

He winced. "I don't know if that's possible."

She shrugged. "We have to because I'm leaving tomorrow morning, and then I'm leaving all this behind. The idea that whatever is going on had something to do with Debbie's death is something I refuse to carry with me for the rest of my life." She shook her head, over and over. "I've already got so much guilt about my mother's death, so it's doubly important that I sort out whatever I can and leave it behind here."

Eric sighed. "So here we are."

"Maybe contact Stefan, see what we need to do to put an end to this." She looked at him and repeated, "So go ahead and call him."

He frowned as he thought about it but didn't pull out his phone.

"It has to be tonight because you know it's hunting already. If we don't become its victims, then it will go after someone else here."

"I had to wonder," he began, "if anybody from here knows anything about it. … I think Samuel knows."

She stared at him and then shrugged. "It's certainly possible, but I highly doubt he understands the implications."

"No, that's true," he agreed. "I'm not even sure we understand those."

"Right," she agreed. "I don't think this is even understandable. I think it's something you just work through, accepting that this horror exists, and, if we're lucky, we'll never see it again in our lifetimes."

"And hopefully 90 percent of the world doesn't even know about it."

"I am a little concerned that there might be a bunch more of these around the world," she shared, staring off in the distance.

"Why would you even say that?" he asked her.

She shrugged. "Snippets of conversations from a long time ago. I don't know that the word *Origin* was ever used or that I ever heard about anything connected to this, but it seems my grandmother had an awful lot of things in her world that weren't quite kosher," she admitted, frowning. "She was a very strange woman."

"What was her relationship like with your mother?"

"My mother was a very soft, gentle woman. My grandmother, on the other hand, was much less so," she shared. "Things had to be her way all the time, and that made it very difficult for my mother."

"And your father?"

"Who knows?" she replied, with a shrug. "I never met him, didn't know who he was, still don't know."

Eric didn't say anything for a long moment.

She shook her head. "It happens, you know?"

"Way too much actually," he replied, with a shrug. "I'm just a little concerned about him popping out of the woodwork somewhere."

She stared at him and laughed. "He hasn't yet, so I highly doubt he has anything to do with what's going on."

"And what about a grandfather?"

"No clue," she said. "I don't know anything about either of them. My grandmother would say men are the devil. So, yeah, she wouldn't have liked you either. As I told you, she wasn't a terribly nice woman."

"No, not the kind of person you go around introducing as your family."

Eden smirked. "No, but she was the only family we had. Even after my mother died, my grandmother just ditched me. I don't even know exactly what happened after that." She raised a hand. "Before you ask, I didn't go looking. I was more than traumatized by everything that had happened, so chasing down my grandmother wasn't anything I wanted to get into."

"Of course not," he agreed. "And you don't have to feel

guilty about it."

She stared at him, "Up until you mentioned that, I didn't think I was feeling guilty, and now it seems as if I can't think of anything else."

He started to laugh, and she responded with a quirky smile. She nodded, adding. "We are fools, aren't we?"

"You're no fool," he declared. "However, you certainly didn't have an easy upbringing, and I think Stefan would say part of that upbringing is because of who you are on the inside."

"Which is?" she challenged.

"A very powerful energy worker and a medium, as we have just seen." He shook his head. "I'm not sure that anything can be done about it, whether you want to develop it more or whether you just want it all to fade away."

"I don't know what I want," she admitted, staring at him. "This may sound silly, but I've heard some of this before, and it's resonating, though I'm not sure exactly how. I accept the fact that I've been influenced by all kinds of trauma in my childhood, primarily surrounding my mother's illness and the way she died. However, I also had the negative influence of my grandmother, who was a little bit of a … I don't want to say, *nutcase*—"

"Oh, do say *nutcase*," he urged, with a laugh. "Let's call it what it is."

She snorted. "But I'm the one who spent time in a mental institution."

"It was probably easier on her if you were there. Then she didn't have to deal with you."

"Maybe," she acknowledged, staring at him. "I never got to go to my mother's funeral either." When he frowned at her, she shrugged. "I got locked up, remember? They decided it would be far too traumatizing for somebody so sensitive as me."

Staring off in the distance, he shook his head. "I don't quite know how that works."

"I don't think anybody knows how any of this shit works," she muttered as she glanced around. She stood to grab her sweater and stated, "So, do we need a powwow with Stefan, or do we just go out there, open up this Origin, and have a battle of worlds?" Looking back at him, a smile curled up her lips. "I hope somebody videotapes it. It would make a hell of a thing to have coffee over afterward."

He stared at her, not sure that he understood the odd mood she was in.

She shrugged. "Sorry. Let's just say, as I keep opening up these memory banks, I'm getting more and more of an idea of what may have happened over the years," she shared. "I presume somebody at that center shut down the memories, put in a block, or did something. I don't know. I should probably thank them. Yet, right now, the removal has been a bit of a shock."

Again, not sure quite how to take it, he suggested, "There is something to be said for someone making a decision for you to wait until you were old enough to handle some of this."

"Maybe," she conceded, "maybe that's what they were doing. I don't know. In the end I guess it doesn't really matter. This is my reality today, and this is the state I'm in right now. If I can do something to confirm my friend wasn't murdered for nothing, I'm happy to do it."

"Look. I shouldn't have mentioned that," he muttered, looking miserable.

"No, you shouldn't have," she agreed, turning on him

with a speed that surprised him. "But you did, and now I have to consider that possibility. It makes me sick to my stomach to think that somebody would pull such a selfish stunt to get me in their grasp. I can't even fathom it. Yet I also know that, if that someone were anything like my grandmother, they would have done exactly that without a thought for my life, as my grandmother would have done the same."

He was nonplussed to hear that, and she shrugged. "We really don't understand what people are willing to do, particularly for the ones they love, until something goes wrong. In my grandmother's case, she was trying to stop the natural order of things and was willing to do whatever it took, no matter the cost, … even to an otherwise innocent child."

At he continued to stare at her in silence, she just shook her head. "My mother was everything in my grandmother's world, and I mean *everything*. I was never a part of my grandmother's world as far as she was concerned, unless she had a particular need."

"Meaning?" he asked.

"Meaning, I wasn't good enough for my grandmother," she snapped, glaring at him.

"Easy now, take a deep breath," Eric suggested. "There are bound to be a lot of things you don't know, and you'll likely find out a lot of them through this process, so it could be really disruptive and difficult for you."

She gave a broken laugh. "It doesn't matter at this point, and I'm really hoping you were wrong about Debbie because that's …" She shook her head. "You just have to be wrong about that."

"I hope I am."

"What you're not wrong about is that this thing will continue to feed, will continue to look for more people until we stop it. If there's nobody else to contain it, then it'll have to be me," she stated, with a fatalistic shrug. "*C'est la vie*. I didn't really want to live any longer anyway."

Alarmed, Eric bellowed, "Whoa, whoa, whoa. Stop that. You dying is not what's happening."

She glared at him. "You don't know that. You can't promise me that."

"No, but I've been a cop for a long time, and I've seen a lot of bad things happen to people. You don't have a clue what some of them will do to *not* die."

"That was something I had to deal with as a very young child. God help my grandmother, but she would have fed me to the wolves if it meant bringing her own daughter back," she declared, with a brittle laugh. "You can't promise that something won't happen to me, and you can't in any way proclaim that I'll be safe."

"But your grandmother isn't around anymore."

"The reality is, you don't know that, and neither do I. Either way, we do need to do this," she stated, as she stared off in the distance. "So, if you won't phone Stefan, I will."

"He's on Speaker right now," Eric noted, holding up his phone.

She stared at it, chagrined that Stefan would have heard the last little bit. Then she realized it didn't matter. Stefan seemed to know more about her than she did anyway. "Did you do any research into my grandmother?"

"We're on it right now," he replied. "And your mother."

"That's good. My mother was a beautiful angel," she stated, a smile on her face. "And my grandmother would say that she deserved the best of everything in the world and didn't deserve me as her daughter. I never really understood what that was all about, but my grandmother was adamant about it."

Stefan added, "Your grandmother was also traumatized herself, facing the loss of her child. So I'm not sure we can give any credence to anything she had to say."

"Maybe not," Eden conceded, "but it's amazing how shit like that stays with you."

"It stays with you because it was stuck in the annals of your mind," Stefan noted, "but it's up to you now to let it go, to get rid of it. Is your grandmother deceased?"

"Yes."

"Are you sure?"

"I've always assumed so. I certainly haven't heard from her, and I was told she was dead, but I was in the mental hospital at the time. So, yeah, I don't really know."

"Wouldn't that be something?"

There was a moment of silence while everybody contemplated that possibility, then Stefan continued. "We'll go on the assumption that she is deceased, and, if she pops up somewhere, we'll know that she isn't." Then he asked Eden, "Would she have tried literally anything to avert your mother's death?"

"Absolutely anything," she stated. "To be honest, she would have cheerfully sold her soul to Lucifer himself. And I get it. It was her daughter, and she absolutely adored her and rightly so. My grandmother felt that, without my mother, she couldn't go on herself. So when they told me that my grandmother had passed on, I just accepted that as the truth. It wasn't hard at all to envision that she wouldn't have had the strength to carry on without my mother."

"Was your mother a powerful healer, psychic, medium,

or something?"

"No clue," she said cheerfully. "She certainly didn't talk to me about it if she was, and I never saw any evidence of it. Of course I didn't really realize what she had me doing either. Anyway, if that's something she was doing, she kept it to herself."

"Interesting," he murmured.

"Yeah, very." She snorted. "Look. I just want to go out there and deal with this, and I want to do it now."

"It's almost dark outside," Stefan noted.

Eric stood up. "So, the witching hour has begun. Thus, if you want to make good on that desire, I guess the time is now." He looked around a bit and added, "I don't suppose we have a backup plan, do we?"

"We do," Stefan interjected, "and that would mean me, but I'm not sure what I can do when you guys are caught up in there."

"What about Dr. Maddy?" Eric asked.

"Dr. Maddy will come if I'm in trouble, as will a few others," he shared. "We do have quite a few who work in this field, even though most have no experience with something like this."

"Then bring them in," Eden suggested. "God knows this is definitely a case of *the more, the merrier.*"

Stefan gave a bark of laughter. "Whenever you guys are ready, I will contact my people."

"You don't want to contact them ahead of time?" Eden asked.

"No need," he said. "They're around and will come as needed at the time."

She had to be satisfied with that. She looked over at Eric and asked, "Are you ready to go?"

He hesitated, then nodded. "Yes." As they were about to walk out, he had the phone in his hand, and an odd look crossed his face. "Stefan, do you think anybody here at the center is connected with Origin?"

"It's hard to say. You've certainly got a few people who could be involved, but this is old energy, very old," he stated. "So, short of somebody being here since forever, and I mean *forever*," he added, "chances are no. They may suspect something is going on, but that doesn't mean they have any actual idea of what is happening there. You can't judge everybody for not being able to see or to do something with this."

"Are you sure?" Eden quipped, as she walked over and opened the door that Eric had closed while talking to Stefan. "Because I really want to blame somebody."

"I know," Stefan noted, "and that's a common issue. But the blame just drops your energy and takes you down to a lower vibration, and that would not be good right now. You need to keep your energy elevated. You need to keep your focus strong, and you need to keep your frequency up."

She stilled as she thought about that. "Now that is something I do remember being told."

"Yes, but did you ever do it?" he asked, his tone quiet but calm. "Because that really is the trick right there. If you go out into something as active and as hungry as this Origin, and you don't have your own energy at a frequency it can't touch, you just became its next meal."

ERIC COULDN'T BELIEVE that Stefan was even saying such things. It was a rough reality for any of them to even think about, yet he made it sound as if this wasn't commonplace but potentially could be out there in many other areas. "You're thinking there's more of these, aren't you?"

"Yes," he agreed, "and we've already established that. The question is whether we can disarm one."

"You might be able to, Stefan," Eden suggested, "but that doesn't mean anybody else wants to try."

"Let's go tackle the beast in our midst," he stated, a gentle smile in his tone, "and then we'll go from there."

She walked out into the hallway and waited, until Eric stepped out.

He looked at her as he pocketed his phone and locked up. "I was half afraid you'd gone on alone."

"No, I'm not that foolish," she muttered, with a headshake. "But I have to admit, it felt a bit foolhardy even being out here in the hallway alone for a second or two."

"Of course," he agreed. "It's scary times, and it's magnified if you're alone."

She shrugged. "It's not even just about the scary times. There just isn't anybody you can talk to about this stuff."

"Did you have any friends who you could talk to?"

"No. I didn't have anybody in my circle to talk to about this stuff," she muttered. "I mean, who does?"

"What about Debbie?"

Eden shook her head. "Debbie wanted to go to psychics," she clarified, "but I don't really see her as somebody who would have gone this far or this deep into that area."

"And yet she wanted to find her mom and possibly talk to her, so that's not far off the realm of possibility."

She pondered that. "Yes, but I don't know that she was driven to this extent."

"If somebody promised her that contact with her mother, would Debbie have gone outside the norm and done something with them?"

"Oh, yes, absolutely," she said immediately, then frowned. "I wonder if that's what happened to her. I don't know. I just don't know. What about the woman who passed away here earlier this weekend? Have you thought about if she had anything to do with it?"

"I've thought about it. I don't know. It's hard to confirm that either way."

Eden didn't know what to say to that.

As they walked down to the lobby of the hotel, Jane, the receptionist, was sitting at her desk.

She gave Eric a bright smile, then looked back at Eden, a bit sheepish. "Oh, good, you're feeling better."

Eden wrapped her sweater around her shoulders and nodded.

Jane continued. "It's almost dinnertime, so I'm glad you're up and moving around. We were a little worried about you."

"I'm fine," Eden replied. "We're going out for a bit of a walk first."

Jane just smiled and nodded as they headed outside.

"What if the staff … or the owners of this place *did* know about Origin?" Eden asked. "Do you think they would close up shop? Or would they willfully … feed it?"

"You do get right to the point with your questions, don't you?"

"From what we know, this Origin has been operating here for a very long time," she pointed out. Eric nodded, as a calm expression took over his face. "So, the question really is, has somebody here been feeding it? Or is it getting nutrients from somewhere else in some other way?"

He groaned. "If we get that far in this nightmare, we can

always ask someone who's closer and in the know."

And, with that, she gave a shout of laughter. The knowledge that, if nothing else, she wasn't alone in this venture, was worth an awful lot. Looping arms with him, she said, "Come on. Let's go fight the ghosties."

And together, the two of them walked out into the waning sun. He led the way to the bench, and, as he sat down there, she shook her head.

"Not here."

Surprised, he stood back up.

"Over there." She pointed to where the woman had recently died.

He looked at her for a long moment. "Are you sure? I mean, that's the place where the woman—"

She nodded but didn't say more.

"Do you want to explain why?"

"I don't know," she admitted. "All I can tell you is it needs to be there."

He hesitated but then nodded. "I guess if I'm trusting you this far, then I better trust you the whole way."

She shrugged. "I could be wrong. If you have a question or disagree, ask away. I may not have the answer, but maybe we'll get some clarity."

He smiled. "We could both be wrong about this." And he chuckled. "Hell, Stefan could be wrong."

"Oh, that's a *great* thought. Thank you for that," she muttered.

He laughed. "I know. It's not exactly what any of us wants to think about," he noted. "But we do have to recognize that whatever this is, things may not always go our way. And nobody's infallible, not even Stefan."

"Are you sure? Because I really don't want to consider that."

As they walked over to where the ill woman had been found—and died later that night in the hospital—Eden stared at the spot and muttered, "It's depressing, isn't it? To think that she died—not here but shortly after being found here—and there's nothing. No memorial, no stone, no flowers, no nothing."

"But she's also not buried here," he noted. "So, no need for a marker. Plus, she didn't die here, and there is the business aspect and all to consider."

She shrugged. "I guess. I just don't want to see this become a killing field," she shared, as she looked around. "And yet it feels as if something's crawling all over my skin." She sat down on the ground, where the terminally ill woman had been found.

Eric winced, but he sat down beside her. She turned her face up to the setting sun, almost as an offering to some God up there. He watched her cautiously. "Is there some system to what you're doing?"

"Yes, I'm opening up." Then she frowned as she added, "And then shutting down."

"Okay, why is that?"

She thought about it and said, "Because that's what we have to do." He didn't say anything more and just watched … and waited.

Finally she turned to him and added, "It's okay. We can do this now."

He wasn't sure what she meant … or if he even wanted to know. Yet he settled in beside her and nodded. "Do you want to tell me what to do?"

"You won't even ask how I know?" she asked.

"No, I just figured your grandmother taught you something."

"I'm wondering if it wasn't my mother," she suggested, "though I don't have any memories of that. It's as if everything got blocked out somehow. That is a terrible thing, but I feel as if I'm not even sure I can remember my mother."

"How do you feel about her? That can shift your view and can give you some perspective."

"I have warm feelings about her, yet all those memories are gone or blocked by something. I don't know why that would be though."

"We can always take another look at it later," Eric offered.

"*Later,* … right," she muttered, her tone bitter. "Everything's always *later.*"

"It doesn't have to be later," he conceded.

"I know. I know," she murmured. "It's fine." But it wasn't fine.

He didn't know how to help her get through whatever these issues were. He just knew that every time they did something together, it formed a bigger, stronger bond between them, and he wasn't sure that she was even aware of it.

If she was, he had to wonder if she was even okay with it because, the more they did of this work, that bond would strengthen. And that was something she might not be too happy about.

Finally she turned, opened her eyes, and smiled. "You ready?"

He winced. "And if I say no?"

"I would say, *Too bad because it's the witching hour.* Plus, we're almost out of time." And, with that, she reached out for him. "You'll need to hold my hand."

Frowning, not at all sure he should even be listening to

everything she said right now, he slowly held out his hand.

She smiled. "Not a good time to question whether you trust me or not."

He looked right into her eyes in the fading light. "Do you trust me?" She opened her eyes wider, and he watched as the question zipped through her, noting exactly when an answer came to her.

She smiled and nodded. "Yes, I do. I don't know how or why, but, for whatever reason, in this moment, we are bonded," she declared, only her words took on a weird sing-song tone.

He sent out a call for Stefan, only to realize he was already there.

It's fine, Stefan replied. *She's slipping into the Netherworld. Let her slip. She needs to bond with the energy. Then she will come back. It might feel as if she's a different person, but she is there and is functioning at a level that I'm not sure we've seen before.*

"She's pretty adamant about doing this. And in a sudden turnabout."

That's a good thing, Stefan noted in a wry tone. *I've never really seen anybody who could slip into a portal like this.*

"It seems she's done it before."

I suspect she has probably done it a lot, but she didn't know what she was doing, and we can probably blame her grandmother for that.

"Why would a grandmother do this to a child? I can't even imagine what that would have required."

"Anything to save the mother presumably," Stefan said, with a sigh. "But that may be a question we never get an answer to."

"I think Eden's even looking for answers from her childhood," Eric shared. "And that is likely part of her journey."

"It absolutely is, and it'll also be part of yours because she's right in one sense. Whatever you guys are doing now will connect you in a way that you hadn't expected."

Just then, the energy around them shifted, while something whistled and roared. Then the wind picked up, and Eric was cast into the center of a maelstrom, with Stefan's last words ringing in his ears.

Look after her. You look after her, and she will keep you alive.

And, with that, Stefan was gone, and so was everything else in Eric's world.

CHAPTER 21

AT FIRST, EDEN heard only deafening silence, saw only darkness, and felt only a cold that seemed to permeate her bones. She couldn't move; she couldn't do anything. She just existed.

She felt everything within her start to fracture, pieces coming off, little by little, as she slipped into nothingness. Such a strange sensation, yet almost familiar. She couldn't react; she couldn't do anything but allow it to happen.

She was content to allow it because, somewhere in the back of her mind, she knew. It was a process as old as time, and, as she separated from one existence into another, it almost felt natural to her. She sensed people around her—bodies, entities, souls, lots of them. She couldn't even begin to sort out how many.

Was it five, or was it fifty?

She couldn't see, couldn't move, couldn't make heads or tails of any of it, and yet it was all here, telling her that, if she wanted answers, they were over there. She only had to go in that direction, and everything would be explained. Yet something was going on in that direction that held her back, telling her no, that this had to be her choice, that it had to be under her control. Otherwise it would not end the way she wanted it to.

She sensed Eric around her, and yet she couldn't see

him. She felt more of an overwhelming acknowledgment that he was here somewhere with her. The fact that it was *somewhere* was even odder since she was nowhere. She was still here, at the same place as always, and yet she was nowhere near where she had been.

She wanted to laugh. Then she wanted to cry. Nothing made sense, yet everything made sense. It was as if all the answers to the universe were right here at her fingertips.

Every question she ever wanted answered was here, right in her grasp. She just couldn't quite reach it, couldn't grasp them.

She had to ask herself some serious questions. *Do I even want the answers?*

Surely she did. Of course she wanted answers.

Can I handle the answers?

She was sure she could do something with this, but the crux of the matter remained the same—that she was nowhere closer to where she wanted to be. And her mind was rolling through an endless up and down, open and closed. It didn't know what to do.

Her mind aimlessly wandered, questioning almost everything about the world that she lived in—or the world that she used to live in anyway.

No. Rein it in, Eden.

The voice was her own, nudging her. She pulled back on that, the world that she did live in. This was not a one-way ticket.

A mocking laughter came beside her.

Eden realized that somebody believed it to be a one-way ticket. Somebody thought she had no way to get back out of here, that it was all about them and not at all about whoever entered this nightmare of theirs. Feeling that sense of certainty within her, she poured more energy into it, building it, strengthening it, so that she had it beside her to pull on, just in case.

"It's useless, you know," a voice whispered into her ear. "You can't fight this. Nobody can. We've tried. There is no fighting it."

Eden didn't want to even look in the direction of that voice, and she absolutely refused to believe it. There was always an answer. Whether she was strong enough to get the answer that she needed or wanted was a different story, but there was always an answer. She knew that.

Somehow she knew that without a bit of doubt. She didn't know how, but voices reverberated in her head from a long time ago, and then she realized it was her grandmother's voice. If Eden were honest, she recognized her mother's voice as well. Somewhere in there, in the past, were the answers she had wanted for so long, answers that nobody was willing to give her.

It was such a strange feeling, a strange sense of home-coming, yet not a homecoming that she particularly wanted or enjoyed. She frowned at that, wondering what the answer was here, and then realized it wasn't so much about the answer as what she would do about this situation while she was here. Somebody else was in control, and it needed to be her. If Eden couldn't do it, she needed to get out, and again she heard that voice from somewhere in her distant past.

Somebody, somebody who had wanted her to do some-thing, had trained her to do something, but ultimately Eden had failed.

She pondered the realities of life, caught up in other people's dreams, hopes, wishes, and needs. She was hit with a tsunami of pain, loss, grief, determination, fury, and fear. It was all there.

It didn't make any sense to her. So much of this didn't, but the emotions were almost impossible to ignore. Something was going on here that Eden only partially understood. She had no idea how this was happening, yet she knew she'd been here before, right here to this edge of the darkness and whatever lay beyond.

You need to take control, child.

The voice was affectionate, and Eden tugged it close, adding it to the whirlwind of energies she had been gathering around her for support.

The maelstrom was peaking and included her mother, her grandmother, and everything they had tried to get her to do. Her mother, who had released her in peace, telling her it was okay, telling her she had done everything that had been asked of her, telling her that her mother was happy to go. Then there was her grandmother, who could not stand to lose her own daughter, who pushed the edge of absolutely everything anybody could possibly believe into existence. Even then it still wasn't enough.

Eden felt the rage and the pain and the sense of failure, the sense of anger and fury that she hadn't been enough. Even as she listened to that voice inside her head, she heard it screaming through the annals of time. She gave herself a hard shake, and, even then, she heard Stefan's voice. "Stefan, you're here?" she cried out.

I'm inside you, he murmured, *and, therefore, I'm here, but I'm not here.*

She laughed, the sound almost freeing. "That makes so little sense."

She could sense the smile in his voice as he whispered, *I know, and that's okay too.*

She wasn't sure. She was almost in a euphoric state, knowing something about where she was, feeling a certainty, a weird freedom that she couldn't quite grasp, yet couldn't let go of either.

How do you feel? he questioned.

"You know how I feel, as I'm sure you feel it too."

Yes, but I want you to tell me.

"Wild, free, painless," she replied in a moment of untethered joy. "It's as if I've always been primed for this. This is meant to be."

And, in many ways, you probably have been primed, Stefan noted. *Can you see anything here? Can you feel what's going on?* he asked, as if trying to direct her somewhere.

However, she didn't understand *where.*

I need you to focus, he said.

"On what?" she asked. "It's beautiful here. Look."

I can't see the same thing you can see, he replied. *I can't see any of it. I cannot feel it. I cannot in any way recognize the same things you sense.*

"But it's so beautiful," she said. "How could you not? So much joy is here."

Joy? he repeated, his tone almost disbelieving, but something else was in his voice. *Tell me exactly what you see.*

"I don't see anything," she replied, "just darkness. Lots and lots of darkness."

And you like that?

"I do," she said, with a smile. "No pain, no worries, just a beautiful, beautiful darkness. It's gorgeous," she whispered.

Listen to me, Eden. This is not for you. You have your own problems to deal with. You aren't ready for this.

"How can you deny the beauty here?" she cried out softly.

Maybe you aren't seeing clearly either, he murmured. In a surprise twist, he asked, *Can I ask you something, and you say the first thing that comes to your mind?*

"Yes," she said, turning around, feeling such a lightness in her heart and soul. "What?"

Who are you?

She froze. "Pardon?"

Who are you right now? he repeated. *I know it's somebody else. I know it's not Eden*, he declared. *Who are you?*

She laughed. "How can you tell it's not me? Of course it's me."

No, he repeated. *Once again you have taken on a persona, taken on an entity, someone who wants to keep you there.*

She laughed. "Maybe it would be nice to be wanted for a change," she replied wistfully. "There's not been very much of that niceness in my world."

I understand," he acknowledged, *but that too is changing.*

"Is it?" she snapped and then sighed. "I'm not angry at you," she shared, "but it's nice in here."

He let out a deep breath. *Is it? Maybe you should show me some of where you're at, some of the places you see, so I can see it too.*

"Can't you see it?"

No, he stated. *I just told you that I can't.*

"Right. It's too bad though," she said. "It's very pretty." She noted that her voice had taken on a weird melodic tone. Then she almost recognized what that tone was. "I don't understand," she admitted, only to have the thought flit away almost as soon as it came to her mind.

I know you don't, Stefan agreed. *Something else is going on here that you don't necessarily recognize.*

"Of course I do," she argued, with a laugh. "It's really

pretty here." Her voice now sounded childlike, almost not capable of recognizing anything around her. It was a little girl's voice, one with pain, one with resignation, fear, not knowing that, whatever this was, it was bound to be bad because it was always bad.

If it is going be bad, Stefan asked, *why do you say it's pretty?*

"Because, if I keep telling myself that it is pretty, then I don't have to worry about how scary it is here," she admitted.

You don't like it there, do you?

Suddenly a buzz filled the air, and everything around her shifted, shimmered, and merged into the same odd darkness. "Now it's getting scary."

And is your mother there?

"She is, but I can't find her. She's already leaving, and I can't stop her. My grandmother will be mad at me."

There was silence, and then he asked, *And what about Debbie?*

"No friends are here," she stated, looking around. And then she frowned because everything around her started to change again and not in a good way. "What is all this?"

What's happening now? Stefan asked.

"The place is changing, shifting in and out. Changing."

Tell me, he urged her.

"Images but different. I don't like them. I don't know them," she explained. "It's not the same anymore."

No, I'm sure it's not the same, he agreed. *Because you're moving through events, through time, moving through passages and maybe some memories of your own. Come back to now.*

"Right," she muttered. "We're supposed to help those people, aren't we?"

Clear the cobwebs, let go of the past, and don't confuse the past with the present. Come back to where we need you, where Eric and I are, Stefan reminded her. *We can discuss your grandmother and your mother later. Come back over here*, he stated, his tone firming up.

"And if I don't want to?"

He hesitated. *People need you here.*

"Right, I'm here for a reason," she declared. "Always for a reason. Always for the same reason. What's the reason, Stefan?"

There is always an opportunity to help someone, he told her. *And, if you're very good at it, there will always be a need.*

"I'm good at it," she declared. "I'm very good at it."

And who told you that?

"My mother. … And my grandmother."

I'm sure she did, he replied. *When you didn't save your mom, she turned, didn't she?*

"Yes, then I became something terrible. Something horrible. And that was hard," she murmured. "And I was only doing what I was told."

Right, Stefan sighed. *Back to these people, … the people who need you right now.*

"Right," she said. As if returning to a more businesslike response, she looked around, checking to see what she was supposed to do. But she felt a weird disconnect now, as if she looked through multiple sets of eyes. She heard Stefan in the back of her head, talking to her.

You're looking through the child's eyes, but you're also looking through your own adult eyes.

That was weird, but it was also very weird hearing Stefan's voice in her head as she tried to maneuver through this strange world that she found herself in.

You're doing fine, he told her, his voice ever soothing and reassuring.

She looked around, the scene changing. Instead of a hospital, instead of seeing her mother as she expected, she now saw a hotel. No, maybe not a hotel, a lodge.

She wasn't sure exactly what it was, but a huge building appeared in front of her. A building with many people, so maybe a hotel. And then she saw the fire, endless, endless fire ripping through the building.

And people running with buckets. Buckets to put out a fire that had already engulfed the bulk of the hotel. And screams of pain and fury.

"The pain is too much," she screamed.

She looked around and panicked because she was inside the fire. She felt the heat. She felt everything twisting through her as she fought the flames.

Stefan interrupted, saying, "It's fine. It's not your pain. Try to detach from it. You're just watching it. Stand firm as a witness."

She heard him, and she understood, yet it wasn't the same as just walking through it and letting it go.

It was a long time ago. It's over and well in the past.

She settled down as she watched, almost in a weird hypnotic fashion, seeing how everybody madly dashed about. She saw people up in the windows, screaming for help.

She winced, hearing the horror in their voices, feeling their pain. A little girl was up in the far corner window, up on the top floor.

And suddenly Eden was right there, right beside her. She reared back in shock. The little girl still stood at the window, screaming, and screaming and screaming for somebody to come save her.

And yet, as Eden held out her hands, she realized the truth. Stefan was right.

It wasn't happening right now. She could watch it all go on around her, like a horrific 3-D movie. As if she'd bought seats to some front-row catastrophe. And yet no hero would step in at the last minute to save all these people.

As Eden looked around, she knew something was here, something important, something that she was supposed to see, to remember, or to do. She didn't know. Frantic now, with the same sense of urgency as the little girl, who was screaming out the window, Eden turned and looked toward the wooden door, which was now burning from the other side.

And then she was in that hallway, staring at all the bedrooms down this long hall, and realized exactly what had happened. Even as she did so, she heard another scream and was inside another bedroom.

She raced toward the little girl, trying to help her, knowing it was futile, but having to try anyway. And just as she got there, a beam in the ceiling fell and hit the little girl. It took her down, killing her instantly. Eden stood here in horror, as she watched the flames sneak toward the little girl's dress, before catching hold. Then, just like a torch, it moved quickly over the small body, engulfing her in the deadly heat.

And, with that, Eden slammed back into her body on the grassy knoll. She opened her eyes, shudders quaking through her. She was alone again.

No, you aren't alone. Eric's right here.

She remembered that she entered Origin with him. He was here beside her now, and yet he didn't appear to be here. She frowned as she stared at Eric, curled into a ball. She put a hand on his shoulder, turning him to face her. "Eric, look at me. Wake up," she said, but he didn't respond. He was in an odd, altered state, but she had no idea where he was or what he was doing.

Panicked, she gave him a hard shake, and then a slap, but she got no response from him. He wasn't reacting in any way. Images from the fire and the hotel collided and merged.

Her mind wasn't putting the pieces together, but she knew without hesitation that Eric was in danger, a danger that neither one of them had even considered. What had she done?

She had dashed off into the fire. Had he tried to follow? She dimly remembered even feeling his presence in a way, and yet she wasn't getting any sense of knowing he was there.

Nothing else felt like him, at least not the same as him. She called out, "Stefan." Almost immediately a strange shimmer appeared in the air around her. She wasn't sure what she was seeing, and it didn't matter. She snapped, "What's happening? What's wrong with him?"

He's back in the energy that you left, he explained. *You came back, but you left him behind.*

She stared at him in shock and muttered, "Oh no, no, no. That can't happen. It's very dangerous back there. He can't be there."

Stefan appeared to nod. *Agreed, but that's where he is.*

She immediately closed her eyes.

This time, the memories were all there. The pain, the fear, the constant terror of what she had to do and what she was doing, as she moved slowly through the hospital, only to get called out by Stefan.

Forget the hospital, he warned, and she realized that, once again, everything she did was being directed, and she quickly moved through to the burning hotel, and there, as she watched, looking for any sign of Eric, she saw somebody trying to help a little boy in the far side of the huge building.

They were on a small balcony, off to the one side. She turned, realizing that Eric was caught up in the same scenario that she was, with him trying to save a little boy. She reached over and touched him.

He looked at her, relief on his face. "Help him," he said. "Help me save him. He'll die if we can't get him out of here," he cried out.

She nodded. "I will help." She wrapped her arms around Eric, and, with a blink of an eye, brought him back home again. As she opened her eyes, he stared at her, wide-eyed, looking down at his hands, even with the smell of smoke still on them. He stared in shock at her.

She nodded. "That was the fire that consumed whatever building had been here at least one hundred years ago and had killed many people," she told him, "and, yes, I brought you back."

Tears welled up in his eyes, and he cried, tears spilling down his cheeks. "Why didn't you help me save him? We could have saved him," Eric roared, the fury and the pain of loss ripping through him at the same time.

She held out a hand. "I couldn't save him," she said. "No one could, Eric. He died well over a century ago."

He stopped his tirade when the words finally filtered through. "What?"

She nodded. "That fire was a long time ago."

And, with that understanding, Eric burst into tears and sobbed for a little boy who had been dead for decades.

IT WAS A while later before Eric finally shifted all the heavy, ugly emotions off to the side and looked at Eden with some calm. "For the longest time, even when I came back, … I couldn't separate from the idea that you couldn't save him. I don't know why I even expected you to," he admitted in bewilderment. "That fire was extreme."

"About that fire, you also saw the lack of firefighting equipment, right?" she asked.

"Yes, not a single truck in sight."

"That's because it was so long ago. They didn't have fire trucks or hydrants. A bucket brigade maybe, but so few people," she noted. She had been quiet for the most part, as he had ranted and raved.

He hadn't conducted himself in a way that he was proud of, but she seemed to be completely unfazed by it, as if accepting that the blame was hers, and that was another thing that got him. He turned and looked at her and said, "You were just accepting everything I was yelling at you. How come?"

She shrugged. "I knew where you were coming from. It was your grief talking. You couldn't help the little boy, and it was tearing you apart."

He closed his eyes as he remembered the panic as he was trying to help the little boy out the door. "I don't understand why I couldn't get the door open. It wouldn't open. I tried."

"Of course you tried, but we all have our own limitations."

"I'm not human enough, am I?" he asked bitterly. "What's the point of doing this work if you can't change something?" When she didn't say anything, he glared at her.

She smiled. "You're asking a question I have asked a million times before," she shared, "and I don't have any answers for you." She sighed, while he sniffled. "I didn't get any answers myself, and nobody has been able to give me any, so I don't know why. I don't know why I had to see that little girl die too," she noted. "Or why you had to see that little boy die and even get caught up in your inability to do anything about it."

"There must be someone who can save them."

"Don't go there. Maybe Stefan can tell us something. I don't know, but I sure wouldn't get my hopes up. That's one of the reasons I absolutely detested the work I was constantly doing with my mother."

He stared at her for a long moment, and just then the phone rang. He answered it, recognizing Stefan's number. "I hope you have some answers for me," he stated bluntly, "because I feel like hell and completely lost."

"I'm sorry," Stefan replied, with a sigh. "Answers are a little thin on the ground right now, and, yes, I do understand, so you don't need to rip me a new one."

"I wasn't—"

Stefan cut him off. "I can feel your anger wafting off you, so don't bother. I understand that it's been brutal and that you weren't in any way prepared for those heavy emotions and the heavy losses."

"It's the loss of a child, Stefan. Many of them. How on earth does anybody find a way to deal with such memories, such images? I mean, that little boy was burned alive," he cried out. "How is that okay?"

Stefan, his voice gentle, said, "I know it makes zero difference to you at this point, but the smoke would have taken him before the fire ever did, so he wouldn't have felt a thing."

"How could he have not felt a thing? It was a nightmare," he cried out, clearly in agony. "How is that okay?"

"It's not okay," Stefan confirmed, his tone soothing, "and yet we all know that it happened a very long time ago, and there's nothing any of us can do to change that. I want to hear a little bit more from Eden."

At that, Eric turned to look at Eden.

"Obviously neither of you have any answers," Stefan noted.

Eric added, "If I thought there was any way to go back in time and save him, I would."

"And then what?" she asked him. "If you could save him, then what? For all you know, he's the one who set the place on fire." When he stared at her in shock, she shrugged. "I mean, it probably wasn't him because of his age and size, but …" Then she fell quiet.

"No, no, no, no," Eric cried out. "You don't get to just go silent. What is it you are trying so hard not to say?"

She didn't answer, and Stefan, his voice gentle, as if he already knew, spoke up. "It would help if we could discuss it, Eden."

"Discuss what?" she asked, her tone hostile. "Discuss the fact that the doors were all locked from the hallway side? Discuss the fact that the fire was lit on purpose? Discuss the fact that those people, including the children we saw and who knows how many more, all died because somebody wanted them to? Discuss the fact that everything that happened there that day was a man-made disaster, a mass murder?" Her voice broke as she cried out, "None of it makes any sense."

She was hyperventilating but still going. "How does knowing any of this help anybody?" she wailed, as she turned to Eric. "Is that what you want to hear?"

He took a step toward her, but she held out a hand, keeping him at bay. "That little boy was murdered. A lock was on his bedroom door from the hallway side, the same as the little girl screaming at the window on the very top floor, whom I saw, whom I was interacting with. I could do nothing for her, and neither of us could do anything for the little boy."

She cried out, "How does going back in time and seeing that absolutely horrific scene do any good for anyone? I didn't need to see that. I didn't need those memories, and I sure as hell didn't need that emotional onslaught." She turned her attention to look at the phone. "Stefan, how is any of that helpful?"

"I don't know if it was helpful," Stefan admitted, "but what I can tell you is, anytime that is shown to people, there's a reason. It's up to us to find out just what that reason is and to solve it."

"Solve what?" Eric repeated, glaring into the phone. "I don't ever want to go through that again."

Stefan sighed. "And maybe you won't ever have to," he replied. "Not everybody wants to do this work, but maybe if you understand what happened to the little boy afterward, you might want to."

"What do you mean—afterward?" he snapped, his tone ominous as he glared down at the phone. "That little boy already went through hell. He should be left in peace."

"That would be nice," Eden muttered, and then she realized what was happening. "Oh God," she moaned, sagging down to a crouch, staring at the phone. "He's in that hole, isn't he? He's in the Origin."

After a moment of silence, Stefan replied, "Yes, I think so."

"He's a prisoner? He's one of many who're in there? We have to help him," Eric roared, as he bounded to his feet. "We have to help him."

"I thought you didn't want to do any of this work," Stefan reminded Eric, with a note of wry humor. Eric turned and glared at the phone yet again, and Stefan added, "Oh, I get it. Believe me that I get it."

"Do you?"

"Yes, I do, but it's not just about one little boy. A lot of other people are in that Origin," he stated, "and we still have to get to the bottom of it in order to shut it off," he told them.

"What do we have to do?" Eden asked, her mind thinking through the possibilities. "Everybody who died in that fire is there, aren't they?"

"Yes, and first things first. I think we need to do some research on what happened," Stefan suggested. "That would give us something to work with here that we didn't have before. It would also help to have the names, ... the names of the people who perished."

"We can do that," she replied, looking over at Eric. "Maybe Eric can get something on it."

"Most likely," Stefan suggested, "somebody at the hotel will have the history, the horrible history, a terrible history. Still, we must find the history of whatever happened there."

"Maybe a few people will still remember," Eric noted.

"I still don't understand why it's feeding, why it needs new souls," Eden shared. "So much here I just don't get."

Eric stared at her. "That you get any of it is beyond me," he muttered. "It's all just so horrific."

"I know," she agreed, "and I understand that, but I also understand that something here needs to be uncovered, and

I'm not exactly sure how or what that'll be, but we have a huge issue here," she declared, "and it definitely needs to be stopped." She frowned. "I don't understand Debbie's involvement either."

"Maybe there isn't any, unless to get you back here to feed Origin," Eric suggested. "Or maybe … Do you know anything about her history?"

"You mean, long-term history? Only the past fifteen years."

"So, maybe it would be helpful to get a genealogy," Stefan suggested. "I do know somebody, so I might reach out."

"There's no *might* about it," Eric barked. "If it's important that we do this right now, we need to make use of whatever we have available in terms of resources to get answers. We came here because of her friend Debbie, but that doesn't mean it's just connected to Debbie."

"Maybe not," Stefan conceded, "but something brought you guys here."

"And," she interrupted, "there is still a connection to your rapist and murderer."

When Eric turned and stared at her, she shrugged and said, "I don't know how. I don't know why. I'm just reminding you of that."

"Christ," he muttered, staring at her. "I forgot about that one."

"I know. I know," she said, "and that's the last thing you wanted to hear."

"It absolutely is, especially if I don't get any more answers than that."

"Sorry, I'm not trying to be unhelpful."

He snorted and collapsed back down, but then, after a moment, he reached out a hand and slid his fingers through hers. "I'm not mad at you."

"Good," she whispered, a sheen of tears in her eyes, "because it feels as if I'm still dealing with a lifetime of people being mad at me."

He shook his head. "Maybe it's time you tell us exactly what your grandmother had you do."

She frowned at him. "You know what she wanted me to do. I told you that already."

"Humor me."

"I sat there in the hospital the whole time, trying to heal my mother of cancer, a cancer that had ravaged her body and had made it almost impossible for her to even smile or to do anything anymore. It's a terrible disease," she whispered, "and it's relentless."

He nodded and didn't say a whole lot for a minute. "What was it that you were supposed to do? Like, how were you supposed to help your mother?"

She shrugged. "I was supposed to heal her any way I could, but the instructions I got were strange, but they were something at least."

"How strange?"

"I was supposed to go to the *between*, to disappear into the nothingness, into the space wherever people were, and ask them to help, ask them for forgiveness, ask them to save her."

"Did she specifically tell you to ask people to help?" Stefan asked, his tone sharp.

"Grandmother had me do all kinds of things. I went in there, trying to do what she would tell me, but terrified because of all the things I heard her telling me to do in the background, things that weren't at all what she told me ahead of time."

"What do you make of that?" Eric asked.

"She was so upset and distressed over my mother's death, or potential death, that she became even more unhinged and irrational as time went on."

Stefan, his tone sharp, spoke up again. "Do you remember what she told you to do? It's important, Eden."

"She said that people were weakest in the hospital, and, although it wasn't a great source of energy, any energy that could be captured for my mother to heal was energy being put to a much better use. I didn't understand what she meant. I guess I still don't really understand, and it was very difficult because she would rant and rave at me every time I came back out, telling me it wasn't enough and to go back in. I hated it in there. It was scary."

Stefan remained quiet, hoping she would go on.

"It was dark. Sometimes a bit of light shone in my world, but, for the most part, Grandmother became completely unhinged, telling me that I had to stay in there and do more."

"It's the *do more* part that I find interesting," Stefan noted, "because it seems she expected you to heal."

"Yes, and for the longest time I was," she noted. "I was able to heal. I tried to avoid getting into those situations, but it was hard for me to not help somebody when I could see that they needed it."

At that, Eric spun and looked at her. "The waitress."

"And it isn't that easy once everything's been … fired up. It takes a while to fire up, and it takes me a long time to shut down," she shared. "So that's just the way it is."

"Now you're starting to make sense," Stefan stated.

"I'm glad you think so," she quipped, "because I don't have a fucking clue. I don't see how I'm making any sense at all," she muttered. "Let's just say that, no matter what I was told to do, I tried hard to do it, but then as the instructions got wilder and wilder, I really struggled."

"You've got to remember all that you can."

"I was little. I was six, going on seven, and all that time that I was working at saving my mother, that was my life. I didn't go to school. I didn't do anything. I was supposedly being homeschooled at the hospital."

"Were you really?"

"I was taught some. My mother always fought to send me out, to send me back to school, but my grandmother would never let me leave, and every time my mother would open her eyes, there I would be. My grandmother was always telling me that I needed to spend every moment with her and that we were connected."

"You were connected because you were mother and daughter."

"Yes, but that wasn't enough for Grandmother," Eden replied.

Stefan continued. "I'm getting a lot of this, but I feel as if you aren't telling me something. You need to remember that to break this."

She sighed. "There's a lot I'm not telling you," she snapped, "because there's a lot that I don't know for shit. And how could I tell people the reason my mother lived as long as she did? No matter how much I fought doing it, if I didn't obey, my life became more and more hellish, until it seemed as if I just couldn't do anything anymore. Sometimes the nurses would come and would take me away, and my grandmother would collapse in grief. Everybody would just put it down to her grief over my mother."

"Which, in many cases, would have been exactly that."

"In many cases, yes, it absolutely would have been."

"But not all?" Eric asked.

"No," she whispered, "not all. Grandmother was obsessed, and I get it. It was my mother after all," she whispered, "but that obsession became almost impossible to live with. If I didn't do everything exactly as Grandmother decreed, it became almost impossible to get away from her."

"And yet you managed … to get away, I mean."

"I would say that my mother put a stop to it," she clarified, "and, by then, I also had an idea of what was going on."

"How so?"

"On the last day, my mother pulled me close and whispered that it was time to stop and that the only way to do that was if *she* could stop it. I wasn't even sure what she was talking about or that she even knew what was going on, though I presumed she did because it was all about her mother. Somewhere along the line, she must have known what my grandmother was doing, what she was making me do. … So, when my grandmother came in that afternoon, she had a little bit of food for me, not much, mostly because she thought I worked better if I wasn't eating, so I was always hungry, almost starving. Sometimes the nurses would bring me extra food because, well, I was a child, and it wasn't really in them to see me suffer. Yet lots of looks came in my direction. That part was difficult for me," she shared. "I mean, how do you explain to people that you're not allowed to leave until you can heal your mother fully, and I knew I wasn't able to heal her fully."

"And why is that?" Eric asked. "I mean, if you were in there and you were healing and all?"

Eden looked at him with sad eyes. "When you take energy from others, and it's good, pure, clean energy, there's still a limit to how it can be used, and my mother did not want to be healed in that way. She would never want to hurt another person."

"I don't understand," Eric replied. When she didn't respond, he felt as if he'd had enough of the games, his frustration bubbling over. "What are you not saying? How exactly did you heal her?"

"I healed her with the energy I took from all the other sick people," she explained. "Because they were sick, the energy didn't go far, but it was as far as I could reach, and, for my grandmother, it wasn't nearly enough."

He stared at her, not sure he wanted to understand, but what she was saying spoke volumes. "So, in order for you to heal your mother, other people had to die?"

"I tried not to take enough to kill them," she whispered, tears rolling down her face. "I tried hard to leave people so they could have their loved ones too, but, if my grandmother thought that I wasn't making a full effort, then, well, let's just say the beatings got worse."

Eric sat back and stared at her in shock.

She shrugged. "See? I'm not the person you think I am, and I know that you really don't want anything to do with me," she added, with a sad smile, "because why would you? Why would anyone? I mean, for all you know, you'll go to sleep one night, and I'll whisk in there and take your energy for someone else," she said in a mocking tone.

"That's not—"

"Don't bother. … I can see it already in your face."

"No," he declared, "you can't see shit in my face because that's not there. What you said is not true."

She stared at him as he went on.

"Am I surprised? Am I shocked that this was even possible? Hell yes, I'm stunned. The fact that your grandmother treated you like that boggles my mind. You were a child."

"You don't understand—"

"Don't understand what?" he asked. "What possible reason could explain that abuse of her own granddaughter?"

She smiled. "It's the most understandable reason in the entire world," she began, "*a mother's love.* Mothers all over would cheerfully sacrifice every other person on this planet, … if it would save their beloved child."

FOR A LONG time after they returned to their suite, Eric didn't even know what to say. Absolutely nothing he had heard or had seen in the last hour made any sense to him, and yet obviously it had happened. He just couldn't understand the driving forces behind it all.

He was still reeling over what Eden had gone through and everything that had happened today, and somewhere along the line, while he'd still been stunned, she'd gotten up and announced she would go lie down. As he sat on the couch, his mind still spinning, Stefan contacted him.

Are you okay?

"Sure," he muttered bitterly, "I guess, but that was way too real. That little boy was screaming in so much pain and terror. Can we go back in time and help these people?"

If that day ever comes, Stefan offered, *I would be the first to make the attempt, but, so far, I haven't even heard of anything like that.*

"And yet isn't there something about dimensional travel and all that good stuff?"

Yeah, and we are working with some of that, he confirmed. *There are always consequences to our actions, and we don't always know what they are until they happen.*

"But what are the repercussions of going back and not having that fire start in the first place? All those people would have lived, right?"

Stefan replied as gently as he could. *And what happens then? I mean, that's how many more souls who lived, who would have reproduced, who would have carried on. Yet other people might not have been born. How much would all of that have changed the world? I mean, at what point in time does messing with any of this make changes in our world that aren't acceptable?*

Eric knew what Stefan was saying, but it was all just so frustrating. "I get it. I can't believe how exhausted all that left me, you know?" he muttered.

I do, and you need to rest, recuperate, and cleanse your system of all that energy so you're not carrying it forward.

"Right now, I don't even know that I want to release it. I just feel so close to that little boy and so grief-stricken."

That's another reason why you need to let that energy go. Because that little boy, regardless of what you saw and how much pain he was in, is long gone, and you don't want to hang on to that energy.

"But he's in there, Stefan. He's in that portal."

I know, Stefan said. *And we might need a little more help to release him and the others. For whatever reason, and maybe that's the part that's so important here, but, for whatever reason, they have been kept in that portal.*

"So, what then? How do we save them? How do we get them out of there?" he cried out. "That's just so wrong."

I agree with you. It is wrong. But we are also still trying to sort it all out.

He groaned at that.

Stefan sighed. *I get it. You want answers, and you want progress, and you want action, and you want it all right now.*

"Damn right, I do," he snapped in frustration. "And I want to know that little boy won't be suffering for all of eternity. How long has he suffered now?"

Maybe that's something you can sort out, he suggested. *Get onto the internet, onto your databases, and do some research on that fire. You'll also need to check in on Eden.*

"Why? Is she in danger?" he asked, turning to look at her bedroom door. "She went to her room to lie down."

Did she though? Stefan asked. *Or did she leave because she felt as if you were judging her for it?*

He froze at that. "Good God." He shook his head. "I wasn't judging her. I'm not in any shape to judge jack shit at the moment."

What you were doing and how she perceived what you were doing could, in this instance, end up being a very different thing.

"Oh, Christ." Eric bolted to his feet. "Do you think she's taken off?"

I don't know what she's done or what she's planning on doing, Stefan stated. *I am just telling you that she's pretty tortured over this whole thing.*

"I can't believe her grandmother would do that."

And yet I understand it, Stefan said. *Agree with it? Absolutely not. But understand it? Maybe. There is no pain like losing a child. And even though the child was an adult, I can see that, for the grandmother, it was completely unacceptable. And to do anything she could to prevent it? That wouldn't be as out of line as it might seem in this moment.*

"Christ," Eric muttered. "The stupid webs we weave, huh?"

She apparently couldn't face life without her daughter. She chose to put everything she had in her to manipulate Eden into saving her daughter.

"But that's ridiculous. Eden was just a child."

And obviously the grandmother must have had some abilities. She fought long and hard with her granddaughter and maybe her own daughter, Stefan surmised. *We need to do more research on that. You need to find more information about the fire.*

"Right. I will do that now," he stated, as he got up. "But, before I dive into that, I'll find Eden and just confirm she's okay."

She's probably gone for a nap, as you mentioned. And tell her that you don't hold her responsible for any of this.

"I don't hold her responsible," he declared, followed by a groan. "Christ, it didn't even occur to me that she would really think that."

Of course she would. She's spent a lifetime believing it herself.

"And yet nothing was her fault," he pointed out. "She was just a child."

Nope, it wasn't Eden's fault. The responsibility is on the grandmother, but you'll struggle to get Eden to believe that.

"That old witch really messed her up, didn't she?"

And remember, all for love. And, with that, Stefan was gone.

Eric sent Eden a quick text, asking if she was okay. And then he would start researching. She sent back a thumbs-up, and he had to be satisfied with that for now.

Then he sat down with his laptop and started going through whatever he could, looking for the corresponding address to this location but one hundred or even two hundred years ago. Who the hell knew what this space even looked like back then? It wasn't like he could check the online land records for ownership. He shook his head. He checked to see if anything was in the archives online regarding this hotel that he could delve into. When he found nothing, he got up and headed down to the front desk to speak to the receptionist to see if any information could be dredged up from there.

When Jane looked up and saw him, she smiled. "Hey, I hope you are having a blast while you're here."

"I was wondering about the history of this place."

"Oh," she muttered, her tone mild, "it's long and bloodied."

"Can you tell me about it?"

"I can tell you some. Like so much of the area, Chattanooga was quite the revolutionary spot when the wars were being fought. Some say that it was a base of operations, so to speak. Others say it was a hospital, a sanctuary. So, a lot of people didn't have a whole lot of good to say about anybody here."

"And was there ever some calamity that happened way back when?"

"Sure," she replied. "Major fires, lots of deaths, lots of fights. I mean, all kinds of it. There was one in particular, of course, that everybody doesn't really want to talk about."

"Which one?"

"Way back when," she began, "the owners, the family at the time, were losing the property. They had spent multiple lifetimes, generation upon generation, building up this property, but the war had brought on such hardship for everybody."

"So, it was around the war time?"

"Hell no, the world wars hadn't even begun yet. It was just one of so many fights arguing about territories. Anyway"—she shook her head—"apparently they were about to lose the property, all of it. So, as the story goes, there was a massive fire, and everybody perished."

"So, someone set the place on fire?"

"*Nah*, they set it on fire themselves."

"What? But why?"

"That is the mystery, isn't it? But there is one popular theory." She leaned closer, licking her lips. "The ultimate reason could be the fact that nothing would be left to fight over. It was almost as if they were sending the message that someone might take the land, but there wouldn't be a single thing left on it."

"Did anyone survive that fire?"

"Unfortunately the entire family living there died, … all in one fell swoop. Now some extended family is thought to have survived, simply by not residing onsite." She gave him a sad smile, backing off a bit. "It was pretty catastrophic."

"And there was literally nobody left in the family?"

She shrugged. "Not the immediate family, not that I know of. As the story goes, basically everybody lived in the same house. It was one of those huge multigenerational family homes. And, of course, back then, it's not as if any firefighting systems were in place."

"And they didn't make it out."

"Nobody made it out."

"I don't suppose you know the name of the family who lived here at the time, do you?" he asked and was met with a questioning gaze. "I'm just … curious."

She laughed. "You wouldn't be the first person to be interested in learning about it," she noted. "I'm not sure that anything good ever comes from disturbing the dead though," she muttered. "Anyway, the family name was Frankberg."

"What happened to the place after they were gone?"

"It was in ruins after the fire, left as it was for a long time, a really long time. Not that anything was left of the original place, other than the land, but then finally somebody bought it."

"You have any idea who that was?"

"Not a clue. I don't even know who they could have bought it from because, at that point in time, who owned this place? The city maybe? The government? There were a couple other disasters way back when," she added. "During the building of the place, a couple younger men got crushed during the process. Their bodies were never recovered. Because of that, it became a memorial for the two men who died, even though there's no actual stones for them."

He stared at her. "You would think that those stones would have been left."

She nodded. "You would think so. Or maybe the families just died away, and nobody was left to protest. I don't know." She shook her head and shrugged. "I just work here."

"Understood," he said, with a smile. "Thanks for that. It's all very interesting, isn't it?"

"It is and it isn't," she replied. "It's kind of creepy in my world."

He nodded. Who the hell wouldn't be slightly creeped out by his interest in the gory details and the bloody history of the place? "Understood." And, with that, he thanked her and started to walk away.

She added, "If you want to do any research, then you should see if the local library has something about it."

He considered that and gave her a wave. "Maybe I'll

look at that."

And as he turned again, she called out, "And will you be staying longer than planned? I currently have you leaving tomorrow."

He frowned as he realized that this was literally the end of the conference, the retreat, where he was supposed to meditate and find out if a killer was here or not. He sighed. "Let me get back to you on that."

"Checkout is at nine in the morning," she pointed out.

"Do you have room if I want to stay a little bit longer?"

She nodded. "A few people will be staying. I guess Richard and Rinaldo will run a few private sessions for them, so they'll be staying on a little bit longer too," she added.

"They offered those as well, didn't they?" he asked her. "That might have been a better answer for us."

She laughed. "Lots of people come here thinking this retreat will be it for them, and then they end up, like you, not attending so much." She flushed, half embarrassed that she'd brought it up.

He smiled and nodded. "At least we tried it."

"And maybe you would do better with the one-on-ones," she suggested generously.

"Maybe, we'll see. Anyway, there's a good chance that, if you have room, we will be staying for another day or two."

"That's for the two of you?" she asked, as she looked down at her books.

"Yes, unless you're short on space."

"Oh no, I think we've got enough room for the two of you to keep your rooms," she noted. "However, the sooner you can let me know for sure, the better."

He smiled, nodded, and headed over to the coffee shop, picked up two cups of coffee, then walked back up to their suite to see if Eden was awake.

When he knocked on her bedroom door, no answer came. He knocked again and again, with still no answer. That's when he got a horrible feeling snaking across his shoulders and on the back of his neck, gripping him tightly and not letting him breathe.

He turned the knob, noting that she never seemed to lock her damn doors. As he stepped in and looked around, he realized with certainty that she wasn't there. He immediately headed out, running back to the same space they had spent far too much time at, calling for Stefan through the ethers. *She's not here. She's not in her room.* His phone rang, and he answered, "Find her, Stefan. And I mean now. Otherwise you know what she's doing. She's going back in there to help those people. But she can't help them, not alone," he yelled.

Stefan sighed. "I know that. But somewhere along the line, she has picked up skills that may well rival anything I have ever seen before. Plus, you basically told her to help them. And, in this case, it's probably not a good thing."

"What do you mean, not a good thing?" he asked, moving faster and faster as he thought about what he had said to Eden. "That doesn't sound like anything I want to hear," he muttered, as he raced along. "I just went up to her room after I'd gotten some of the history on this place."

"What did you find out?"

"There was a massive fire way back when. Apparently the family that had been here for generations were about to lose the place entirely. And I suspect they set the building on fire, just so nobody could have it for themselves, and everybody perished."

"Right," Stefan muttered. "So that would follow."

"Sure, maybe it follows. Or maybe," he added, "it's a completely different scenario."

"And maybe it is," he murmured. "All I can tell you is, you need to find Eden and fast."

CHAPTER 22

S HEER INSTINCTS TOOK Eden back outside to the same spot where that poor sick woman had fallen. The Santino brothers had created a place of vigil for the woman. Eden lay down, her body literally trying to mimic the position that the woman had been in. Meanwhile Eden had to wonder if her death really was from natural causes or if something else was going on.

Eden slowly relaxed deeper and deeper into the space around her, feeling the cool moist air and the grass beneath her. She knew why she was here; she just didn't know if what she was doing was the right thing or not.

She had tried to help a lot of people for what seemed like forever, seeing somebody who needed it and working her way up to create the opportunity for a casual touch or a pat on the back so she could deliver a shot of healing energy, all because of her history. Because, if people found out what she had done in the past and why, they would hate her more than she hated herself already. And that was saying a lot because there wasn't much in her world that she could forgive herself for.

Eden knew some people would say she had nothing to be forgiven for, but they were wrong.

So many messed-up thought processes were in her world that she knew it was almost impossible for her to get past them all. But she had to, if only to realize that this energetic nightmare currently going on was a very similar thing. Something the men around her probably didn't recognize. The fact that she did revealed a lot about what she had been through in her own world.

She knew she needed to stop Origin, before it took more.

And her next thought was even scarier. What if she failed? Like she'd failed to save her mother?

She closed her eyes and let her energy slip away as she entered another world.

Such a weird, freeing feeling. A separation from self. A letting go of the physical world.

A complete release of everything as she had known it. Freeing and in many ways terrifying. She let it go, moving past the other, sliding on down in a way she didn't understand.

Freedom called out to her. She slipped from her body and started moving toward the nothingness of space around her. The absolute nonexistence of anything, including self.

As she let it go, she moved higher and higher up in frequency. The frequency of the all-knowing. Letting go of everything that was in her mind, in her tortured soul, in her guilt-ridden heart.

Knowing that she could have saved more people if she had been allowed. If she had had the strength, the courage to buck the system, a system she didn't even understand at the time.

Somewhere in there, she knew she had to forgive herself. And, to forgive herself, she had to let go.

The problem was, she was okay with letting go … permanently. Coming back was the hardship because she didn't want to. She didn't want to come back to this world of pain and suffering and ugliness that she had seen so much of.

She had done a lot of studying over the years, trying to figure out in what way she could atone. Only to realize that, in this lifetime, there was no atoning.

And yet if she could do this—

If she could do this one thing, maybe she could regain forgiveness for all the things she'd done that had hurt others, even though she hadn't meant to.

It was heartbreaking, absolutely devastating for her to see how she had hurt others, yet she cared about goodness, life, choice, growth, spirituality, heartfelt moments, coming from the heart, living in those spaces where goodness could happen. *Allowing* for goodness to happen.

One needed to be in the space, open and yet elevated to as high a frequency as possible.

It sounded right. Something that she had often done for her mother's sake, only to feel her soul crushing under the weight of what she was doing as she fell endlessly in vibration, down to the point to do what she had to do. Take energy from the dying.

Screaming for forgiveness, even as she worked hard to help her mother, knowing it was taking away from somebody else who also deserved life. Those were tricky moments in her history. Those moments of *How could you* heartfelt screams to her grandmother that she knew her mother had heard and had understood the torment Eden was going through.

How did all that bring her to this moment?

Could she do this? It wouldn't make up for all she'd done, but it would help. And it was something she desperately wanted to do.

It wasn't helping people, but it was helping the universe, the soul, the energy of everyone around them. She just had to pull it off, once and for all. She closed her eyes, her inner eyes, and sank deeper and deeper and deeper into the goodness all around them.

All around her.

A goodness that she always felt she never deserved. A goodness they would snatch away from her in a heartbeat as soon as people knew. But Eden knew that atonement had to happen.

She just didn't know how.

Just then she heard a voice beside her, and she shifted, only to see another woman standing there, glowing, yet with an oddly gray cast to her.

"Atonement. That's a good word for it," the gray lady murmured. "You can help us. We need the help. You can become one with us."

Eden stared at her, confused, not sure who this was. And yet, at the same time, half recognizing her. "Who are you?" she whispered.

"I am Helen Frankberg, the one you came to see," she declared. "I am the one who did everything she could to save her family, only to lose it all."

Something was right, and yet something was so very wrong about her words. Not necessarily a falseness to it, but maybe a false take on it. "You are hiding behind your words."

Helen shook her head. "You don't understand," she declared. "Everybody would have ended up with no place to live."

"What are you talking about? Who are you?"

"I am no one. And we had no place to go. Nothing was

left for us. They were taking it all."

"Who?"

"Bad men, so much bigger, so much stronger, so much uglier than anything we could have imagined. And I knew my daughters would suffer. Suffer like no woman should have to," Helen shared. "My son was just a child, innocent. I did the only thing I could. And I know you don't believe me, and you will judge me for it. But it doesn't matter."

"What doesn't matter?" Eden asked, trying to slow down the woman's story and to get more clarity.

"I will do it all over again," she cried out, while a wind picked up behind her. Passion, love, truth, and necessity rolling through her voice, she repeated, "I'll do it again if I have to."

"Easy," Eden murmured to her. "Just take it easy."

Helen laughed. "There is no easy in life anymore," she stated. "Once you go down this pathway, there is no easy. I know not why you are truly here, but that you are my good fortune because it's getting harder and harder to keep everyone here. It's as if their consciousness is rising, and they're struggling to leave, even though I've warned them how dangerous it is out there. I can't keep them contained for much longer."

Eden winced and nodded. "I can see that. They are souls wanting to move on," she told the frazzled woman. "And you're tired."

"I'm so tired," Helen cried out softly. "So tired. I'm doing everything I can to keep us together, to keep us safe. And yet, it seems as if they don't get it. They don't understand."

"It's because they understand safety in a very different way than you. And I think it's been slow to come, but, over time, understanding what's happening, or maybe not understanding, just as part of their soul journey, slowly realizing that this is not how they are meant to live."

"None of us are meant to live this way." Helen's voice cracked, hard and deep. "Do you think any of us want this?"

Eden stepped back ever-so-slightly, as Helen's energy slid through the space around them with a lack of emotion that was both awe-inspiring and disconcerting. Eden's energy disappeared farther and farther into the nothingness.

"You can't keep going," Helen told her. "You'll be lost forever."

Eden smiled at her. "It's not that I'll be lost forever," she clarified. "Instead I'll be found."

"No, no, no, no, you don't understand. You must stay and help me. I can't do this anymore," Helen cried out, the pain and agony in her heart so horrific, with such a strong need that it was all Eden could do to not stop in place. "You are strong. You can keep my babies alive in here. You can keep them safe."

"I know you can't keep up these guards," Eden pointed out, as she reached out with the gentlest touch to stroke Helen's energy, moving it, softening it. "You're so broken from all this."

Helen started to cry, her pain, her sorrow, her exhaustion, trying to stay ever vigilant in keeping everyone safe.

Eden heard voices around her, clamoring voices saying that they wanted to leave, that it was time to go, that they were safe, and they could leave now, but Helen shut them down immediately. Obviously everything in her life had been so hard, still was, and it was crushing her. She was at the end of her rope and didn't know how to go on.

Helen was so determined to protect everybody that she was losing them all, but it was a slow poisoning process. She was trying to keep everybody safe, and nobody was listening. Yet they were all bound by the same rules Helen had set out. Until she released them, there was no setting them free, no letting them go, no joy of release for any of them.

Helen stared at her. "You're not here to help, are you?" she asked, her voice gaining in outrage. "You think you can save them? You think you can take them away, can expose them to all that nastiness where they will be hurt, where everybody will punish them for who they are?"

"No," Eden countered, "I'm not here to do that at all. I'm here to release them so they can go on as the souls they were intended to be, as the people they were intended to be. You cannot keep them here forever, and it's poisoning you."

"It matters not," Helen cried out. "I care not what happens to me. It doesn't matter. I only care that they are safe."

"And they will be safe. I promise you that they will be safe, but it's time for them to move on to another space, to another time."

Shaking her head, Helen visibly trembled. "No. ... You're just like the others. You are lying, trying to trick me. They tried to get my house away from me, take our livelihood away from me. Take my children from me."

"Why did they come for you?"

"Jealously. They couldn't stand that I was making money here, that we were okay, that we were fine together. They didn't like that. But we are fine here now. I made sure of that."

"No, that's not true. You're not okay at all," Eden argued, her voice soft, gentle as the wind. "By doing what you did to try and keep everybody safe, it's tearing you all apart, and you're having to bring in more people."

"Of course. That's how business is run," she stated. "You

must have more people to keep it going. So, that's what I'm doing. I'm not hurting anybody."

"That is also not true," Eden told her. "You are hurting people who don't deserve this."

"Of course not," Helen snapped. "People just want to take it away from us, to break us up, take what's ours, make us suffer," she cried out.

So much outrage and pain filled Helen's tone that Eden could only imagine, given the time frame that Helen had lived in, how hard it would have been to fight against those determined to steal from her, determined to take everything that mattered. Eden whispered, "I'm not here to take anything from you. I'm here to help."

"No, no you're not," Helen snapped. "Help is not what you're here to do. You just want what I have worked so hard for."

"No, I don't," she repeated, "and yet I understand. I understand that, for you, this is a war that just won't quit. It's a life that you've been in hiding over, even though that life is long gone."

Helen stared, her eyes wide, her hair flying, as if in a breeze.

Eden continued. "You know it, deep down inside, and you know it well. You couldn't bear the idea of anyone else taking it from you, so you set that house of yours on fire. And, just like that, you torched every family member, young and old alike, sending those you loved beyond that lifetime and into a new one. With tears rolling down your face, you made sure that not one of them could escape that fire, so they could all travel with you away from the world that was so harsh. No way you would let them go, not to what those men wanted to do."

Helen's face crumpled. "You have no idea what they would do to my girls, even to my little boy," she wailed. "I spent my whole life, everything to protect them, but they were coming the next day, and I had no way to stop them. I had no way to fight them. The only thing I could do was take away the things that they wanted."

"The house," Eden noted.

Helen nodded. "The house and more, of course. … The house, the children, my dignity." She sighed, then nodded. "That's what they really wanted. That's all they wanted—everything," she muttered, with a broken laugh. "And when I say *all*, I mean all. As long as they could get every last thing from me, they were satisfied. I know not who these men even were or where they came from. I just know that they came, took, and destroyed, with every word, every blow, every punch. I wasn't strong enough to protect those around me. I couldn't let my poor children suffer."

Eden heard both the fear and the resolve in Helen's tone, yet still filled with pain and horror. Eden marveled in wonder, in this space of nothing physical, in this space of nothingness, as the tears ran down poor Helen's face, her torment so real, so profound, and so exhausting as she continued to keep her children safe.

Nothing could be done for her, except to try and get her to understand that those times were long gone.

What Helen hadn't accounted for was the effort to keep them here, the effort that she had expended to try and keep them safe—albeit her version of safe, not realizing that it came at a price, and that price required more energy, always more lives, and if she couldn't create it herself, it had to come from everyone else around her.

Eden understood, based on her own grandmother's fear,

just how deadly that was. To families, to anybody in this world who couldn't seem to get past it, who didn't understand that there was so much more to life than what their fear was giving them for an existence.

Helen cried out, "You don't understand."

"Maybe I don't," Eden conceded, "and maybe it's something that you need to explain to me, but I can't have you taking more lives, hurting more people, to save everybody in this space. It's not where they belong. It's not where you belong. They are spirits now, and they need to be free. You need to let them go, in love, in joy, where they truly will be safe. You saw your world as dangerous. You made a choice, right or wrong, and that choice has led you to this moment in time," Eden explained, "and that moment has now led you here. Now you and your family can find that peace."

It looked as if Helen was ready to acquiesce, when suddenly she gathered up an enormous amount of energy and roared, "No!" With a sudden wave of her grasping claw-like hand, she reached out and grabbed Eden's energy in an electric grasp.

"You are only here to take, like everyone else. It's what you do," Helen cried out, in anger, in pain. "You hurt others. You take from others. Now you want to take from me. You do not want to help me," she yelled. "You couldn't even help the ones you wanted to help. You only want to take from me, and that I will not allow."

And with that came this heavy, ugly *whoosh*, and a weird thick energy came crushing down on top of Eden, blackness all around her, and then she knew no more.

ERIC REACHED EDEN'S body, just as a shockwave seemed to

hit her, and she jolted, jerked, and thrashed near the Origin portal.

He cried out as he dropped down at her side, but Stefan warned him immediately, *Don't touch her*, just as Eric's hands were about to grab her and shake her. Eric froze.

Don't touch her, Stefan warned again. *Something's going on, and we don't know what, but I need you to not put your hands on her.*

Eric stared around. The place was secluded, not the same place where the poor sick woman had fallen. Eric didn't know what the connection was, if there was a connection, but he didn't want to hang around to wait and see. "I'm going in after her," he declared, with a resolve that surprised even him.

He didn't have any experience in this, but it didn't matter. If somebody was after Eden, then Eric would go in and would ensure they didn't succeed. She'd had enough shit in her life, enough people making her do stuff she had no desire to do. Somebody with a skill like Eden's shouldn't be forced, pressured, or coerced to do the bidding of others, but he also understood that it was all about survival of the fittest. In this case, he could only hope that she was strong enough to endure whatever was happening to her.

Stefan's words of warning were in his ear, as he lay down beside her, close but not touching.

Stefan noted, *You do understand.*

"No, I don't. I understand nothing," he declared. "I just know that I can't let whatever this is be something she faces alone. That's all she's ever done was face this shit alone," he snapped, "and that ends today. She learned on the go, and I guess that's what I'll do too."

With that, he closed his eyes and shut off all communication. He drifted off into the Netherland, the land of nothing, the land of energy, wiping out distance and time. He knew there was a whole massive eternity to explore. He had to keep pulling his energy back, as everything inside him wanted to drift off into a million other directions.

Little voices and thoughts tried to set him off on a different course, not necessarily deliberately but because they could, because they always had. Learning to discipline the mind was a whole different ball game, one he hadn't spent much time worrying about. Now he realized that had been a mistake.

Shifting his energy deeper and deeper, another voice popped in. This time it was Stefan.

Don't worry about what you can and cannot do. Just follow my voice, he instructed. *We'll go together and see what's happening to her.*

Grateful for the company, and realizing that Stefan was the better hand at this, Eric followed Stefan, using his voice as a guide to continue deeper and deeper into this unknown morass of energy, energy that seemed to suck him in, almost with a giddy joyfulness as he rode deeper.

Stefan said, *Enjoy it, relish it, and realize this is not the time to explore, but you can come back here anytime you want, particularly after this run.*

"And I want to," he stated. "I really want to because something is incredibly freeing about being here."

Exactly, it's where you get to de-stress and to let go of everything that's taken over your world, Stefan explained. *I'm here a lot, so is Dr. Maddy, and so are many of our friends and energy workers. It's a space where you can just let go*, he shared, *and be who we were always intended to be.*

"But, if it's so freeing, why is Eden stuck here?"

She's not here. It's just a halfway house, … if you want to call it that. We are people of the energy. We are workers of the light, Stefan said. *We always have been, always will be, but you must make the journey back here to find it yourself. Having found it now, you can come here as you wish.*

"And that is something I'll take you up on later, … after we get her back, safe and sound. You were telling me—"

Origin is buried under the beauty. It's a black hole.

"And this place?"

It's more a sanctuary for energy workers, a safe space.

Stefan didn't say anything more, but, as they pushed deeper, Eric sensed a hesitation inside Stefan. "Don't bother," Eric said. "I'm not going back. I am here with her, regardless."

Are you sure that is something she'll want?

"It doesn't matter," he replied. "She'll take the low road and say she doesn't need me, that she can do it without me, and maybe she can. However, I don't think there's ever been a time when that woman has had somebody watch her back. Maybe it's time for that to stop too."

Absolutely, Stefan agreed. *Yet you also must understand that, for every step she takes like this, there could be a dozen you have to take to follow her. She's been walking in this world for a very long time. I'm not even sure how she managed to get up so high and then drop so quickly to do the work she was doing. It's one thing to help someone. It's entirely another to go up into this space and help somebody, while hurting someone else in the process,* he noted.

"It shouldn't be possible."

I'm not sure how she was managing, but I suspect her grandmother had a lot to do with it—or her mother. Nothing we know for sure.

Eric shook his head. "I asked my partner to pull up her mother's file, and he just sent back a message a little bit ago. saying that her mother committed suicide."

Suicide? Stefan reared at that.

"I know. It makes no sense."

Now that I've had a moment, it probably makes more sense than anything, he offered. *I suspect the grandmother was fighting a battle the daughter no longer wanted to fight, and watching her own daughter, Eden, be tormented by her mother was something Eden's mother couldn't handle. It makes a certain sense that she took herself out of the game because she couldn't stop either one of them.*

They drifted deeper, and Eric felt Stefan become part of him, one with him, their energies overlapping, intermingling, sliding through and apart as they separated and thinned, as they went farther into the nowhere, the nothingness, where everything was just space and eternal energy. "I feel. I know." Then Eric's words just stopped.

Don't worry about what you feel. Don't worry about what you think or don't know, just continue, Stefan urged him. *Don't think. Let it go. Let it all go. Losing control is the only way forward.*

Eric wasn't sure what any of that meant. Stefan probably wasn't sure either, but, for everything he said, there always seemed to be something else he wasn't saying. It was both scary and irritating. However, Eric trusted Stefan to get him to Eden, and that was the important thing. He felt Stefan in his mind as they drifted, their thoughts no longer cohesive. There was an odd lightness, a nothingness to his existence.

There was no body, no frame, no sustenance, just a central floating sensation, and a weird sense of going home. That phrase almost knocked him out of place. Only Stefan's steady guidance kept Eric in the same state as he floated on.

You are going home, Stefan confirmed. *We all are going home, but you need to stop thinking so much. It's sending you off track.*

With that and half a smile, acknowledging that all thought meant he was conscious and aware, when he should be the alternative, Eric drifted back into the same state he had been, letting all of it slide over and around him. When he came to with a sudden hard jolt, he opened his eyes and realized that he was somewhere now. Where, he didn't know, but *there* was something.

There, in front of him, standing in an odd-looking space, was Eden. She looked over at him, her eyes widening, and she shook her head frantically.

He realized that she couldn't hear him. She could see him, and something was going on in her world that she didn't want him to see. She kept trying to push him to leave, and then finally he heard her in his head.

"Leave," she ordered. "You don't want to be here."

He frowned and asked, "Can you stop this?"

She stared at him, tears in her eyes, and shook her head. "I don't think so."

He stared out. "I'm not sure what exactly went wrong or why, but … I don't believe you. You are stronger than this."

She shook her head. "No, I'm not," she cried out.

Yet now he sensed a little child's tone to her voice, a sense of her having gone back in time, to where she was not able to do what everybody wanted her to do. His heart broke for the little girl who was even now struggling for her autonomy. "Yes," he argued, "you can do it, for your sake, for everyone's sake, but mostly for yours, so that you can have a life after this, so you can have something normal."

Tears filled her eyes, even though he knew she didn't exist in a physical form. She stood in front of him, opaque, and yet, in a weird way, solid.

She stared at him and whispered, "I wish you hadn't come."

He closed his eyes and nodded. "Maybe, … but I had to. I had to know you were okay."

"Why?" she asked. "You think I'm a monster."

He winced and shook his head. "No, I've never thought that. You were a child being forced to do things other people wanted you to do, and you didn't get a say in the matter," he explained. "And, since you've been released from that prison, you've done nothing but try to help everybody else, trying to atone for something that you weren't responsible for in the first place."

"Yes, I was responsible, and so many people were hurt," she cried out. "Some of them were dying anyway, but some of them weren't or might have had a chance at least. My grandmother would tell me which ones, and she wouldn't listen anytime I tried to tell her that I couldn't or that they wouldn't or that it was too hard." Eden shook her head, tears down her cheeks now. "She would get so angry, and I had no way to stop her."

"Listen to me. None of that matters right now because we need to get you out of here. Your guilt is what's holding you here," he stated, knowing instinctively that her own negative energy was restraining her. "Whoever this is, whatever has been done here—"

"Helen Frankberg, a mother of thirteen children," she interrupted and added, "and she's done it out of love."

He stopped and stared. Then he slowly nodded. "The mother of the boy?"

"Yes, the one from the fire."

"I guess in a way that makes sense," he muttered.

"It's not her fault because it's her reaction to what was done to her. Her children who burned in that fire? Helen's just been trying to keep them safe," she told him in a pleading voice. "You have to understand that."

"I understand that," he replied, "but do they? Do you?"

"They don't," she noted, "not any longer. They're fighting, fighting against her, fighting against their prison," she shared.

"Of course they are," Eric agreed. "They need to be set free."

"I know," she acknowledged, as she stared around. "I feel as if Helen's locked me up somehow too."

No, the only thing she's locked up is your ability to see through this. Stefan's voice slid through them both.

Eden glanced all around, looking for Stefan. "Stefan, you're here too?" she asked uncertainly.

Yes, of course I am, he said. *We are all here in one form or another. You are here, but you are only kept prisoner by your guilt, by your fear, by your belief that you deserve to be punished.*

"But nobody blames you for what happened," Eric pointed out compassionately. "No one."

Eric's right. Nobody, alive or dead, blames you for what you did, Stefan confirmed. *You were a child, and, as a child, you had no ability to fight your grandmother's wishes. That's what you must remember. You aren't being blamed for this by anybody but yourself.*

Eric saw her tears wash through her—literally, as if a light were passing through her. In amazement, he stepped forward and whispered, "Sweetheart, we need to put a stop to this. We need Helen to see that she's holding these people against their will, and her fear's stopping everything. Everybody would be free if she would just let her fear go."

Eden smiled. "That makes sense, doesn't it? ... If she would let them go, they would be free."

Exactly, Stefan agreed. *So, it's something that we must help her to see. They need to be free, and if not—*

When the resounding roar to the side buffeted Eric sideways and backward, he turned to face the new arrival. Sure enough, it was an older woman, worn out but still feisty. She looked exhausted from whatever she had been fighting, yet she was still willing to go on.

"This is Helen," Eden explained. "And she's petrified that any change will cause her to lose her children."

"Of course," Eric said, studying the woman, noting that she no longer had any reasoning ability and was literally living on her emotions of fear and distrust, all bound up in the love of a mother for her children.

Stefan reached forward with a calming energy, just giving Helen a slight touch. It sapped her energy, and she bolted backward, crying out. Then she lunged forward, as if looking to find the foe that had so easily caught her.

Almost immediately Eden grabbed her arm. "Please don't."

Helen turned on her, spitting with a fury that the others couldn't see but could still recognize for what it was—an absolutely overriding terror of what would happen to her and her children.

Stefan spoke to her telepathically. *Take it easy. Your children are safe.*

Helen spun around, looking for the source, not recognizing where it came from, who it came from. "Who are you? Why are you here? What do you want?" But fear trembled through her words, and nobody could blame her for what she had done or why she was still here.

Eden called out to the ethers, "It's okay. Come forward." Slowly, other forms, other energies, just tiny overwhelming energy pockets, floated out of the dark shadows.

Eric was stunned as he looked around to see how many were here. Surely they weren't all from the same house.

Eden explained, "Helen had thirteen children. Think of it. The bad men buying this property were gonna use all her children and even Helen, one way or another." She shook her head, grimacing, her tears coming again. "Thirteen children this woman has spent decades trying to protect. It's literally the love of a mother that brings us here."

That may be, Stefan conceded, his voice ever-so-gentle.

Eden could see the energy around them lightening up, something within the space around them softening, gentling. She didn't know what Stefan was doing, but some weird resonance was going on around him.

Eric glanced backward and then forward.

Helen seemed confused, yet almost more fearful because Stefan's energy was new, was different, and was something she couldn't explain. She roared, "Stop! Stop now or I'll kill her."

Eden stepped forward, approaching Helen. "I understand how you would react with fear when confronted by more strangers," she explained, "but we are here to help you. You've been lost for so very long and exhausted from the fight, from protecting your family. We know that, and we're here to help."

"There is no help," she declared, staring at Eden suspiciously. "How could you even think that you could help?"

"I can help," Eden announced. "Your children are tired. They are also looking to be free."

Many of them were around her now, most nodding in agreement. Some came closer. Some stayed far away, as if they wanted nothing to do with Helen. "I promise they will be safe," Eden told Helen.

"You can't promise that," she snapped. "Nobody can make that promise. I did everything I could."

"I know that," Eden said. "I know that, and, in the process, you have done amazingly well. You have kept them safe all this time, but now it's time to let them go. You can't keep doing this. You're worn out. You're exhausted."

"I can," she cried out. "I will. Don't you understand? … I must."

"I understand. I know you will continue to do absolutely everything you can, but I'm here to tell you that the fight is over. It's okay to let it go. The war has been won. Your house is gone, but those men never got it, and your children can now move on. That's what you want, isn't it?"

She stared at her and whispered, "I want them safe."

CHAPTER 23

"I KNOW YOU do," Eden stated, her voice as warm and caring as the gentle energy floating closer and closer to Helen. Eden could only imagine that Stefan was sending the energy of love to Helen, but Eden wasn't sure. She'd never seen anything like it before. It was purely amazing to even see it now, but there was something about it, something magical and healing to it all.

Then she realized it wasn't Stefan's energy. She didn't know whose it was, but someone was here, someone full of love and caring, someone who wanted to help. "Where's your mother?" she asked Helen.

The older woman sighed, then shrugged. "I don't know. I lost her in the house fire." Her voice broke with that statement. "I was trying so hard to protect her, but I don't think it worked."

"No, I don't think so," Eden noted. "And do you think your mother would forgive you for that?"

Helen shook her head, tears in her eyes, and whispered, "I don't see how. I can't even forgive myself."

Eden didn't say anything, but she turned to consider the energy here, so full of some raw emotion that she couldn't place it. "I think your mother would forgive you. I think maybe she was already worn out and in such a different form that you didn't recognize her here beside you this whole time."

Helen stared at her in shock. "What are you talking about?"

Eden pointed to the energy at Helen's side and asked, "Is that your mother?"

Helen spun to see the same energy that Eden was looking at. She gasped. "Mama!" And then she burst into tears.

The two energies blended into one in an almost superhuman hug, a soul revelation coming together, two parts into one, as they blended in perfect harmony.

As soon as she did that, Eden tapped both energies, one with each hand. She felt Eric doing the same on the other side, and then two other warm loving energies wrapped around them both. She knew it was Stefan and whoever had come with him.

They were being filled from the inside out with love, a love that expanded and expanded and expanded. Suddenly another energy pushed into the circle, one of the children, and then another and another, until finally the circle was so big, so huge, and so full.

Eden lifted her head toward the infinity all around them and whispered, "And so it is." And, with that said, followed by an almost magical clap, some resonating explosion came from within, and she lost consciousness, falling once again to the grass that she lay upon.

When she came to, she took several moments to recognize the blue sky and the sun dawning on the horizon. She sat up and looked around, a little groggy, a little worn out, and a lot disoriented. As she turned, she found an old man, squatted in front of her.

He looked at her with a frown and asked, "Are you okay?"

She realized it was Samuel, the gardener. She nodded slowly. "I think so."

He shook his head. "It's really not a good idea to be sleeping out here," he shared. "Somebody passed away recently, right after falling down about here." He looked around and sighed. "I don't understand what the two of you were even doing here."

She smiled. "Yeah, I'm not sure we do either." She nudged Eric awake. "I guess just the beautiful morning, and since we both weren't getting much sleep recently, we just … passed out for a bit."

He nodded, but he stood up, stared at her, and added, "It would probably be a really good idea for you to go home."

"Yes, it probably would," she agreed. "And maybe it would be time for you to go home too, Samuel."

He stared at her in surprise, his brows wrinkling.

She nodded. "It's over."

"Is it?" he asked warily, not sure who or what she was talking about.

"Yes," she said, "it is. You have been guarding this place for a very long time, but they're safe now, all of them, and they're going home where they belong." He stared at her in shock, but there was that little bit of hope in the back of his gaze, and she nodded again. "That's what we were doing."

He crouched beside her, his gaze turning to look from her to Eric, who was just now waking up. "Are they really?"

"Yes," she stated, "they're really safe."

"She was my great-great-great-grandmother—I don't know how many *greats* actually," he admitted. "A little bit off her rocker, a little bit too possessive, a little bit too …" He stopped and shrugged, then added, "She loved very deeply."

"She did indeed," Eden confirmed, "but even she is home and now safe."

He closed his eyes as the tears welled up, and he whispered, "I was told to watch over her and the others. I'm so tired."

"I know you are," she agreed, "but it's over."

He slowly looked around the gardens, tears in his eyes. "She picked a lovely place."

"She did, except for taking other people."

He nodded, turning to her. "Some I could save over the years. Some I couldn't. …"

"Like the terminally ill lady who came to the seminar and fell in the gardens and died soon afterward at the hospital?"

He sighed, then nodded. "That goes for you too. Sometimes we can help, and sometimes we can't," he shared ever-so-gently. He tilted his hat at her. "Thank you for saving them." And, with that, he walked away.

Even as he did, she wanted to call him back and ask a million questions. Yet, as he strode off into the sunrise, he seemed to walk literally into the horizon, and she knew that he was gone, really gone—as in he too had returned from whence he came.

Eric stared at her and asked, "Did that just happen?"

"Which part?" she quipped, with half a laugh.

He pointed to the horizon, where Samuel was nowhere to be seen.

"Ah, the caretaker, … yes." She nodded. "That did just happen. It seems we released not only souls bound on the other side, but at least one soul bound on this side too," she pointed out.

"Good God," he muttered, "do we even know what that place was or if Helen created it or if someone else did? If so, why?"

"Nope, and I didn't really have time to ask him," she admitted. "I figured we had enough to worry about without getting into that."

He chuckled softly as he slowly made his way into a sitting position, then managed to stand up. "Wow, I'm not sure what that was, but wow."

She smiled. "It was definitely something."

He turned to her. "Are you okay?"

"I will be," she declared. "In a way, this probably needed to happen to me for a very long time, and, once I deal with the fallout, I think I'll be just fine." He eyed her carefully, as she looked over at him, shaking her head. "I'm fine."

He smiled. "I hear you. I'm just worried."

She smiled as she reached out a hand, and he helped her to her feet. "Thank you for being worried," she said, "and for caring. It's been a very long road."

He wrapped her up in his arms and muttered, "Does this solve everything now?"

"Nope, it doesn't, but it does solve a lot of it."

"And Debbie?"

"Yeah, Debbie's a whole different case," she stated, "and, for that, we'll need to talk to the men."

"What men?" After they turned and headed to the hotel, she told Eric, an odd tone in her voice, "I don't want to stay here much longer."

"It's definitely not as peaceful as it was." Then he stopped, as if listening to something, and clarified, "No, that's wrong. It's more peaceful now."

"It is, but I still don't want to stay," she muttered.

"You want to go back home to solve Debbie's death?" Eric asked.

"I'm not exactly sure what happened to Debbie, but I do know that it's connected to your murder-rapist cases."

He stopped and stared.

She turned back when he didn't keep up with her and held out a hand. "As I mentioned, we need to talk to the men."

Even as they got closer to the hotel, they saw the two brothers loading up their luggage, ready to leave. They stopped and stared as the two of them walked over.

"What happened to you two?" Rinaldo Santino asked, with a snicker. "You look as if you slept outside."

"It's not that we slept outside, but maybe we had a nap," she clarified. "Not to worry. You'll have a lot of time to have a nap yourself, … once you're in jail."

He froze and stared at her in shock. "What are you talking about? I don't have anything to go to jail for."

Richard turned to his brother, then back to her, and asked pointedly, "What are you talking about?"

"She's just bitching," Rinaldo snapped, spitting mad. "You really need to get some help," he declared as he turned to Eden. "You do know how sick you are, right?" Then he turned to Eric. "You need to get a leash on her, or I will."

"*Right.*" She nodded. "As if someone could touch me without having their hands broken. As for my *bitching*, I do know. And it might be time for me to get some therapy. I mean, Debbie's death has been rough on me, you know?"

"Yes, it's been difficult. I'm so sorry," Richard interjected, frowning back at Rinaldo.

"I'm sure you are. She was a very special person," Eden replied with a smile, but tears filled her eyes as she nodded.

"You know that, right, Rinaldo?"

"Yes, she was a very special person," Rinaldo agreed, his tone soft and silky.

"Then why did you kill her?"

ERIC STARED IN shock, watching as the color drained from Richard's face. Rinaldo, on the other hand, looked more pissed than anything. He glared from one to the other. Richard stood rooted to the same spot, while his brother started to back up.

Eric stepped forward, grabbed Rinaldo, and brought him to stand beside Richard and Eden. He looked at Eden with a big question in his eyes. "You want to explain that?"

"The reason you haven't caught the rapist is because it wasn't just one. It was two."

Eric swore as she went on.

"They were picking their victims as they could, as they wanted and needed. Not necessarily even from their roster of people who attended these retreats. But they had to be careful, so they cast their nets wide. Plus, they had the perfect cover. It allowed them to travel from city to city, where both brothers were always present."

"Is that true?" Eric asked, but Rinaldo continued looking pissed, while Richard remained rooted in place, yet his eyes were glassy now.

"If you check the list of rapes versus the locations of their retreats, you'll find a lot of matches," Eden suggested. "They have been quite busy, if that's what you want to know. Plus, you likely didn't widen enough to check other cities, other states."

"I want to know more because I'll need more than location matches," Eric pointed out.

She nodded and turned to Richard. "Richard, it's time. It really is." His bottom lip wobbled, and she nodded. "You know it's time. You can't keep this up."

"I didn't kill Debbie."

"No, you didn't," she stated, patting his hand. "He did." She turned to look at his brother. "He did it because you were falling for her in a way that would have changed everything, and he couldn't have that. He liked what you guys were doing. He loved the games, the chase, and the fact that, because both of you were involved, the police were always in the dark and way too far behind," she shared. "So, yes, it's time to come clean. Why not just get it off your chest? He killed Debbie because you loved her."

He turned to his brother and cried out, "Did you? Did you? How could you do that?" He stared at his brother in horror.

Rinaldo snapped, "How could *you*? How could you fall for that tart? How could you take everything we were doing and throw it all away, … just like that?" He snapped his fingers. "You know that tart would have ended our ruse, and no way could this end like that. The ruse was the best part of living right now," he declared. "And you would throw it all away for a sorry piece of ass."

"I loved her."

"You *wanted* her is all."

"I still don't understand how she died though," Richard added, turning to Eden. "He didn't have any weapons or anything to kill her, not when traveling recently."

"No, he didn't. But you do use drugs, don't you? Hard-to-detect drugs? Debbie had a weak heart, since she was a kid. Almost died several times. She was on heart medication already. As long as she took it religiously, she seemed completely healthy otherwise. Pretty easy to find a drug that would interact negatively with her regular meds to stop her heart."

When Richard stole her a sideways glance, she knew she had hit the nail on the head.

"She really loved you. She was ready to throw away absolutely everything in her world to spend her life with you—until your brother decided that her story had to have a different ending," she stated, with a sad look for Richard. "I'm so sorry, but you're both going to jail for a very long time."

CHAPTER 24

Two Weeks Later

EDEN STOOD AT the grave site, staring at the new headstone she'd managed to get delivered and put in place for Debbie. The mercurial Deborah Lee Kingston, her best friend, only wanted to love and to be loved back.

Instead she found a killer. Eric told her how the interview went, how Rinaldo got jealous that Richard was getting so close to Debbie, and it affected the brothers' extracurricular activities, making Rinaldo unstable enough to lure Debbie to talk about Richard, insinuating that he was mentally unstable. Right about the time that seminar was ending, he offered her a glass of wine, mixed with his chosen special time-release pills. She never knew what hit her. The bastard followed her ride home, then carried her away in a suitcase, still alive but unconscious, intending to rape her, but she died soon afterward. So he set up the suicide theory when he got her back home again.

Even as Eden stood here where Debbie had been buried, a sense of calm filled Eden, the same sense of peace that she'd felt earlier, after freeing everyone from Origin. She desperately needed that peace both here and back then, when she thought about that chaotic night and all the pain that everybody had gone through.

Debbie had been subconsciously healing from her abusive boyfriends, until the fight with Eden. That fight had separated Debbie from her healing energy, making Debbie even more vulnerable. Eden refused to believe Debbie died because of her, but Eden might have contributed.

Eden reached out a hand, her fingers immediately grasped by Eric, standing at her side—the one person who stood with her through all the shit. Not counting Stefan of course.

"Are you okay with this?" Eric asked quietly, with a nudge toward the gravestone.

She smiled and nodded. "Yes. I think she would have liked it."

He laughed. "I'm sure she would have preferred being alive."

"I'm not sure that was even a choice."

"According to Stefan, some things we just can't change, no matter how much we may want to," he shared with her. "Her medical history stated she'd been ill for a very long time and had lived longer than anyone thought, all possible because of you. And, because of you, we had the tox screen widened to include heart-specific drugs, good and bad, and that definitely helped to lead us to the brothers. They knew the evidence was solid, so they cooperated, gave us statements."

"I know that Debbie was a *live in the moment* gal, and, in many ways, I don't think she would be all that upset at the way this turned out."

"Particularly now as you also know the part about the why."

She continued. "Yes, I do know now. However, I wish I'd known back then, before she ran off into the arms of a rapist-murderer duo. I was doing my darndest to help her, but she wasn't making it easy. I doubt she even realized how bad her heart was. From what we found out in her medical history, she wouldn't go to the doctor, wouldn't get the offered treatment. Not much anyone can do if someone refuses any medical help."

"Other than your brand of healing," he pointed out. "However, in this case, it was not to be."

She smiled, then nodded. "I guess I can't really change people, can I?"

"No," he agreed, "you can't, and you shouldn't have to. People are people, and they'll make their own decisions based on a variety of things."

She nodded. "I wonder how Richard would feel if he only knew that Debbie had a heart issue and wasn't expected to live very long."

"I don't know that he would have changed anything. I think in many ways he did love her, but he didn't get a chance to get that far because of his brother," Eric theorized. "Even if he had managed some semblance of normalcy, in the end, he was just as guilty as his brother. Even if he didn't kill Debbie himself, he still participated in the rape and murder of dozens of women across half-a-dozen state lines."

"Destroying families," she murmured.

"Not just families but those we love, those we take for granted, those who love us, their needs, our needs," he added. "Sometimes I think it's just a big mess."

"Sometimes?" she asked, with a laugh in his direction, "More like all the time."

He wrapped an arm around her and asked, "Shall we?"

Nodding, they headed out of the cemetery where Debbie was buried. It was a quaint little place that Eden knew her friend would have loved. If one had to be buried somewhere, this was a better place than many.

"She didn't have any family left," Eden muttered. "It always feels sad to be at a grave site with nobody there."

"You were there for her," he noted. "Don't ever forget that."

She didn't say anything because sometimes, well, … sometimes it just hit her harder than others. Sometimes it was just life. She wasn't sure what she would even do from here, but life had resumed somewhat of a normal state. They'd had to give multiple statements, but both Richard and his brother had ended up providing written confessions.

As Eric told her, the anger between the brothers had erupted time and time again, each one needing the other in a very twisted relationship that they wouldn't get out of anytime soon, if at all. So, for that, she was glad. If there was one positive thing to have come out of it all, it was the knowledge that the brothers couldn't continue doing what they had been doing to so many young women.

As for Helen, the woman who had tried to save her family by torching her large home and boarding house with all of them in it, they hadn't heard anything else from her. According to Stefan, everybody who had been caught up in that nightmare had well and truly moved on to where they belonged.

As for Eden, she was seeing a therapist and was working on all that guilt she'd kept inside for so long, finally letting it go in a healthy way. She was also working as a volunteer for Dr. Maddy now in her spare time, although Dr. Maddy was trying to convince her to come work for her. Eden wasn't sure how that would work, but Dr. Maddy declared that Eden was too strong of a healer to be wasted in an office job, designing book covers and fashion ads. So, if she wanted to do something positive and healthy for everyone, then Dr. Maddy would very much like for Eden to do that at her facility.

"Have you thought about Dr. Maddy's proposition at all?" Eric asked.

Eden turned to him and shrugged. "I was just thinking about that. I haven't decided, but I must admit it would be a lot more fulfilling than what I'm doing."

He smiled and tucked her a little closer. "I think you would be fabulous at it," he stated.

"I don't know. It's weird stuff."

He burst out laughing. "It's definitely weird stuff, but, of all the people who do weird stuff, I think Dr. Maddy would be the one who I would want to work with the most."

Eden had to admit that Eric had a point. From what she'd seen, Dr. Maddy was incredibly gifted and was so very open and so very capable of teaching things that nobody really understood, except for maybe Stefan. Eden had entered a wild and wonderful world that she hadn't really known existed, and yet she'd been walking in that world for a very long time.

"Coffee shop?" he asked, as they both headed to his car.

"Sure," she replied with a gentle smile.

"And then what?"

"And then home," she said.

She'd moved in with him a couple weeks ago, and she was still getting used to it. After a lifetime of being alone, living with him had proven to be educational, inspiring, and, at times, downright irritating. She looked over at him and smiled.

"You'll get used to me," he quipped.

"If you say so," she muttered, as they walked to his car.

"Hey, we're doing great together," he pointed out. "I mean, neither one of us are exactly easy to get along with."

"Whatever do you mean? I'm perfect," she teased. When he burst out laughing, she grinned at him. "Okay, maybe not perfect," she corrected, "but I come from the heart."

He nodded, leaned over, grasped the side of her face, and kissed her gently. "That you do," he agreed, "and that is worth everything."

It wasn't long before they parked and soon were inside the coffee shop. She stopped for a moment and smiled. He looked over at her with a questioning expression.

She shrugged. "Something is very freeing about my life right now."

"Good." He nodded. "That's how it should be."

"Maybe. It just feels as if I always had secrets before. It's exhausting keeping secrets. I always had to keep everything locked down and quiet. Now … it just feels different."

He smiled, then led her over to an empty table closer to the back wall, and she nodded. "One day I want to sit up closer to the front," she shared, with half a laugh.

"Maybe someday I will too," he noted with a smile. She stopped, looked at him, and he nodded. "I always sit at the back."

"It's just one of the safest things to do, I guess," she murmured. "I hadn't really considered the things we do automatically."

"No, because, for us, we will always do certain things because we feel they are necessary, and staying safe is one of them," he explained. "That's okay too, so don't worry about it."

She laughed as she took her seat. The waitress came over, and they ordered coffee. She nodded and took off.

Eric leaned in and said, "My partner wanted to stop by and say hi, if you don't mind."

"Cody? Sure," she said. "He probably wants to know if a complete nutcase has moved in with you."

He burst out laughing. "Maybe," he muttered, shaking his head. "On the other hand, I've also told him a whole lot about you."

She looked at him in alarm. "All good things, but nothing about, you know—"

"Nothing, I promise," he vowed. "I wouldn't dare. Besides, I couldn't explain it if I tried." He smiled. "I will continue working with Stefan though."

"Oh, good," she said, looking at him in delight. "I mean, you did great in there."

He laughed. "I hardly did great. I didn't really do anything. You were the savior of the hour, and I was just along for the ride."

She shook her head. "All the work that we did, that was Dr. Maddy and Stefan," she stated. "I can't even imagine how much time they have spent working in that space."

"It's absolutely incredible to think about all that they're doing, which is why I think it's seriously cool that you'll be working with her."

"I haven't accepted her offer yet," she pointed out.

"No, but it sounds as if that is what you want to do."

"Yes, I do," she shared. And in all honesty, every time she thought about it, it became a little more defined in her mind. "It is definitely something I would love."

"In that case, you know what your answer is."

"I haven't talked to her about money though," she began, "and it seems crass to do so."

"I'm sure that, from your perspective, it is. From hers, I

would think she would be very pragmatic about it. You need money to live on. She needs your skills, or at least your raw talent, raw energy. … Is that how we say it?" he asked, with a chuckle.

"I don't know," she confessed. "As long as it's enough for me to live on, then I'm probably good to go," she added, "It could mean moving closer to her to really be able to learn, but I do need to have that conversation with her. It could be temporary too. I don't really know how that could work yet."

"Of course," he noted, with a bright smile. "Personally I'm just thrilled for you."

"You could always join us," she suggested. "I know Dr. Maddy mentioned how there is plenty of room for more and that you have … *untapped resources and some intuition that you're not using to your true potential.*"

"Maybe," he muttered. "Down the road perhaps. I don't know. Right now, I don't quite want to give up what I'm doing," he told her. "Putting guys away like the Santino brothers, that's pretty important too."

"It's very important," she murmured. "It still drives me crazy to think about what they did."

"I know," he muttered, "but that's not something we'll dwell on."

Just then came a shout from the entrance to the coffee shop.

Eric looked up, smiled, and waved at Cody. "Over here."

She looked over to see a big, burly man somewhere in his mid- to late thirties, wearing a big grin on his face as he sat down beside them. His gaze was frank and assessing as he looked her over.

She smiled at him. "Hi, I'm Eden."

"Hi, so you're the woman who's tied him into knots."

She nodded. "I am. And you must be the partner who's always annoying the hell out of him."

He burst out laughing, looking at Eric. "I like her already. Straight to the point, clear-cut, and honest," he declared. "That's pretty amazing."

She looked at him closely, assessing his energies. "You're just worried about him," she noted, "so it's easy to be honest."

He stared at her in surprise, as he narrowed his gaze. "Don't tell me that you're into that weird woo-woo stuff that he is."

She burst out laughing. "I just might be."

"Oh, God help us," he muttered, groaning. "It'll make both of you insufferable."

"*Nah*," she replied sarcastically, "I'll just be a fly on the wall."

"Which is so far from the truth," Eric noted, giving a chuckle to Eden. Then he faced his partner. "Besides, what do you care if it brings us good things?"

"Like what?" Cody asked, with an eye roll.

"Like helping us on our cases," Eric pointed out, followed by a laugh, "like she did already."

"Oh, that came from you, did it?" he asked, eyeing her with interest. "That was a big one. Got anything else to help us with?"

"I don't know," she said. "You got any other cases?"

"We always have cases," he replied, with a snort. "That is one of the sad facts of our lives. There is never a shortage of those."

She winced and nodded. "I can see that," she agreed, but then she was struck by something. She frowned as numbers danced through her head. "I have no idea what this pertains to or why I need to tell you, but all these numbers are slamming through my brain right now."

"What's going on?" Eric asked.

"Oh, God, they're hurting me."

"What kind of numbers?" Eric asked.

"License plates, but one in particular," she replied, feeling some sense of that, "but I don't really know what this means." She reeled off a series of numbers, and Cody froze, staring at her.

Eric asked her, "Do you have any idea what those are?"

"No, I don't," she admitted. "Why?"

"Because it's the license plate to Cody's truck," Eric revealed.

"Yes, my truck," Cody snapped, "and it was stolen last night."

Eric frowned at him in shock.

"Yeah, I didn't even get a chance to tell you," Cody noted. "It was taken right out of the driveway." He turned to her and asked, "Do you know who did it?"

"I don't know anything about who did it," she replied cautiously, "but I can tell you where it is." He frowned at her. She shrugged and continued. "It's parked at a hotel close to here, and some guy, whoever he is, he took it from your place and is sleeping it off." Then she frowned and added, "But he's due to wake up anytime now, so you better hurry."

Cory bolted to his feet. "If you're right, God damn, that's amazing. But if you're wrong"—he smacked the table hard—"we'll have a talk." And, with that, he took off.

Eric eyed her in astonishment.

She shrugged. "What am I supposed to say?"

"Are you serious? Is that what you saw?"

"Yeah," she said, frowning at him, puzzled. "I mean, it does happen—unfortunately a little too often now that I know what this energy stuff is more about."

He let out his breath with a big *whoosh*. "Any idea who it is?"

"No, I don't do names very well," she conceded, "but it will be whoever is registered to that room. I don't know his name." She shrugged. "I just know he's there sleeping it off, whatever that means in his case."

"Probably a bender," Eric guessed. "Somebody'll wake up with a hell of a hangover and a lot more besides if my partner gets a hold of him."

She nodded. "Yeah, probably, but wait." She frowned. "It's also somebody he knows, and I would say they know each other pretty well."

He stared at her and shook his head. "Oh no, don't tell me it's his brother-in-law."

"I don't know if it's his brother-in-law or not," she stated, staring at him. "Don't know anything about him. Seems it was more of a lark than anything, and they go way back, so … no clue."

Eric shook his head. "Next time, maybe just don't tell him."

"How can I not tell him?" she asked in astonishment. "Particularly in this case. Plus, he bloody well asked for it."

He laughed. "I know. Never mind. We'll figure out our gifts as we go along."

An hour later Eric got a phone call from Cody. "What the hell? It was your brother-in-law, right?"

Silence came from the other end of the call. "Jesus, did she get that too?"

"Yeah, she sure did, but after you left."

"Damn, he's in the drunk tank right now. I have my truck back, and thank God there's no damage to it," he shared, "but, boy, will we have a serious talk." And, with that, he slammed down the phone.

Eric looked over at Eden and shared, "Cody's a little pissed."

She smiled and nodded. "He is a lot pissed, but that's okay. As I mentioned, they go way back."

He laughed. "That they do."

"So, it'll be fine," she murmured.

He didn't say anything but reached across the table for her hand. "You're really special, you know that?"

She shrugged, almost embarrassed at his words.

He could see it too. He laughed. "Finish up your coffee. It's time to go home."

"Are you sure?" she asked. "We just got here."

"Yeah, I'm sure. We haven't spent anywhere near enough time at home," he declared with a big grin, as he waggled his eyebrows at her.

She groaned and whispered, "I hardly think it's that time of day."

"I don't think the time of day makes any difference," he stated on a laugh. "Besides, time alone is what I'm after. I don't care what we do, as long as it's just us."

And, with that, she smiled. "Now that I can agree on." Within minutes, they were back home, stretched out together on the couch, just holding each other.

She let her eyelids drift closed, and he whispered, "Just don't leave me, okay?"

Her eyes flew open. She stared at him, not sure where that was coming from. "No, I won't."

"Promise me," he said. "Whatever that was, ... it was

pretty damn scary."

She nodded. "I know, and it was scary for me too. But I promise, I'm not going anywhere."

He held her close. "I'm holding you to that."

She hugged him tightly to her. "Good, please do. It's been a pretty rough life on my own."

He leaned over and kissed her. "Past tense. All that's over now. We have each other, and we have a whole world ahead of us to learn about and to share our lives—*together*," he added. "That's all we need. We can work out which city, which state, none of that matters. What matters is us."

She agreed, then leaned over and gave him a big kiss. "You're right. Just us together."

This concludes Book 28 of Psychic Visions:
A Mother's Love.

Read a sneak peek Remnants: Psychic Visions, Book 29

Remnants: Psychic Visions (Book #29)

Devon Blue never planned to be a mother—especially not to her best friend's twins. But, after cancer stole their mom too soon, Devon stepped in. Now her paycheck barely stretches far enough, her nerves are frayed, and the offer of a dream home feels like salvation. Maybe even fate.

Detective Camden Hartwell doesn't believe in fate—but the woman next door tests his resolve. Strong yet weary, Devon makes him want to protect her ... and not just from the world outside.

The twins start changing subtly as ghostly figures appear just beyond the fence line, their safe new beginning turning sinister. Whatever haunts the property isn't inside—it's waiting for them outside.

Please continue reading for a sneak peek...

EVON WALKED OVER to the front porch and stared out at the street and beyond to the houses there. She wanted this house something awful, but she still wasn't at all sure she could manage it. She felt as if she was even here on false pretenses in a way since her finances were so tight. She couldn't see a way to make this happen. The house was old, and it was small, yet the quaintness to it made her feel like she was home.

The twins came racing over. "Can we stay? Can we have it, please, please?"

The Realtor had called Devon out of the blue as she was coming home from work, saying that she had a house for her to look at. Before she could say no, she was persuaded to come, maybe because she'd had a crap day and had been too tired to put up much of a fight. The twins were with her. She'd just picked them up from school, and now she wandered around the empty house with them.

The Realtor walked over and asked, "What do you think?"

"Well, … sure, if I had the money, I would absolutely love to buy this," she stated. "I just don't think I can make it work."

"Part of the reason I brought you over here," said her Realtor, "is because they're not asking much. A very old couple owned it, but they've passed away, and their son is also of an age where he's going into a home himself and can't look after it anymore, so he's letting it go cheap."

"Yeah, when people say *cheap*," she began, with a wry look at her friend, "you and I both know that *cheap* is like … in the eye of the beholder, as they say."

Madeline interrupted her with an opening sales figure that had Devon freezing on the spot.

"Seriously?" she asked, when she could breathe again. "You must be joking."

"I'm not joking. Now you know why I wanted you to come, and to come now, because I don't know who else they may have told. The family sis looking at listing it with me, but they want it sold fast, and they don't want any headaches with it. They just want it gone," she explained. "As far as I can tell, there's absolutely no reason *not* to buy it. The interest rates aren't likely to get any lower than they are now, so it's a really good time for you to get into this. You need a great home for the twins, and they would stay in the same school. So, basically it's perfect."

"It is perfect," the twins screamed in unison as they raced toward her again. "Can we get it, please?"

Devon didn't know what to say. She looked over at her Realtor friend, still hesitant, and added, "I'll have to talk to the bank."

"And you'll need to do it fast," she insisted, "because I'm serious. This won't last."

"I know it won't," Devon muttered, followed by a groan. "Nothing ever lasts at these kinds of prices."

"Exactly, which is why—"

"I know. I know." Yet she felt horribly pressured.

Still, she got where Madeline was coming from. Devon's lease was coming due, and it was keeping her awake at night.

The rent had gone up considerably, and she wasn't sure she could afford the new rates. The mortgage payments on this house could potentially be a lot cheaper than her growing rent, and the money that Tabitha had left her could also help in a big way. She frowned as she thought about it, then checked the time on her phone. "I'll contact the bank in the morning."

"You did apply for a loan already, didn't you?"

"I did," she confirmed, "but I'm not sure they were very happy with my application."

"Times are tough for banks right now too," Madeline noted, "so I wouldn't worry about it. It's just that I need you to do something about it fast, or this will be gone, and everything else will be tens of thousands more. And honestly, the way the market is, things are just going up and up."

"I know it."

"So, jump on it. I need you to get settled in a home where the rent won't keep rising. I need to know you're safe and that the twins have a place where they can be safe too." Her voice cracked with emotions at that comment, and Devon understood.

The three of them had been friends for a very long time, and Madeline didn't have any children, although she'd really hoped to, but ended up divorced before it happened.

Tabitha had children, and then her husband had passed on. Worse yet, Tabitha died soon afterward, after being diagnosed with breast cancer. So now Devon was looking after Tabitha's twins, hoping rather desperately to find a place for them all. This home would probably be her best option.

She nodded determinedly. "I can only contact the bank and see what I can do about it."

Madeline added, "I have a broker I work with a lot. I'll get her to call you. Just get your documents ready. We can make an offer on this place, if you're sure you want it, and that gives us some time to confirm we can get the financing."

"Yeah, I hear you."

"He really does want to sell and hoped it would go to somebody who could use and appreciate it," she noted. "The family was here before he was even born."

She winced at that because that was always the thing. People who had raised families in homes really wanted them to go to people who would take care of them, knowing that a lot of work was needed. "Yeah, believe me that I can see that, but I'm not at all sure I'm the person to fix it up," she admitted, looking around the place. "That takes money."

"In this case, it's more about elbow grease," Madeline clarified, with a laugh, "and you and I both know we can do a lot of that ourselves."

Devon laughed and had to agree. "Yeah, we did projects on Tabitha's place God-only-knows how many times. But that time has come and gone," she added, trying to ward off the tears that once again threatened to overcome her.

"Good," Madeline replied, rubbing away her own tears. "We need to get you settled so I can at least know that I've done all I could do for her and the twins."

"I hear you," Devon muttered, "but I'll still be stuck with a mortgage that may be more than I can afford."

"She left you money for that, didn't she?"

"She did, but it still isn't that much."

"I understand." Madeline chewed on her finger, considering that. "Think about it overnight. Contact the bank first thing. I'll tell the seller that you're very interested and perfect for the house, but you aren't positive you'll get the financing, and you need a little bit of time. Now, if another buyer turns up in the meantime, I don't know that we can do anything to stop it."

"*Right*," Devon muttered, sighing. "Obviously, if they need to sell, they need to sell, but see what you can do. I'll take the twins home and get my paperwork together and do what I can."

But she knew in her heart that the banks were not very friendly, particularly since she was now a single mom raising twins, and the last time she contacted them, she wasn't all that stable, financially speaking. She didn't understand how someone could ever get stable financially when banks won't lend the money to buy a house and to start building equity, but it was an old argument. You had to look good on paper, and, if you didn't, the banks didn't want to talk to you.

Loading up the kids, she started her car and took one last look at the house.

The kids were screaming, "We really, really want to move in there."

She turned and looked at them. "But why? It's just a house."

"I know it's just a house," Tabby admitted, who was named after their mother.

"But I think it's our house," Toby clarified, dead serious as he stared at Devon.

"If it is, then it will all work out," Devon suggested. "I'll contact the bank in the morning, but, anytime I have tried in the past, they haven't been very open to it."

"It'll be different this time," Toby declared confidently.

"I hope so because I know you guys really want it, and I would love it as well. I'm ready to go in this direction if it works out, but I can't make any promises because I know what happened before."

"Yeah, but what happened before won't happen again."

Toby spoke with such confidence that she had to laugh. "I hope you're right."

He just smiled at her, and his expression had an almost otherworldly look to it. She looked away, tears coming to her eyes. This was not how she had expected her life to go, honest to God, but it's the one thing she had been able to do for Tabitha. Finding out her cancer was terminal had been bad enough. Then learning that her cancer was far too advanced for treatment to do any more than make her last days bearable just made it heart-wrenchingly horrible. Tabitha had vowed to take full advantage of every day she had.

The one thing Devon had been able to promise her friend was that she would look after the kids. They were eight, so she had at least ten years to ensure they felt loved and were fed and looked after. She had known them since birth, so, in many ways, it was the best answer for everyone.

The kids, although they had been absolutely devastated at losing their mom, seemed to accept it, taking it far better than she or Madeline had. Devon took one last look at the house in the rearview mirror.

Toby spoke up. "See? You really like it too."

"It doesn't matter if I like it or not, Toby," she clarified. "I have to get the bank to agree. Without being able to borrow the money, I'm not sure we have much of a chance."

He smiled. "No problem."

She hesitated, then asked, "And you know that how?"

He looked at her with the wisdom of the ages and announced, "Because this is meant to be. Nothing can stop this from happening, not even you."

Something about his tone sent chills up and down her spine. It was almost as if he had ordained it, and it had better come to pass … or else.

Find Book 29 here!
To find out more visit Dale Mayer's website.
https://geni.us/DMSRemnants

Simon Says... Hide: Kate Morgan (Book #1)

Welcome to a new thriller series from *USA Today* Best-Selling Author Dale Mayer. Set in Vancouver, BC, the team of Detective Kate Morgan and Simon St. Laurant, an unwilling psychic, marries all the elements of Dale's work that you've come to love, plus so much more.

Detective Kate Morgan, newly promoted to the Vancouver PD Homicide Department, stands for the victims in her world. She was once a victim herself, just as her mother had been a victim, and then her brother—an unsolved missing child's case—was yet another victim. She can't stand those who take advantage of others, and the worst ones are those who prey on the hopes of desperate people to line their own pockets.

So, when she finds a connection between more than a half-dozen cold cases to a current case, where a child's life hangs in the balance, Kate would make a deal with the devil himself to find the culprit and to save the child.

Simon St. Laurant's grandmother had the Sight and had warned him that, once he used it, he could never walk away. Until now, her caution had made it easy to avoid that first step. But, when nightmares of his own past are triggered, Simon can't stand back and watch child after child be abused. Not without offering his help to those chasing the monsters.

Even if it means dealing with the cranky and critical Detective Kate Morgan …

Find Simon Says… Hide here!
To find out more visit Dale Mayer's website.
https://geni.us/DMSSHideUniversal

Author's Note

Thank you for reading A Mother's Love: Psychic Visions, Book 28! If you enjoyed the book, please take a moment and leave a short review.

Dear reader,

I love to hear from readers, and you can contact me at my website: www.dalemayer.com or at my Facebook author page. To be informed of new releases and special offers, sign up for my newsletter or follow me on BookBub. And if you are interested in joining Dale Mayer's Reader Group, here is the Facebook sign up page.
http://geni.us/DaleMayerFBGroup

Cheers,
Dale Mayer

About the Author

Dale Mayer is a *USA Today* best-selling author, best known for her SEALs military romances, her Psychic Visions series, and her Lovely Lethal Garden cozy series. Her contemporary romances are raw and full of passion and emotion (Broken But ... Mending, Hathaway House series). Her thrillers will keep you guessing (Kate Morgan, By Death series), and her romantic comedies will keep you giggling (*It's a Dog's Life*, a stand-alone novella; and the Broken Protocols series, starring Charming Marvin, the cat).

Dale honors the stories that come to her—and some of them are crazy, break all the rules and cross multiple genres!

To go with her fiction, she also writes nonfiction in many different fields, with books available on résumé writing, companion gardening, and the US mortgage system. All her books are available in print and ebook format.

Connect with Dale Mayer Online

Dale's Website – www.dalemayer.com
Twitter – @DaleMayer
Facebook Page – geni.us/DaleMayerFBFanPage
Facebook Group – geni.us/DaleMayerFBGroup
BookBub – geni.us/DaleMayerBookbub
Instagram – geni.us/DaleMayerInstagram
Goodreads – geni.us/DaleMayerGoodreads
Newsletter – geni.us/DaleNews